MW01043238

The Season for
Strawberries

The Season for Strawberries

A NOVEL

Dorothy Brown Henderson

WOOD LAKE

Editor: Ellen Turnbull
Proofreader: Pattie Bender
Designer: Robert MacDonald

Library and Archives Canada Cataloguing in Publication
Henderson, Dorothy Brown, 1945-, author
The season for strawberries : a novel / Dorothy Brown Henderson.
Issued in print and electronic formats.
ISBN 978-1-77343-143-7 (softcover). – ISBN 978-1-77343-144-4 (HTML)
I. Title.
PS8615.E5226S43 2018   C813'.6   C2018-901911-5   C2018-901912-3

This book is a work of fiction. Names, characters, the village of Milburn Corners, and incidents are either the product of the author's imagination or used fictitiously. Any resemblance to actual persons living or dead, events, or locales is coincidental. However, the places mentioned in the novel – Owen Sound, Sauble Beach, Lake Huron, Tobermory, Inglis Falls, and Toronto – are real places in Ontario, as is Winnipeg in the province of Manitoba. All are rewarding to visit. The concepts of religion based on the work of Ninian Smart are taken from *The World's Religions,* Cambridge Press, 1992.

Text Copyright © 2018 by Dorothy Brown Henderson
Cover Art Copyright © 2018 by Sara Gallagher
All rights reserved. No part of this publication may be reproduced – except in the case of brief quotations embodied in critical articles and reviews – stored in an electronic retrieval system, or transmitted in any form or by any means, electronic, mechanical, photocopying, recording, or otherwise, without the prior written permission of the publisher or copyright holder.

Published by Wood Lake Publishing Inc.
485 Beaver Lake Road, Kelowna, BC, Canada, v4v 1s5
www.woodlake.com | 250.766.2778

Wood Lake Publishing acknowledges the financial support of the Government of Canada through the Canada Book Fund (CFB) for its publishing activities. Wood Lake Publishing acknowledges the financial support of the Province of British Columbia through the Book Publishing Tax Credit.

Wood Lake Publishing would like to acknowledge that we operate in the unceded territory of the Syilx/Okanagan peoples, and we work to support reconciliation and challenge the legacies of colonialism. The Syilx/Okanagan territory is a diverse and beautiful landscape of deserts and lakes, alpine forests and endangered grasslands. We honour the ancestral stewardship of the Syilx/Okanagan people.

GOLD

Printing 10 9 8 7 6 5 4 3 2 1
Printed in Canada

This book is dedicated to my husband, John, and to our three children, Sonya, Joel, and Daniel, and their families, who have all shared the richness of life with me.

This book is also dedicated to the many wonderful people who, over the years, have been part of our community life – in all its ups and downs.

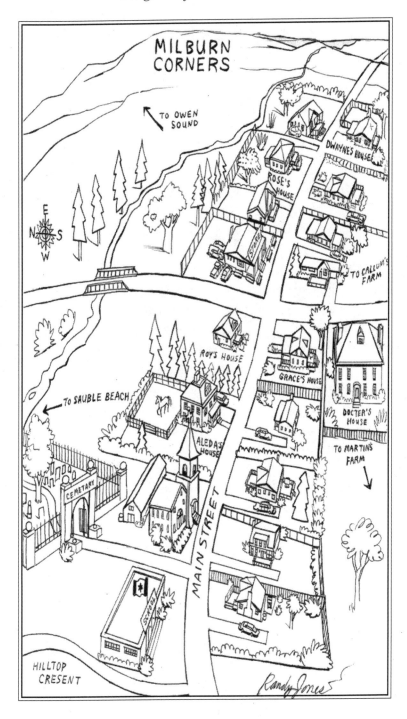

For everything there is a season,
  and a time for every matter under heaven:
a time to be born, and a time to die;
a time to plant, and a time to pluck up what is planted;
a time to kill, and a time to heal;
a time to break down, and a time to build up;
a time to weep, and a time to laugh;
a time to mourn, and a time to dance;
a time to throw away stones,
  and a time to gather stones together;
a time to embrace, and a time to refrain from embracing;
a time to seek, and a time to lose;
a time to keep, and a time to throw away;
a time to tear, and a time to sew;
a time to keep silence, and a time to speak;
a time to love, and a time to hate;
a time for war, and a time for peace.
... it is God's gift that all should eat and drink
  and take pleasure in all their toil.

– *Ecclesiastes 3:1–8, 13* (NRSV)

1

Accident

May 2002

 LEDA VASTAG STOOD IN HER screened front porch eating an afternoon snack – slices of spicy Hungarian sausage and a dill pickle. Although it was only 4 p.m., the sun had slipped behind the steeple of the church next door, casting shadows onto the parsonage porch. Aleda shivered; although it was May, there was a late spring chill in the air of southern Ontario.

Moving to stand in a shaft of sunlight, Aleda wiggled her toes. Despite the coolness of the day, she had dressed in sandals and capri pants. It was the beginning of a holiday long weekend and the day had seemed to call for apparel that signalled the beginning of the summer season...or so she thought.

As she ate, she waited for the yellow school bus to pull up to the curb by the village store. When she saw it roll in, she set down her plate and watched the five teenagers from the village scramble down the steps, backpacks hooked over their shoulders. They stood waiting on the curb until Dwayne, shoulders slouched, slowly walked down the steep bus steps. The six teens talked for a few minutes in front of the store until Savannah and her friends turned west, walking toward the green mailbox, moving past Roy's house toward Aleda's and the new subdivision beyond where they lived. Dwayne, who lived with his grandmother at the other end of the village, turned away, head down, sagging brown backpack dangling from one shoulder.

Aleda opened the screen door and moved down the steps, wandering toward the maple tree in the centre of her front lawn. She folded her arms and stood smiling as the youth came toward her. Savannah was laughing and gesturing to her friends, swinging her head from side to side to include everyone. When she spotted Aleda, Savannah raised her arms high above her head and waved them back and forth, swaying and wiggling her fingers. Aleda stood waiting, wanting to wish the teens a happy weekend.

Before she had time to call out a greeting, Aleda heard the screech of car brakes. The young people swung around and watched as a vehicle accelerated up the knoll behind them and tore out of the village. Confused, they stared at the speeding car until something caught their attention on Roy's front lawn. There was a black dog lying motionless on the grass. It had been struck by the car.

For a moment, it was as if time had stopped. Everyone stood frozen near Aleda's maple tree. Then, all at once, they began to run together toward Roy's house. Roy had been brushing dry winter leaves from the edge of a perennial bed, but now he dropped his broom on the driveway and hurried toward the front of his lawn as Aleda and the five teens arrived, panting.

They edged over to where the dog lay whimpering. It was a medium-sized black dog of no distinct breed, and as Aleda, Savannah, and Roy crept closer, it began to growl, and drew back its upper lip in a snarl. They stopped, staring down at the injured animal.

"Don't see no blood." Roy's voice was quiet, calm, measured. "That's a good sign, I think."

"What should we do, Roy?" Aleda could hear the panic in her own voice.

"Not sure," Roy replied. "Can't think of who to call."

Aleda bent forward. She could see that the pupils in the dog's eyes were dilated in pain.

"What about the humane society?" she asked.

"Don't know. Not sure if this is their sort of thing."

The commotion had attracted Grace, who came rushing from her house across the street, wiping her hands on her floral apron.

"This dog was just struck by a speeding car. We don't know what to do." Aleda's heart thumped against her ribs, and her voice, even to her own ears, sounded higher than usual.

"We have to get this dog to the vet at Rockford," Savannah said, taking charge.

"Do you think so? Should it be moved?" Roy peered at the dog as it continued to alternate between whimpering and growling.

As they stood looking down at the injured dog, no one noticed a rusty grey truck pull over in front of Roy's house. A man hopped out of the truck, strolled over to the huddled group, and said, "What have we here?"

"This dog was hit by a speeding car and tossed into Roy's yard. We know it's hurt, but we have no idea who it belongs to, or what we should do."

The man crouched in front of the whimpering dog, speaking in a low quiet voice.

"Easy boy. Easy boy." He gently swept his hand across the dog's head and down its spine, but as he reached the end of the spine, the dog picked up his head and growled, showing its teeth. The man looked up at the anxious group huddled around the dog.

"I'm not sure, but I think it's his leg." Turning to Roy, he asked, "If you have an old blanket, we can get him to the vet, if one of you will help me."

"I'll go with you," Savannah offered immediately, taking the woolen plaid blanket that Roy had retrieved from the trunk of his car.

When the dog had been carefully laid on the seat of the truck, Savannah hopped into the back of the pickup and sat leaning against the cab. Aleda, Grace, Roy, and the other teens stood watching as the truck eased away from the sidewalk and headed east to Rockford.

Aleda felt her knees shaking, and Roy looked pale, but it was Grace who voiced the questions. Whose dog is it? Should they call the police to report the speeding car? Had anyone spotted the car's license plate? Who was the stranger with the grey truck? Should they have let Savannah ride off with a complete stranger, and isn't it unsafe to travel in the open back of a pickup truck? Isn't it illegal? And who was going to pay the vet bill?

"We have to follow them, Roy," Aleda said. "I'll get my van and pick you up." She turned back toward her house, walking as fast as her shaky legs would allow. She ran up the porch steps, grabbed her keys, jumped into her van, and drove down the street toward Roy's house, clutching the steering wheel tightly to steady her hands. As Roy hurried around to the passenger side of Aleda's van, Grace returned to her house to finish the apple pie she had been preparing.

When Aleda and Roy pulled into the parking lot at the veterinary clinic and spotted the grey truck parked in the spot closest to the front door, Aleda blurted out, "Oh, thank God for small mercies!"

"Don't kid yourself, Aleda. This is a big mercy," Roy said, and the two of them hurried into the waiting room.

Savannah and the man were sitting on opposite sides of the room. The girl was flipping through a magazine and the man sat with his arms folded, staring at the wall posters. Savannah jumped up and threw her arms around Aleda.

"Oh, thank goodness you came," she said, trembling.

Aleda gave Savannah a firm hug, patted the girl's shoulder, and sat down beside her. "The dog?"

"It's with the vet. She said to wait here while she examined it and took an x-ray."

Roy turned to the man who had come to their rescue. He reached out his hand and said, "I'm Roy Gregory. Thanks for helping out. I'm not sure what would have happened if you hadn't come along."

"Not a problem," the stranger replied, rising to shake Roy's hand. "Name's Martin Hart. I've a place up near the town line and just happened to be coming through when I saw the commotion on your lawn."

"Ah. Yes, I recognize you now. You're Rose Hart's boy, and you come up for the summer. Haven't seen you for some years, son," Roy said.

Aleda looked at the man who Roy had called son, thinking that the stranger was clearly close to her own age. Then she dropped her eyes and the four waited in silence.

After what seemed a very long time, Dr. Patel emerged from the examining room and looked around, surprised to see four people in the waiting room.

"Hello," she smiled. She looked at Aleda and asked, "Are you the owner?"

Aleda began to explain the situation, but Dr. Patel said with a wave of her hand, "Oh, yes. Martin here has told me about the accident." She paused and cleared her throat. "Well, there are a couple of things. First, this is a very lucky dog. She does have a broken leg, but it is a nice, clean, closed fracture. The skin was not broken at all. With a cast and a quiet life she should be as good as new in five or six weeks." Dr. Patel looked at Aleda and Savannah. "The other thing you should know is that this dog is going to have puppies."

Aleda and Savannah stared at the veterinarian, absorbing the information.

"Also," the vet went on, "there's no dog tag, which suggests that whoever owns this dog might not have been taking the best care of her, and certainly didn't keep her fenced in and safe. There's some evidence that the dog wasn't fed well. She's very thin. Since you don't know whose dog this is, I was wondering about the matter of…" Dr. Patel's voice trailed off.

"The bill?" Aleda asked.

"Well, it is a consideration. If you can't find an owner, there is always the option of having the dog put down," Dr. Patel continued slowly. "But, of course, we don't like to do that if there is any other choice. It's just hard to find someone willing to adopt a pregnant, malnourished dog with a broken leg."

13

Savannah jumped up. "No! Just give us a little time. We'll find the owner! We can do it, for sure. I'll put up posters around the village. My dad was born in Milburn Corners, and he knows most of the farmers around here. We'll phone them, or I'll ride my bike and ask around until we find the owner."

Aleda stood silently, her lips pursed, wondering if her church's benevolent fund could be stretched as far as covering the veterinary bill for a stray dog. Then she heard her own voice, as if it belonged to someone else, say, "I will see that the bill is paid. Are there papers I need to sign?"

By the time Aleda had dropped Roy and Savannah at their homes, it was 6 p.m. Walking into the kitchen, she felt suddenly weak and hungry. Opening the fridge door, she squinted into the nearly empty space, searching for leftovers, something easy. She grabbed the fry pan, spooned in some butter, and when it had begun to sizzle she popped bread into the toaster and broke two eggs into the hot pan. Aleda ate quickly and was mopping up a stream of egg yolk with a crust of toast when the phone rang.

"Aleda, it's Dr. Patel calling. I just want to let you know that the dog is doing fine. We've put on a cast, and she is eating and drinking well."

"Oh such good news, Dr. Patel. I'm sure Savannah and Roy will be relieved to hear that."

"We're happy to keep her overnight," Dr. Patel continued, "but, really, she'll be ready to leave here tomorrow. Can that be arranged?"

Aleda hesitated. She would need to talk with Savannah, but she replied, "I'm sure that can be arranged."

Later, when the sun had gone down behind the old stone shed, Aleda headed down the steps of the back veranda. She could hear Tracker shuffling about in his stall, waiting for her to come. As she walked through the shed door, she called out to the horse in a soothing tone, "Hello old boy, come boy, dinner boy." She heard the horse's soft whinny and wondered if the horse had grown fond of her or, well, if not fond, at least accustomed to her? Or was he merely hungry?

The shed smelled of horse: fresh manure, musty straw, dust, and ground meal. Lifting the lid to the wooden bin, Aleda filled a silver scoop with crushed oats and entered the stall to dump the meal into the horse's bowl. Tracker turned his great shaggy head toward the bowl and began to eat. Aleda stroked him, running her hand along his sway back, rubbing his dull coat, now sprinkled with grey hairs. When the horse had first come to live in the church shed, as they were learning to like each other, Aleda discovered that Tracker liked to have his forehead rubbed. Now all was silent except for the crunching of ground oats and the slow, soft strokes of hand on horse hide.

Aleda spread some fresh straw in Tracker's stall, then stroked the horse's neck. He turned and nuzzled the pocket of her capri pants, waiting for the treat they both understood would follow the oats. Aleda pulled the apple from her pocket and held it out to the horse. She listened as Tracker ground the apple between his worn teeth, then she murmured, "Good night old soul, sleep tight old friend," before giving him a gentle slap on the rump. She closed the shed door, making sure that the latch was secure, then turned back toward the parsonage.

By the time she had washed her dishes, Aleda could see the moon low on the horizon. She pulled on a pair of sweat pants and a fleece jacket and walked out into the backyard, looking up into the darkening sky. One or two stars had begun to appear and Aleda squinted, trying to recognize a pattern. She inhaled deeply – sweet clover, soon to be the first crop of fresh hay from a nearby farm. The frogs were sending a continuous *riddup-riddup* from the swamp at the edge of the village. Aleda sat down onto a wooden cottage chair, damp with dew. "Oh, why didn't I bring out a blanket and a cup of coffee?" she mumbled to herself. She jumped out of the chair and walked back across the lawn, then ran up the back veranda steps and into the kitchen.

Aleda had plugged in the kettle and was reaching for a mug when the telephone rang. Who on earth is calling at this time of night? she thought with irritation. She glanced at the call display and her annoyance increased. Grace Stone.

When Aleda met with her friend and mentor, the Right Reverend Dr. Robert McKay, for her monthly pick-me-up, as Aleda liked to call it, she often told a story about Grace. Sometimes Aleda put an amusing spin on the story – it helped her feel more kindly toward Grace – but usually the story had an irritated edge. "Every minister has burdens to bear, so why should I be different?" she would say in a resigned and petulant tone of voice. Or she would say, "Every minister has a contentious parishioner who challenges and pushes." But often Aleda, with a sigh, would say simply say, "I guess every church has a Grace."

"My dear," Robert would say, leaning forward, a gleam in his eyes, "every church has grace," and Aleda would look down into her coffee mug, feeling ashamed yet not able to drop her annoyance with the woman who seemed to delight in making Aleda's life difficult.

Aleda let the phone ring six times before she answered, hoping to convey to Grace that she was busy – editing her Sunday sermon, or polishing her toe nails, or taking a bath, or watching a thriller on television.

"Did you notice there's a light in the doctor's house?" Grace had not bothered with any pleasantries.

"A light?"

Aleda's first thought was of vandalism. After all, it *was* the first night of a long weekend. Was it possible that the teens had broken into the doctor's house? Everyone in Milburn Corners knew that the grand old Georgian house on the hill had been empty for four years.

"I was out in the backyard while my dog did her business and I just happened to glance up the hill and the light was on in the front room of the doctor's house!"

Aleda could hear the excitement in Grace's voice. There weren't many things that Grace enjoyed more than gossip, scandal, or mystery. I won't give her the satisfaction, Aleda thought, grinding her teeth. She took a deep breath.

"Well, I suppose there's a logical explanation," Aleda said in a calm voice.

"But shouldn't we at least check it out?"

Aleda paused. She realized that Grace was right.

Throughout the entire first year of her ministry in Milburn Corners, Aleda had worked hard to convince the older members of her congregation that the youth were an important, even essential, part of the church. Surely the boys wouldn't have the audacity to break into a house with a case of beer to celebrate the long weekend. That would ruin all the bridge-building she had done. Aleda felt annoyance merely imagining the possibility.

Aleda massaged the bridge of her nose, easing the tight sensation that warned her that her blood pressure had risen. "Yes, well, I'm sure it's nothing," she said to Grace. "I'm sure there's a logical explanation." And before Grace could say anything more, Aleda said with politeness and restraint, "Thanks for calling. Have a good night," and hung up the phone.

Snoopy old busybody, Aleda thought uncharitably. She stared at her wavy reflection in the steaming kettle, then pulled out the plug and whisked the mug and coffee filter back into the cupboard. Turning to the side counter, she grabbed a wine goblet and poured herself a glass of Merlot, filling it to the top. Then she stood on her tiptoes and looked out her kitchen window, but she couldn't see the doctor's house for the spruce trees that lined the side of the parsonage.

Grabbing her old pink afghan from the wicker chair in the front porch, and carrying her wine glass, Aleda stepped out the back door and walked to the edge of the veranda. With care, she set down the wine and the blanket and hopped up onto the edge of the wide flower planter, steadying herself by holding on to the eavestrough. Staring through a gap between two spruce trees, Aleda could see that Grace had been right. There was a light on in the doctor's house.

Aleda jumped off the planter, picked up her wine, and walked to the cottage chair. She lined the chair with the blanket and sat down carefully, pulling the sides of the afghan around her legs.

As she took a sip of wine, she thought, this is nonsense. It couldn't possibly be the boys. Michael and Jacob are both such responsible kids, and Dwayne, well. Aleda sighed. Why is it that I always sigh when I think of Dwayne? she wondered.

From the time that she had arrived in the village, Dwayne had been a worry to her. She had tried so many times to have a good conversation with the boy. She could sense that Dwayne was a bit of a lost soul; sullen, withdrawn, and – what? Depressed? Certainly unhappy, Aleda thought. She sighed again. No, if the boys had wanted to do something daring, Michael and Jacob would not choose to break in to an empty house, and Dwayne wouldn't have the courage to initiate such a thing. Besides, they wouldn't have turned on lights. No, it couldn't possibly be the boys.

Somehow Aleda could not imagine *her* girls – Savannah, Ashley, Victoria – doing anything as stupid as breaking into an empty country house either. No, my girls will be doing something positive and productive – maybe finishing their homework, or babysitting to earn a little extra money. Or maybe they are eating popcorn with their parents, watching a classic movie.

Aleda took another sip of wine. The stars were popping out and she leaned her head against the chair, looking up into the clear sky. It seemed as if the stars were being switched on one after another. I wish, she thought, full of self-recrimination, that I had taken time to study the constellations. I wish I were the type of person who could stick with things.

Then she wondered why she was so hard on herself, thinking, perhaps, that this was one of the pitfalls of living alone. She worried that she was becoming too self-focused, too self-critical, too introspective. But then, maybe it's not that I can't stick with things. Maybe, instead, I'm the type of person who is meant to enjoy the grand drama, the broad spectrum, the great curves and arches of life, and that is why I tend to flit from one thing to another. I just can't wait to taste all of life.

Aleda smiled now, and, in that small moment, alone in the dark of her backyard, she savoured the fact that God had given her – she was sure of this – a flamboyant personality. It was true, she told herself. Even as a child she had the ability to turn the ordinary into something extravagant. It was just who she was. She sat smiling, pulling the afghan around her arms.

Feeling the dew begin to settle on the grass, Aleda pulled her bare feet from her sandals and tucked them into the afghan. Suddenly, this small act of self-comfort unsettled her and she felt herself on the verge of tears, sorry for herself in some inexplicable way. The whole village is preparing for a holiday weekend and I am sitting alone, wrapped in a blanket drinking wine. If only I had invited Margie for the weekend. We could be sitting here drinking wine together, remembering high school days. If only she lived closer. But Margie was busy with her teenage girls and her career as city librarian.

How different would things be if her parents were still alive. She might have invited them to Milburn Corners for the weekend and the three of them could now be huddled together in the quiet of the backyard, wrapped in blankets and watching stars.

Her parents. How little she understood about them and their student days in Hungary. She remembered how hard they worked after arriving in Canada – her father in the steel mill and her mother cleaning houses. She also recalled how cherished she had felt as an only child, learning to cook, perched on a stool beside the kitchen counter rolling cookie dough with her mother. She remembered sitting on her father's knee, learning facts about the world from the encyclopedia that her father had saved to buy.

"How do you know all these things?" she asked her father once, looking up into his face as they sat in the tiny kitchen in the house on St. Mary Street.

"Oh," he said with a grave face, "your mother and I were students at the university in Budapest. We had to leave, but we never forgot that we need to keep learning."

Aleda's mind then drifted to Ben — beautiful, gentle, funny, enchanting Ben — with whom she had believed she would share the rest of her life. Aleda felt bitterness rise in the back of her throat. I wonder where Ben is now.

Aleda remembered when she met him. As students were gathering in the rotunda of the college, she had glanced across the room toward a beautiful, blue-eyed man. His shirt was rumpled and loosely tucked into a pair of baggy pants, and, when he spotted Aleda, he had smiled and edged his way around the group of students gathered in front of him.

It had been a wonderful year. She and Ben had shared laughter and meals, theological debates and research. He had been her first lover and the man whom she really had never gotten over. Ben. Beautiful Ben. Where are you now? Tears rolled down her cheeks as she took another sip of wine. She pressed her hand against a sharp pain in her chest when she recalled how everything had ended. No, it was better that he was not in her life.

I shouldn't drink when I'm in this mood, she thought. Wine makes me morose. I'm 42 years old, single, and really, does my work matter? She took another deep, shuddering breath.

At that moment, Aleda heard a rustle from the corner of the yard. I hope it's not a skunk, she thought, jumping up. Grasping the wine glass between her hands, she turned and squinted into the dark hedge. Seeing nothing, she pushed her sandals on and began to move toward the grass alley between the house and the imposing red-brick wall of the church, the only way to access the front of the house from the backyard. This space seemed harmless in the daytime, but at night it was eerie and damp with trapped night air. She strode with haste through the alleyway and could see the circle of white cast by the sole street light in Milburn Corners – an old-fashioned Victorian lamppost standing in front of Roy's house. From the front lawn she had a perfect view of the doctor's house. A light was shining in the front room of the house.

She stood under the maple tree until she saw another light switch on in a front upstairs room. Relieved that it was not the village boys, Aleda began to stroll down Main Street, her eyes on the house. She crossed the street before she came to the street lamp, staying in the shadows as long as possible. Then, to avoid walking in front of Grace's house, she crossed back again.

When she reached the village store, she had a clear view into the living room. She could see a woman on crutches swinging herself forward in an awkward motion. The woman appeared tall, slim, and attractive – maybe 45 or 50, Aleda thought. She watched as the woman leaned her crutches against the French doors of the living room and hopped into a back room. Another person was moving around in a front bedroom, stopping to snap open the window and let in the evening air.

After watching for a while, Aleda turned back toward home, following the same criss-cross pattern to avoid the street light.

Grace Stone, dressed in a yellow nylon nightgown, stood in her living room behind her sheer curtains, her house in complete darkness. Ah, she thought. The minister did go. And, of all things, she went walking through the village at night with a glass of wine in her hand!

2

Tracker

HERE ARE MANY THINGS THAT ministers do not know about their parishioners, and often this is quite a good thing. Aleda did not know, for instance, that when the church Board had a vote on whether or not to invite Aleda to be their minister, Grace Stone had written a large *No* on her ballot.

Grace had also been the only person to say aloud what some others may have been thinking: "We've never had a woman minister here in Milburn Corners, and I don't see any reason why we can't find a nice man. Besides, she's single. Ministers should have families."

Neither did Grace consider Aleda to be truly Canadian. She was Hungarian, an outsider in Grace's eyes, someone from a country that had fought against the Allies in World War II. It didn't seem to matter to Grace that Aleda had actually been born in Canada. Her parents had come from Hungary, and that was proof enough to Grace. Aleda was a foreigner.

Grace did not like change in general, but one in particular had grated on her nerves. The previous minister had persisted in efforts to change the name of the church from Milburn Corners Presbyterian Church to Milburn Corners Community Church.

"We have young families in the new subdivision," he had said at every meeting of the Board. "While all of us are proud of our Presbyterian heritage, it doesn't mean much to the younger generation. But a community church! Well, everyone understands community."

In the end, the Board had agreed, worn down by the arguments and continual bickering. It was a bittersweet victory though, for it had also worn down the minister and in June of that year he announced his resignation, packed up his family and belongings, and moved to a city church.

Thankfully, Aleda said later to Robert, she had had little awareness of these matters when she came to the village. "It's better to be more than a little ignorant about these things at the beginning," she said. "Then you come into the community without preconceived ideas. It's a chance to start fresh. It's like having a clean slate."

On Saturday morning of the long weekend, Aleda wakened and tried to rouse herself. She sat up, took a long drink of water from the glass on her bedside table, slapped her face gently. Then she plopped back down, her head buried in the pillow, her legs smothered in the tangle of bedclothes. Aleda was not, as she told friends, a morning person. She was groggy and thick-headed for the first hour of her day. It didn't matter if she rose with the sun or at noon; Aleda found it difficult to wake up. She had learned, though, to set her alarm for 7 a.m. It seemed the whole village got up early and it often happened that her doorbell rang early in the morning. Would she like a basket of tomatoes? Did she know that her porch light had been on overnight? Had she remembered to pick up a loaf of bread for Sunday communion?

Aleda stretched, still reluctant to get up. Then she struggled out of bed, headed to the bathroom, tugged off the oversized T-shirt that she wore as a nightshirt, stepped into the shower, and let the hot water flow over her skin and waken her to the day.

After her shower, Aleda dried herself and wrapped the damp towel around her wet hair. She stood naked in front of the mirrored shower doors and looked at her sturdy strong body; her firm round breasts, her skin tone that tended to brown, her long arms, and her compact muscular legs. She smoothed her dark straight eyebrows, touched her wide cheek bones, and ran her fingers over her nose and her wide curving lips. She leaned forward and peered at the two lines that ran vertically between her eyebrows. As the years passed, these lines had seemed to become deeper, especially when Aleda was worried or troubled. She removed the towel from her head, shook her head to loosen her short curly dark hair and thought, it's a good body, a good, solid, serviceable body – maybe even a beautiful body.

Back in her bedroom, Aleda pulled on jeans and a T-shirt. She padded down the stairs in bare feet, turned into the kitchen, and plugged in the kettle. Her day was about to begin, whether she was ready or not.

After breakfast, Aleda turned toward the back door and pulled on her red rubber boots.

When Aleda had first come to Milburn Corners and realized that most of her congregational members were farmers, she had asked Roy a question that was worrying her. Roy had been digging dandelions out of his front lawn when she walked past to pick up her mail.

"Roy," she called out, "there's something on my mind, and I could use some advice."

"What's that, Aleda?"

"It's the men of the church."

He tilted his head, a puzzled look on his face.

"Yes, the men. It's been easy for me to get to know the women. They come to the Ladies Guild, and help out in Sunday school, and make the funeral lunches, and bring flowers. But I don't like to bother the men. They have so much work to do on their farms. I don't feel as if I know them at all. Some of them I can hardly call by name."

"Well," Roy said.

Aleda waited, her eyebrows raised.

"Well," Roy repeated. "Maybe what you need is a pair of rubber boots."

"Rubber boots." She stared into Roy's face for a moment.

"Have you met Dr. Patel, the vet?" Roy asked.

"Not yet," Aleda had replied, "but I've heard about her."

"That's the first thing she does when she gets to a farm. She gets out of the car, takes off her shoes, and puts on a pair of rubber boots. It's a signal to farmers that she means business and that she's ready to muck around anywhere, anytime, in the manure, or barn-yard, or mud."

"So you are suggesting…"

"Can't hurt. Git yourself a pair of rubber boots and when you go to call at a farm just put 'em on. The men'll invite you out to see something. You can count on that."

"But Roy, surely farmers are far too busy to stop work and visit with a minister," she had protested, thinking that they might not want to be interrupted.

But when she began to drop in to farms while wearing her rubber boots, she had discovered that the men who belonged to her church seemed happy to pause in their work and show her how they had renovated a milking parlour or added a new ground cover in a no-till acreage. Perhaps, she thought, the boots *are* the secret to success.

In later weeks she came to realize that perhaps her rubber boots were as much a surprise to the farmers as they had been to Roy. One day, when Roy had come to the back door with a bale of straw for Tracker's stall, she had said, "Hang on a sec, Roy. I'll just grab my boots and open the shed door for you."

"Land's sake, Aleda! Where on God's good green acres did you git them boots?"

"Roy! You yourself advised me to buy some rubber boots, did you not? And I've been having great success in getting out into farmer's fields and barns."

Roy stood staring down at her feet. "But bright red boots, Aleda? I didn't know you could even buy bright red rubber boots." And for a few minutes, as they stood beside the bale of straw, Roy and Aleda gazed back and forth between their feet, Roy's in dark blue rubber with a rust-coloured sole, the kind that all farmers buy at the Owen Sound Farm and Country Store, and Aleda's in scarlet.

Aleda tromped out to the shed to feed Tracker.

"Good boy, atta boy, good morning merry sunshine," she said as she brushed his back and flanks.

In the mornings, it was Aleda's little secret – or so she thought – that she let Tracker out of his stall and into the backyard of the parsonage. She told herself that sunshine and a bit of exercise were good for him. The backyard was fenced on three sides, the only open space being the end of the grass alley between the house and the church. At first Aleda thought that she might put a gate there, but she worried that it would draw attention to the fact that she was letting Tracker into the backyard. Perhaps someone would complain and there would be another stormy Board meeting. So instead of a gate, she drove her van across the opening, sometimes lifting the tailgate as if to suggest that she had just unloaded some groceries or was preparing for a trip to the landfill site. The van blocked Tracker's escape route – not that he ever seemed inclined to stir from his favourite spot facing the swamp in the north end of the yard.

I'm probably the only minister in Ontario who has an old horse for a pet, she thought, smiling. When she remembered last October's Board meeting though, her smile faded. Aleda had asked if anyone would accompany her to a seminar on how to make the church a more welcoming place. One by one, the Board members made polite excuses.

"How about you, Norm?" Roy had asked.

"Nope. Have a run on Saturday. Gotta go down to Toronto. The Brubachers up on the town line have a horse that's too old for ploughing. They don't want to dispose of it themselves, so I'm trucking it to Toronto for rendering."

Sitting at the battered boardroom table in the church hall, Aleda stared at Norm, her mouth open. Rendering. What a heartless, cruel end for a noble animal. She had never before considered that large animals such as horses would have to be buried or disposed of when they died. But rendered? Although she had never known her grandmothers, wouldn't that be like shoving your beloved grandmother off a cliff because she had become too old to do much?

"But why?" she asked in a flash of anger. "Why have they decided to send the horse to be rendered?" The lines between her eyes deepened as she frowned.

Norm shrugged. "What else do you do with an old horse?"

The following morning, Aleda rose earlier than usual, pulled on her jeans and a T-shirt, and turned her van toward the town line. By 11 a.m. she was the proud owner of an old horse called Tracker. She had only needed to say to Ezekiel Brubacher, "How much money do you have to pay to ship an old horse for rendering?" and add a few more dollars, and Tracker was hers. Ezekiel promised to keep the horse for an extra week until she found a place where she could keep it.

On the way home, speeding along in her van, Aleda said in a loud and startled voice, "Good grief, Aleda! What have you done? What kind of a pastor has a pet horse, and an old one at that? What on earth will people say? How on earth am I going to explain this one?"

When Aleda was a child, she had begged her parents for a pet. She would have settled for a cat, a dog, or even a gerbil, but what she really wanted was a horse. When she told her parents that she had decided to have a pet horse, they smiled at her, puzzled and surprised. Mama and Papa, after fleeing for their lives during the Hungarian revolution in 1956, had struggled to establish a new life in Canada. The thought of their forceful, persuasive, and bright young daughter keeping a horse on their narrow strip of lawn only brought smiles to their faces.

The special meeting of the church Board generated more gossip than any other meeting in the history of the church.

"Do you know what the new minister wants to do?" Grace asked Ethel Aylmer, the village storekeeper. "She wants to keep an old horse as a pet, and she wants to keep it in the stone shed at the back of the church! Can you believe that?"

It was an out-of-the-ordinary request and raised many questions. What if there was a smell? Aleda countered that the shed had probably been used for sheltering horses in earlier times when people came to church in sleighs or wagons pulled by horses. Did people complain then about smell?

What about manure, and where will you get straw and hay?

Aleda dismissed many concerns with an impatient wave of her hand. "Manure? I've been meaning to do some work on those flower borders anyway. Roy, you said you would help me, didn't you?"

It had been a long meeting, and it left everyone unsettled. In the end, it had been Roy who said, "Now, now. Our minister has new ideas, and what can it hurt if she has an old horse for a pet? That church shed just sits there empty anyway."

The following week, Ezekiel Brubacher delivered Tracker at dusk, as Aleda had requested. As Ezekiel backed the horse out of the trailer Aleda suddenly was overwhelmed with what she had done. She felt both fragile and frightened when she saw the size of the horse. She had forgotten how big horses were and she perceived in that moment that her love of horses had been mainly on a fantasy level.

Ezekiel led the reluctant horse through to the shed that opened into Aleda's back yard. But the frightened and stubborn horse refused to enter.

Ezekiel called to Aleda, "Here, take this rope and pull." He walked to the back of the horse and gave it two sharp whacks on the rump with a cane. The surprised horse jumped forward into the shed, almost pushing down the equally startled woman.

It would take weeks before Aleda and Tracker could be easy with each other. Aleda had not counted on this. Finally she had a pet horse, but the horse did not seem to like her, and she was not sure that she liked Tracker either.

When Aleda had finished freeing Tracker and then washing her breakfast dishes on Saturday morning, she wandered into the screened porch at the front of the house. From this vantage point, she could see a black car in the curving driveway of the doctor's house. She was curious about the people in the house and the car. Reaching for her novel – an historical novel set in the outer Hebrides – she settled into the wicker chair. She had read to the bottom of the first page when the telephone rang. She groaned and heaved herself to her feet.

"Aleda. Roy here."

"Hi, Roy. What's up?"

"Well, it's Grace, you see. She just came across the street to remind me that we should call the police to report that speeding car that hit the dog yesterday." Roy paused. "You want to do that, Aleda, or should I?" Aleda massaged the skin on the bridge of her nose.

"Oh, good point Roy. It slipped my mind. Don't you worry about it. I'll give the police a call." When she placed a call to the number listed in her telephone book, she was told that they would send Constable Brennan in the afternoon to get a statement. Aleda had just hung up and was preparing to return to her novel when the telephone rang again. Aleda recognized the voice of Eadie's daughter.

"Reverend Vastag, Aleda, it's Mother. She has been taken to the palliative care unit at the hospital in Owen Sound."

"Oh, I am so very sorry to hear that. I knew that your mother was unwell, but I'm sure we all hoped that things would improve."

"She's pretty upset today," Eadie's daughter continued. "And she is so fond of you. I was wondering if you might go for a bit of a visit."

"Of course. Of course."

Aleda sighed, closed her book, and set it back on the seat of the wicker chair. Might as well go right away, she thought, picking up the keys for her van.

It was noon when Aleda drove back into Milburn Corners. As she pulled into the parsonage driveway she put her hands on her cheeks and gasped. Jumping from the van, she tore down the grass alley, knowing what she would find – an empty backyard and an empty shed. She had forgotten about Tracker, enjoying his freedom in the back yard, when she left in the van to visit Eadie.

Dazed, Aleda sat down on the steps of the back veranda and looked around as if hoping that Tracker might magically appear in his usual spot, shaggy head resting over the back fence and tail swishing back and forth. Aleda got up and walked into the kitchen. I need a cup of hot, strong tea, she thought. As she plugged in the kettle, she noticed the red message light blinking on the telephone.

Aleda pressed play and heard Grace reminding her to make an announcement at church the following day about a special meeting of the Ladies Guild on Tuesday night to plan the annual strawberry social. And she was wondering what had happened to that dog. It didn't look like any dog from the village. And by the way, had she found out yet who's in the doctor's house?

The kettle whistled and Aleda reached for the tea canister. As the tea steeped she gazed out the window at Roy's lawn. She felt as if she might cry.

What is wrong with this day? It is going completely haywire. It is the Saturday of a long weekend. Much of the county is at the beach having fun but I have a sermon to finish for tomorrow. I have a dying parishioner to worry about. I have just promised to pay the veterinary bill for a stray dog that needs to get picked up from the clinic today, and now I have a lost horse. Should I laugh or cry?

She glanced at the clock, then grabbed an old backpack hanging on a hook by the kitchen door and popped some sugar cubes into a zippered pocket of the pack. Then she walked out to the shed, and took Tracker's seldom-used halter and rope off a hook and stuffed them in her backpack too. She walked to the end of her driveway and stopped. Left or right? If I were an ornery old horse, which way would I go?

When Aleda met with Robert for her monthly coffee date, he would often ask her to tell him about her life and work. On more than one occasion, when she had agonized over what later seemed a trivial matter, he would ask her what her instinct was, and tell her to trust her gut.

Now his words came back to her and she thought: Swamp. Tracker always stands facing the swamp. If Tracker were to run away from home, he would go to the swamp.

Aleda headed down toward the old bridge and the swampy area of cedars, marsh marigolds, bulrushes, and reeds. There was no sign of Tracker – no horse buns at the side of the road, no hoof prints in the gravel. But as she neared the bridge, Aleda thought that the tall, dry winter grass looked slightly bent and broken. She stopped, crouched, and peered closely. I think he went in here, she thought, and turning off the road, she began to follow the curve of the creek. Within seconds, Aleda lost a sense of the trail. She stopped for a minute, rubbing her sweaty forehead and shooing away mosquitoes. Then a rustle and a dry brushing sound caught her attention. Was that the thud of a hoof? She hitched the backpack more firmly onto her shoulder and rounded the curve.

There, standing in a little grove of cedar trees in front of her, was Tracker. Aleda stopped, eased the backpack off her shoulder and retrieved the sugar lumps and the halter.

"Atta boy, good boy, come on old boy," she murmured as she approached the horse, which stood switching his tail. With one hand she held out the sugar, and with the other she slipped the halter over his head. Then she grabbed the rope, hooked it through the halter, and got ready to lead Tracker home.

But wait a minute, she thought. How ridiculous will this look? The entire village already thinks I'm idiotic for rescuing a bad-tempered old horse. I'll be the laughing stock of the entire church – maybe the brunt of jokes made by everyone in the whole municipality – if I'm seen tromping home leading my recalcitrant pet horse.

"No way, Tracker," she said aloud. "You got yourself into this mess. Well, I guess I have to bear some responsibility. But you, my old friend, will have to wait here in the swamp until it's dark so no one will see us going home."

Aleda tied the end of the rope to a stout limb on the biggest cedar tree, then trudged home to retrieve Tracker's winter blanket. She jumped in her van and drove back to the edge of the swamp and retraced her steps, then threw the blanket over Tracker to protect him from the worst of the mosquitoes.

The phone was ringing when Aleda walked back into the house.

"Aleda, it's Dr. Patel calling. I just want to let you know that the dog is doing well and is ready to go home."

"Dr. Patel," Aleda said slowly, "we so appreciate your help, but, the thing is, we just haven't found the owner yet. Would it be possible for you to keep the dog at the clinic for one more day? It would give us another 24 hours to find the owner."

Aleda heard the hesitancy in the veterinarian's voice. "It's just that with the long weekend there's no one here at the clinic. We're on call, of course, for emergencies."

Aleda took a deep breath. "Would you let Roy or Savannah or me go into the clinic to check on the dog?"

"No, no, that won't be necessary." Did Aleda hear Dr. Patel sigh? "But please, the dog needs to be out tomorrow. We have two dogs coming in for surgery on Monday and we need the space."

"Thank you, thank you."

Okay, Savannah, we need to work some magic here.

Aleda picked up the mug of cold tea, added two ice cubes and headed to her office. Sitting down at her computer she pulled her open Bible toward her and sat staring at the opening words of her sermon on the computer screen. Why do I always leave this to the last minute? she demanded of herself, impatient and irritated by what she considered her most annoying character flaw. The words wouldn't come. Aleda sat staring at the screen for a few more minutes then suddenly stood up. All she could think about was her horse tied to a cedar tree in a mosquito-infested swamp. Waiting for darkness to descend made her anxious and restless. Aleda walked out of her office to the top step of the back veranda. She pulled on her red boots, walked to the shed, grabbed a fork, and began piling manure from Tracker's stall into a wheelbarrow. When she had finished, she cut open a fresh bale of straw and spread it around the stall. She swept clean the floor in front of the oat bin and brushed the cobwebs off the window. Seeing that it was still light outside, Aleda wheeled the manure out into her backyard and shoveled it onto her perennial beds, just as she had seen Roy do a few days before.

By the time Aleda had finished, the sky had begun to darken. She returned to the house, set her boots outside the back door, and walked upstairs to the bathroom. Her dirty clothes fell to the floor as she turned on the hot shower. After patting herself dry and towel-drying her hair, she changed into black jeans, a black long-sleeved shirt and black running shoes. I'm ready when you are Tracker, she said to herself, and began to hike down the road once again, heading to the swamp.

Tracker stood with his head bowed, swishing his tail back and forth. To Aleda, he looked despondent and forlorn. Ha, she thought a little aggressively, maybe you learned your lesson, old soul. She untied the rope and led Tracker along the edge of the swamp, up onto the gravel shoulder and toward his shed. If this weren't so ridiculous, Aleda thought, it would be funny, but at least we're not doing it in broad daylight. Really, though, how *can* one horse make so much noise just walking along?

Aleda felt an anxious ripple in her stomach, worried that people would be out walking their dogs or sitting in their front porches, but to her relief she met no one. She and Tracker walked through to the backyard and, without any urging at all, Tracker entered his stall. Aleda bumped open the oat bin, filled the silver scoop, and dumped the ground meal into Tracker's bowl.

"That's it, old boy," she said, giving him a little slap on the rump with the flat of her hand as he began eating. When Aleda had settled once again in front of her computer, it was after ten.

I've got to finish this sermon, she thought. But now, instead of feeling the pressure of a deadline, she sighed in relief. She had managed to lead Tracker home to safety without anyone noticing.

What she didn't know was that half the people in the village had peered out from behind their curtains at the sound of a horse's clip-clop on Main Street and muttered to themselves, "Why is that daft woman taking her old horse out for a walk at this time of night?"

3

Interruptions

I T WAS ALEDA'S CUSTOM TO RISE early on Sunday mornings to open all the church doors. First she unlocked the heavy wooden front doors with the large century-old key. On warm days, she hooked the doors back to let in fresh morning air. Then she strolled to the west side of the church and unlocked the door by the parking lot. At the back of the church she unlocked the third door, the one by the cemetery, the door that opened into the church kitchen.

Aleda felt a private satisfaction from this habit of walking alone and opening the church doors on Sunday morning. It was as if she were flinging open the doors in an elegant sweep of hospitality, inviting the world into the church. Or maybe she was letting out all the stuffiness that sometimes came with church.

Even though she aspired to introduce the members to the third millennium, and to give the old church a refreshing and breezy atmosphere, Aleda was also aware of how deeply she appreciated history, and how much she carried the past in her bones. She knew with certainty who she was. As the only child of Hungarian immigrants, she had grown up on the stories of the robust and independent Magyars who had swept in from the Asian steppes 1,100 years before and settled in the Carpathian Basin. These people, *her* people, were determined and brave, protective of their language and their ways. These Magyars, her spiritual and physical ancestors, kept alive a desire in the young to wear traditional clothing, to cook in the old ways, and to tell and re-tell the stories of the Hungarian people's revolt against Soviet control in 1956. Yes, if there was anyone who appreciated history and tradition, it was Aleda. Had she not won the church history prize three years in a row while studying at the seminary?

At the same time, Aleda realized that the village young people had a very different appreciation of history and tradition. She wondered what they knew or understood about World War I or World War II or even the Vietnam War. She was quite sure, too, that the young people did not share her personal angst over the terrorist attacks on September 11 which, the previous year, had crashed down the World Trade Centre towers in New York City and hit the Pentagon. The young people may have heard about wars and disasters and no doubt saw images on television, but these teenagers, Aleda felt quite sure, lived with intensity in the hopefulness of present time, and looked with eagerness to the future, untroubled by the past.

Or was that true? she wondered. What about Dwayne? When Aleda looked at Dwayne, she saw a troubled soul. Dwayne: a pudgy, shy, and uncommunicative boy who seemed to be unhappy. No one knew where Dwayne's parents were, or how it came to be that he lived with his grandmother. Am I the only one who worries about Dwayne? Aleda wondered. Clearly it is my duty, my responsibility, to help him in some way. But how?

Doris Blanchett walked up the church steps, carrying a vase filled with blousy red peonies.

"Good morning, Aleda," she called out cheerfully. "What a glorious day! Will you look at these peonies? A new early variety that blooms in May, imagine that. First of the season! Aren't they beauties? I'll just set them here on the altar."

Doris settled the fragrant bouquet in the middle of the communion table and adjusted a drooping bloom. Aleda nodded and smiled but winced inwardly. She remembered the voice of her former systematic theology professor declaring, "In the Reformed tradition, we do not have an altar. We have a communion table. *Communion table.* In Reformed tradition we leave the table bare. *Bare,*" he would repeat, with a sweep of his hand, as though clearing off a table. "When we celebrate the Lord's Supper, that, *that* is the only time we dress the table! Then we bring out the polished silver and the snow white, crisply-ironed linen and, in love and respect, we drape the elements that are central to our Reformed faith. The communion table is to remain *bare* except for the glorious feast of our Lord!"

Aleda sighed and thought, sorry professor. She glanced at the bouquet of peonies on the communion table. It had seemed like theological pettiness to object when the Ladies Guild had purchased a bronze Celtic cross and a green and gold liturgical cloth to decorate the communion table. Now it seemed the communion table had also become the repository for flowers.

Turning toward the pulpit, Aleda slipped her hand into the side pocket of her cassock and checked to see that she had tucked a paper tissue into it. Grinning in a small secretive way, she wondered for the hundredth time why preaching made her nose run. Someday when I meet a psychiatrist at a cocktail party... As she felt for the tissue, she touched the envelope she had grabbed on her way out the front door that morning. Someone had left it tucked into the frame of the porch window. She glanced at the envelope and ripped it open.

Rev Vastag:

I came by to get a report on a speeding car that caused an accident. I understand a dog was injured and you witnessed the incident. Since you weren't home, perhaps you might call the police number again when you are free.

Sincerely, Constable Neil Brennan

Aleda inhaled sharply. In her search for Tracker yesterday she had forgotten that a police officer was to drop in for her statement.

"Aleda! Is something wrong?" Savannah looked up the side aisle where she was setting up the music stands.

"No. No. Just something important that I neglected to do, but I will see to it after worship."

Savannah's eyebrows were drawn together in worry. "Have you heard anything more about the dog's owner?"

"Not a thing, unfortunately. You?"

Savannah shook her head. "I'm starting to get really worried. I mean, what will we do if we can't find the owner?"

Aleda patted the girl's arm and said, "Don't worry. I'm sure it will work out," but privately she fussed. They had until 5 p.m. to find the owner of that dog.

Everything was ready for worship. People from the village and families from the farms around Milburn Corners had arrived and stood chatting on the front lawn before settling into the pews where many of their parents and grandparents had also sat. The youth took their places behind their instruments. Suddenly Savannah jumped up from her stool and clapped her hands together.

"Oh! I'm so stupid! I forgot to pick up Dwayne. I'm sorry Aleda. I was so busy thinking about that dog that I totally forgot to get Dwayne! Do I have time to run to his house and get him?"

The youth in the praise band and Dwayne were the only teen-agers who lived in the village. Savannah, with persistent cheerful-ness and energy, had taken Dwayne under her wing. She made sure that Dwayne was included in the conversation while they waited for the bus and lent him CDs of her favourite pop singers.

When Savannah and Aleda developed the idea to form a praise band for the church, Savannah had organized her friends. She and Jacob were in the high school band. Michael took guitar lessons and was quite good. Ashley didn't play an instrument, but she could play tambourine or shakers. As for Victoria, well…she has a great singing voice. There was just the problem of how to include Dwayne.

In the end, because Savannah insisted on picking him up, Dwayne agreed to be the sound technician, setting up the micro-phones, turning on and monitoring the sound system. After a few weeks, Aleda had asked Dwayne if he would also consider another small but important Sunday morning task. Would he ring the church bell?

For some time – perhaps for more than a century – the church members in Milburn Corners had a tradition of ringing the large iron bell five minutes before worship. It was a way of signalling that worship was about to begin. It was a way of calling in the straggling groups from the lawn outside. It was a nostalgic link with the past. To the people of Milburn Corners, it would not seem like Sunday without the pealing of the church bell at ten twenty-five.

Now, as Savannah looked at Aleda, anxious for permission to pedal her bike quickly down Main Street to get Dwayne, Aleda glanced at her watch and shook her head.

"Only two minutes left before it's time for worship," she said. "I'll ask the usher to ring the bell today."

When people had settled into their pews, Aleda smiled and welcomed them. She explained the theme of worship for that day, then read some announcements that were relevant to their life as a community. Then Aleda asked, "Are there other announcements that anyone would like to make?"

Immediately, she noticed that she had goofed. Grace had reminded her to announce the Tuesday meeting of the Ladies Guild, but Aleda had forgotten. Well, she thought, feeling a flush creep up her neck and into her cheeks, every woman in this congregation knows that the Ladies Guild meets on the third Tuesday of the month, and every woman in the church knows that this is the meeting when they finalize plans for the annual strawberry social. After all, Aleda thought indignantly, the strawberry social has been going on for years.

There was a stir of movement from the far side of the church. Aleda watched as Grace rose from the pew where she always sat, under the old clock. Aleda groaned inwardly, then slowly sank down into the red upholstered chair behind the pulpit.

"Now ladies," Grace began, "I notice that our minister forgot to make an announcement about the Ladies Guild meeting this Tuesday at seven-thirty sharp. It's very important that all ladies are present because we have to keep working on the annual strawberry social. I was just up at Spence's farm this week and the strawberries are in bloom. It promises to be a good season for strawberries." Without pausing Grace continued, "Now, I know it's been the custom that I chair the strawberry social, but that doesn't need to be the case. If any of you would like to take over, you just need to say so. Now, in the past, Margaret has always done the coleslaw, and I'm sure she could use some help with chopping all that cabbage. And we usually get the sliced ham from Georgian Meat Market, so I think we'll just do that again this year, unless somebody has a different idea. It's a good idea to pick it up when it's on sale, because the meat is our biggest cost. We asked the bakery in Owen Sound to donate 12 dozen rolls again, so we will need someone to pick them up. And Doris always makes the budayda salad."

Aleda sat staring into the empty space at the back of the pulpit. Why does this entire village pronounce *potato* as *budayda*? she wondered for the hundredth time. If I were to preach a sermon on potatoes, and pronounce it very distinctly as *po-tay-toe* a dozen or a hundred times, would people learn to pronounce it correctly? The problem is, Aleda pondered, I can't think of one reference to potatoes in the Bible. What on earth would I use as the text for the day?

"Oh, and I almost forgot, there's the matter of the strawberries, too." Grace drew out the word strawberries into three long distinct syllables. "We always pick them up on the Saturday morning of the strawberry social at Spence's farm on the town line, so we will need a volunteer to collect them and then stem them and cut them in half. And, of course, there are lots of the younger women who are now working out." ("Working out" was the village euphemism, Aleda had learned, for women who worked at jobs outside the home.) "The younger women can bring two pounds of butter, or supply the serviettes or some cream for whipping. So make sure you come out to the meeting on Tuesday night. There are a lot of things to be worked out, and it's important that we make money to keep this church going."

Grace sat down with a plop.

Aleda had a quick desperate thought. How could she possibly transition that announcement time into a worshipful ambiance, a time of grace, awe, wonder, joy, and mystery? But as she sat in that liminal moment, to her delight the band picked up their instruments and began to play the soft sweet melody of "Spirit, Spirit of Gentleness" and Victoria's crystal-clear soprano filled the sanctuary like the voice of an angel.

After the service, Aleda shared coffee and muffins in the church basement with the people she was growing to know and love. She then returned to the sanctuary and gathered up her sermon notes and Bible from the top of the pulpit, and turned off the lights. She stood for a few minutes in the empty church, still warm from its host of worshippers. She felt suddenly too tired to move. Why is it, she wondered, that I am so weary after the Sunday service? I could work all day in the hot sun and not be as tired as when I finish leading a worship service. She shrugged to ease the tension in her neck, pulled the wooden doors closed, locked them with the heavy key, and crossed the lawn to the front door of her home. She kicked her dress shoes into the hall closet, padded down the hall to the kitchen, and slapped together a peanut butter sandwich, not bothering to cut it. Then she walked to the front door, locked it, and set up her custom-made sign.

If you are looking for Aleda Vastag
and see this sign,
it means that Aleda is unavailable.
Knocking on the door will not help.
Please call again.

When Aleda had first come to the village, she had complained to Robert in a good-natured way that although she appreciated how the village people were so friendly and helpful, they never seemed to leave her alone. Inevitably, someone knocked on the door to tell her about a parishioner who needed a pastoral visit, or did she need a bushel of pears? Would she be interested in buying a ticket to the fall fair?

"Well, why don't you get a sign that would signal to your congregation that you need some space and privacy?" Robert replied.

In the end, that is what she had done.

Climbing the stairs to her bedroom, munching the last of her peanut butter sandwich, she changed clothes and stretched out on her bed. A stray dog to settle, a visit to make at the doctor's house, a call to the police station, the strawberry social; but first, a nap.

Her limbs felt heavy with fatigue but sleep eluded her. Her mind raced from one thing to another. Who was to pay the vet bill? Should she call into the doctor's house today or leave that visit until tomorrow? Where had she put the note with the phone number for the police station? And then, there was that matter of the strawberries.

Last week Savannah had proposed a way to raise money for the high school band trip to the music festival in Ottawa. The idea was simple. The Ladies Guild needed strawberries. Her friends needed money for their band trip. Savannah would persuade Spence's Strawberry Farm to allow the teenagers to pick strawberries at half price. They would then sell the berries to the Ladies Guild at full price, the amount they would pay Spence's farm anyway. The youth would wash, stem, and cut the berries in half on the morning of the strawberry social. All in all, it seemed to Savannah to be a win-win situation. But Aleda, with years of Ladies Guild experience in her background, had a sense of just how fast this proposal could go wrong. Sighing, the sleepless Aleda swung her legs over the side of the bed and stooped to lace on her running shoes. What she needed was a stroll through the cemetery and a brisk walk on one of the country roads.

Shortly after Aleda had arrived in Milburn Corners her friend Margie had driven north from Hamilton for a visit. Aleda proposed a drive through the countryside, a quick visit to Owen Sound, and a spin out to Sauble Beach, but before starting out, she took Margie on a tour through the church and shed. When they stepped out of the shed door near the cemetery gate, Aleda had exclaimed with a grand gesturing wave, "Look at that, Margie! Isn't that the most beautiful cemetery you've ever seen?"

Margie shook her head and said, smiling, "Are you serious?"

"But look!" Aleda had exclaimed. "Such an incredible archway into the burial grounds," and both women stood gazing at the ornate iron grill with the words *Community of Saints* written on it in raised lettering. When Aleda moved toward the archway as if to enter, Margie had grasped her arm.

"Wait! Doesn't it give you the creeps to wander around the graves and to have a cemetery practically in your backyard?"

Aleda had laughed. "Oh good heavens, no. I find it comforting and peaceful. It helps me remember the continuity between the living and the dead. Besides, there are such interesting things on tombstones. Do you know what I found on one?"

Margie shook her head.

"In 1894, a mother called Maisie buried a daughter named Sarah. The baby had lived only a few days. Then, in 1895, she buried another little daughter also called Sarah. And, guess what? In 1896, there was a third baby, also Sarah. The next year, the mother was buried beside her three little Sarahs. Amazing, don't you think?" Aleda folded her arms and looked through the archway, swaying a little. "Maybe the mother died of a broken heart."

"Perhaps," Margie had replied dryly, "they might have had the common sense to call the babies by different names. The name Sarah seems to have brought them bad luck."

Aleda had asked Roy how it came to be that the cemetery was named *Community of Saints*.

"Not sure, really," Roy had replied. "The thing I know is that my dear wife is buried there, and just about everyone in the village and from the farms around here have a loved one buried here. It's a great comfort to walk in here or sit down on that bench under the oak tree and feel close to them."

"Ah, yes, I see. Community of saints – the saints on earth and the saints in heaven. The living and the dead."

"Oh, they're not dead. We just can't see them for a while."

Aleda wandered among the gravestones reading names and dates, pausing to reflect on a verse here and there. Although her own parents were buried in Hamilton, Aleda liked to imagine that this was their final resting place. She often sat on the wooden bench under the century-old oak tree in the centre of the cemetery, re-membering happy times with her parents. She ran her hand over the polished surface of the wooden bench, noting that someone took great care to keep it in pristine condition. Once she had said to Roy, "This cemetery is not only beautiful, it's also a place to restore the soul."

"Land's sake Aleda," Roy had responded. "You said that so true."

When she felt her energy return, Aleda walked out of the cem-etery toward the centre of the village and up the hill toward the doctor's house. If I see signs of life, I'll pop in, but if there's no car, I'll walk by and mind my own business, she thought. As she rounded the top of the hill she could see that the driveway was empty. She admitted to herself that she felt both relieved and annoyed. Hav-ing to engage with a stranger might deplete her fragile Sunday afternoon energy, but if she avoided a call today the task would have to stay on her to-do worry list.

As she walked past the driveway, Aleda noticed someone stretched out on a lounge chair in the shady arbour at the back of the house. The tall blond woman whom Aleda had seen through the window on Friday night sat reading a magazine, her crutches propped beside her. Aleda paused, then strolled up the driveway toward the arbour and cleared her throat. The woman looked up, startled.

44

"Hello," Aleda called out. "I'm sorry to disturb you."

"No, no, please." The woman gestured to an empty chair on the other side of the arbour. "I'm afraid I'm not able to…."

"No, no, really. Please, please, don't try to get up." Aleda walked toward the woman, her hand outstretched. "I'm Aleda Vastag, the minister of the local community church."

"Oh, I see," the woman responded. She paused and then gestured again to the chair. "Please sit down. I'm Laura Browning, and as you can see, I have a broken ankle."

"Yes, I'm sorry," Aleda said, but the woman waved her hand as if she didn't need or want to hear expressions of sympathy from someone who was a stranger to her.

After chatting with Laura for a few minutes, Aleda said in a cheerful voice that did not match her mood, "Well, I must be on my way. Sunday afternoon walk." The brief conversation with the woman had felt uncomfortable – and Aleda realized that she had intruded where she was unwelcome. She regretted coming up the driveway.

"I wish you a speedy recovery," Aleda said as she turned to leave.

"Oh, is there something you came for? A donation for the church perhaps? My parents were technically Anglican but we were never churchgoers. I believe my father made regular donations to the local church though. Did you come for a donation?"

"Oh, no, no," Aleda assured her, shaking her head. "I just popped in to say hello."

Then, as if it came from someplace outside herself completely, Aleda heard herself say, "Well, we do have this strawberry social coming up at the church on June 22. Would you donate two pounds of butter?"

Aleda walked toward the town line. Two pounds of butter, she berated herself. Where had that come from? Asking a stranger to donate two pounds of butter to a strawberry social she had no interest in and certainly would not attend. Aleda scuffed the loose gravel on the side of the road with the toes of her running shoes, angry with herself.

In her short conversation she *had* learned, though, that Laura Browning was a high school teacher from Toronto, that she had broken her ankle playing basketball with students, and that a friend had driven her to Milburn Corners but had returned to Toronto. Laura was the younger child of the former community doctor, and the house to which Laura had returned had been unoccupied since Laura's mother died four years ago. Laura had not explained why she had come to Milburn Corners with her broken ankle.

The sun shone on Aleda's face and arm and hinted at the warmth to come. It would be, as all the people around reminded her, a great season for strawberries. But the kindliness of the sunshine did not alter Aleda's mood. As she walked along, she realized that she had been feeling discouraged, depressed, and vulnerable, and didn't know why. But then it came to her. That's it, she thought. I've always considered my ministry to be good and worthy, but lately – it was painful for her to admit this – she had come to doubt the value of what she was doing with her life. It seemed to her that others – firefighters, police, nurses, even ordinary citizens – were doing things that made a vital difference. Heck, even Margie as a city librarian helps people choose books that change their perspective and turn their lives around. And what would we do without the constant work of the farmers? These farms feed the world, and what do I do? I'm caught up in fussing over strawberry socials and building bridges between the generations in my church.

As she walked along another painful reality formed in her mind: the trouble with Dwayne. Dwayne has come to symbolize my powerlessness, she thought. I want to help him because I can see that he is so unhappy, but I don't know how to give him what he needs. I try to reach out to him, but it is never enough. Dwayne, the most unlikeable of teenagers.

Aleda walked past the Richardson's tidy farm. Rail fences surrounded a front pasture full of grazing Holstein cows, and she could see a chain link fence around the barn protecting a flock of sheep. Then she noticed two properties farther south, almost across the road from one another.

On her left was a weathered clapboard house set well back from the road. To the side of the house were small huts that might once have housed chickens. The barn, long neglected, had caved in on one end, exposing bales of blackened hay. It was impossible to see if the house was abandoned, but where there had been a lawn there was now long grass and Scotch thistles. In the laneway leading to the house the grass had grown so long between the ruts that it would make a rustling rumble under any vehicle that entered.

The property on the opposite side of the road had a small old barn, patched along the side with new wood. The house, a red brick Ontario cottage, looked like most of the farm houses in the region, but without any additions. It stood alone, lost in an expanse of newly planted cornfields. Aleda glanced from side to side at the two properties. *Perhaps it's time to turn around and walk back home*, she thought.

As she was making up her mind, two things happened. From the laneway with the long grass, she watched in astonishment as a little boy began to walk, then run, toward her. At the same time she observed some movement from the laneway of the farm house on the opposite side of the road. She swung her head around and saw an old grey truck rumble down the lane and turn toward her.

The boy, his brow sweaty, stopped in front of Aleda, gasping for air. She stood gazing at his dirty T-shirt and red shorts, a size too big, which he tugged up with his left hand.

"I think Martin knows where my dog is. Do you know where it is?" he demanded, breathing quickly. "I've been looking for my dog since Friday." Aleda was taken aback by the assertiveness of this small child.

The pickup had stopped beside them and the man, who Aleda now recognized as Martin, jumped out of the cab.

"Hello again," he said, smiling at Aleda. "I guess Callum here told you that we think we have found out who owns the dog we rescued Friday."

Aleda shook her head and glanced at the derelict house, turning back as Martin said to both of them, "Well, what are we waiting for? It's time we get that dog back home where it belongs. Hop in."

How is it, Aleda thought as she slammed shut the truck door behind her, that I could be walking along a country road on a warm Sunday afternoon of the long weekend in May, brooding over morose things, and a minute later find myself in the cab of a rusty truck with a man I barely know and a forceful, dirty little boy, and we are hurtling down a dusty country road to fetch an injured, pregnant, mongrel dog that has a large unpaid vet bill.

"Are you sure you'll be able to look after Buddy until she's mended?" Martin was asking Callum.

So the dog's name was Buddy. Slightly odd name for a female dog about to have pups.

"Oh, yes. I know how to care for Buddy, I do. Maybe my dad will help."

Aleda glanced sideways at Martin who was staring straight ahead at the road.

"I was wondering," Martin said slowly, "if it might be better if we made a bed for your dog in my back kitchen. Buddy will have to stay very quiet until the broken bone is healed. I could keep her still and comfortable in the daytime. You'll be in school all day and won't be able to do that, right?"

Martin glanced down, tilting his head, trying to see how the boy was responding to his suggestion. When Callum didn't answer, Martin said, "You could come across to look after her every morning and every night. You could keep her water bowl filled and feed her. What do you think of that idea?"

Callum still said nothing, but Aleda could see that he was considering the suggestion.

"I don't think my dad would like that," he answered finally.

"Let me talk to him," Martin said. "Maybe your dad will agree if I tell him that I will pay the vet bill."

Aleda stared at Martin. This sunny bright Sunday was not proceeding as she had anticipated. Not at all.

As Aleda, Martin, and Callum prepared to leave the clinic, they saw that it was impossible for all of them to fit into the cab for the return trip.

"I'll drive the dog home," Martin suggested to Aleda. "You and Callum wait here for me and I'll come back to pick you up." But the dog was licking Callum's hand and the boy refused to leave the dog's side.

Martin shrugged. "I'll take the boy and dog home and then come back for you."

"If you don't mind, I'll start walking home. It will do me good."

She had walked only a few minutes when a passing car slowed to a stop. It was Roy.

"Land's sake!" he called out. "What on earth are you doing walking so far from the village? Hop in. I'll give you a lift home."

"Thanks, Roy. I appreciate the offer, but it's such a beautiful day and I need a good long walk."

"Well, suit yourself. Are you sure?"

Aleda gave him a wave and said, "See you later, Roy. And thanks for stopping."

Within ten minutes, Martin had returned. He made a U-turn and pulled the truck up beside her. "Hop in," he called out, reaching over to open the truck door for her. "My wife would be appalled to hear that I'm picking up pretty hitchhikers," he grinned.

It was late afternoon when Martin dropped Aleda at her home. She walked up the steps into the porch, unlaced her dusty running shoes, rolled off her socks and tossed them into the closet, then sank down with a weary groan into her wicker chair. She sat for a few minutes, feeling a little dazed, re-living the day with all its twists and turns. Then she walked into the kitchen, picked up the phone, and left a message sharing the good news about the dog for Savannah.

I know what I'll do now, she thought. I'll cook myself a Hungarian dinner.

Tonight Aleda longed for breaded meat. She remembered her mother making *rántott hús*, three bowl dinner, so many times. She dug around in the freezer, pulled out two pork cutlets, and set them to defrost in the microwave. While they thawed she sprinkled flour in a flat bowl, beat two eggs in a second bowl, then poured a generous pile of dried bread crumbs into a third. She patted dry the cutlets, flattened them with a meat pounder, then dipped them into flour, then egg, and finally into the breadcrumbs. She slipped the chops into a pan of shimmering hot oil on the stovetop. As the rich aroma of *rántott hús* filled the kitchen, Aleda inhaled and smiled, then started on the bread fried with garlic.

Aleda set the table with a red cloth and napkin and reached into the cupboard where she kept a few bottles of Merlot. She rustled around in one of the kitchen drawers until she found a candle and matches. Then, when all was ready, Aleda settled in her chair and bowed her head in a moment of gratitude for her meal: two breaded pork cutlets, fried garlic bread, and, to ease her conscience, some slices of fresh cucumber. She took the first bite. Delicious, absolutely delicious. Raising her glass, she said aloud, "Thank you, Mama. God bless you, Mama."

Aleda had almost finished her first cutlet when the doorbell rang. "Damn," she said loudly, setting down her fork. "Can I not be left in peace to enjoy my dinner?"

She rose and padded to the front door in her bare feet. Opening the screen door, she gasped. Standing on the front step was a police officer in full uniform.

"I'm sorry to startle you."

"Startle me? Officer, you scared the shit out of me," Aleda stammered. "Oh sorry, sorry. Pardon the language."

The officer shuffled on the step, his mouth open. "I didn't know ministers knew words like that," he said, smiling a little now. "I'm out on patrol and saw your van, so thought that I should drop by and get that statement about the accident and the dog. I'm Constable Neil Brennan."

"Oh of course, of course. Please come in." Aleda turned toward the kitchen, but when she pulled out a kitchen chair for the officer, he began to apologize.

"Oh, I'm so sorry. I'm interrupting your dinner." His eyes lingered on the pork cutlet and garlic bread, then on the wine bottle and candle. "Glad to see that you know how to…" His hand swept out over the scene.

"Cook?" Aleda said.

"No," the officer said, smiling again. "That you know how to eat in style. Me, mostly I gobble something down in front of the television. It's not good."

Aleda tilted her head, noticing the faint trace of Irish lilt in his voice.

When Constable Brennan had finished asking questions, he snapped shut his small book and said, smiling again, "This should make an interesting report. No description of car, no license plate, no report of damage other than a stray dog's broken leg. Just lots of village witnesses."

"I'm sorry! I'm sorry!" Aleda was now genuinely embarrassed. "I've wasted your time and I apologize. It's just that someone suggested we call." Her mind flashed to Grace.

"Hey," the officer said, leaning forward, "in your line of work, don't you have times when people completely waste *your* time?"

Aleda looked up into his brown eyes framed by laughter lines. For some reason that she did not understand, she felt an overwhelming urge to blurt out the worries that had plagued her of late; her unease over whether her work had any real significance. Surely, she thought, being an officer of the law must be a tremendously meaningful career.

Before she could say anything though, he said, "Sometimes those wasted moments just turn out to be the best things that have ever happened."

He slowly rose to his feet, reached out to offer a handshake to Aleda, and said in a light-hearted voice, "Constable Neil Brennan at your service, ma'am. If there is anything you need in the way of protection, Reverend Vastag, please call on me."

"Aleda. Please call me Aleda."

"I'm sorry to have interrupted your dinner."

"No, really. It's me who is sorry for not being more helpful."

"Then we're both sorry," the constable said, laughing, and he hesitated for a moment as if what he really wanted to do was to sit down at the table and share dinner and wine by candlelight.

Aleda watched as the police car disappeared over the knoll, then headed back into the kitchen. As she was lifting the re-warmed food from the microwave, the telephone rang. Sighing, Aleda squinted at the call display. She expected to see Grace Stone's name, as she had no doubt seen the police cruiser in the driveway. Instead, she was surprised to see that the number belonged to Savannah's family.

"Hello, Aleda," Savannah said in a rushed, excited voice. "I hope I haven't interrupted your dinner."

Aleda held her breath for a moment. "No. No. It's fine." She picked up her wine glass and took a sip.

"That's absolutely cool that you found the owner of the dog. I'm so excited. Is everything okay then?"

After Aleda told her the story about Martin, Callum, and the dog, Savannah added, "Oh, by the way, the girls and I were wondering if you would like to hang out with us tomorrow at Sauble Beach?"

Aleda set down the wine glass. Her girls – her wonderful, responsible girls who buoyed her spirits and gave her such hope for the future – were inviting her to hang out with them. Aleda was not naive about this. She recognized that none of their parents were free to drive them to the beach and they needed a ride. Still, they *had* invited her.

"I'll pick all of you up at your house at 10 a.m.," she said, and hung up the phone. Then she turned back to her meal.

4

Beach

OR ONCE, ALEDA WAKENED EARLY and hopped out of bed, the anticipation of going to the beach for the day flooding her with energy. She fed Tracker his morning oats and looked up at the sky. Sunshine filtered through the spruce trees, but Aleda could also see wispy bands of stratus cloud through the limbs. She heard Roy's voice in her head: East wind brings rain. Aleda crouched down and peered through the branches at Roy's flag, which rippled in the wind. Aleda looked overhead again. Sunshine and mostly clear sky. She turned back into the kitchen and gathered bread and butter, ham and cheese, pickles and potato chips. She stacked soft drinks into a cooler.

Savannah, Ashley, and Victoria were waiting for her when she swung into the paved driveway of Savannah's home. The girls flung their backpacks into the rear of the van and they all set out for Sauble Beach on Lake Huron, excited and full of chatter.

Following directions from the girls, she drove to their favourite spot and parked. Then they walked together, clutching bags, the cooler, and a blanket, toward the water's edge. Aleda spread the blanket on a dry stretch of the wide sandy beach and noticed that the wind had picked up from the east. Savannah and Ashley, eager to be first in the water even though it was still chilly, whipped off their sweatshirts and dashed toward the water's edge. Victoria, always more shy and hesitant, stood with Aleda on the beach watching as Savannah and Ashley ran into the water, squealed, turned around, and ran out, then turned back again to the lake, jumping as each wave splashed higher on their bare thighs.

Aleda stared. She thought of these girls as innocent, fragile, and child-like, but now, seeing them in their tell-all swimsuits, she felt very protective of them. For a fleeting moment she wondered if she might have been able to be a mother after all, had that been her lot in life. What on earth do parents think when they see their daughters in swimsuits like these?

After braving the cold lake water, the girls lay covered in towels, eating the ham and cheese sandwiches that Aleda had prepared. Aleda was pouring herself a cup of coffee from the thermos when she felt the first moisture on her skin. The rain began as a mist, and as the clouds darkened, bigger drops arrived, soft and gentle. The girls began scooping up shorts and towels, leftover sandwiches, the blanket, and the cooler.

For a few minutes, the girls and Aleda sat in the van, pulling on shorts and shirts, eating the sandwiches, and watching the windshield wipers go back and forth. "Not much point in staying on," Aleda said, looking up at the sky. "This rain looks as if it has settled in for the day." She waited a moment. "Is there anything else you want to do on a rainy afternoon?" she asked, rather longing for her chair on the porch, her novel, and a mug of warm tea.

"We could go shopping," Savannah said, brightly. "The malls are open in Owen Sound."

In the early evening, after depositing the girls on Savannah's driveway, Aleda headed home, shaking her head and smiling a little. Well, not how I might have opted to spend a free day, but then how else do you find out what's important to teenage girls? You listen to their conversation; you hear what they laugh about; you drag along from store to store looking at the watches, jewellery, and clothes they admire.

Later, when she told Margie about the day with the girls, Aleda said, "You know what amazes me most about these kids? How much they talk about their parents. I thought teenagers were supposed to hate their parents."

"Well," Margie said rather smugly, for she had two teenage daughters and believed that this gave her the right to be an expert on young people, "they push back against their parents all the time. It's their way of becoming themselves. But I sometimes think that my girls need me now more than when they were pre-schoolers. They like me to be home when they get in from school, even though they just plunk their bags in the hall and go right to their rooms. I think there is a certain stability that comes from knowing Mom and Dad are still there for them."

"You could be right," Aleda said, although she doubted her friend's words. "It just surprises me."

And her mind went to Dwayne. If it's true that parents are so important in the lives of teenagers, what does it mean for Dwayne that there are no parents to butt up against, to argue with, to be there for him when he needs them? Perhaps his grandmother fills that role. But even as this thought came into Aleda's mind, she dismissed it. Dwayne's grandmother couldn't replace the two parents who seem to have disappeared from his life.

It was the first time in 24 hours that Aleda had thought of Dwayne. And now her memory of that day last March that Dwayne had erupted in church was as clear as if it were yesterday.

It had been a sunny, crisp morning, a day when the remaining snow lay pocked with patches where melted snow had frozen over during the night, forming crystal patterns. Though the ground was cold, there was softness in the air that hinted of spring. It was a bright and hopeful morning, perhaps not the best morning to deliver the punchy sermon she had prepared, but still, a day when hope would triumph. Or so Aleda had anticipated.

Earlier in the week she had smoothed out her copy of the Owen Sound *Sun Times* and set it aside. Was she the only person who was worrying about the war in Afghanistan? Was she the only one who had just set aside the daily paper after reading that Operation Ana-conda had killed 500 Taliban and Al-Qaeda fighters? Did this worry and scare anyone but her?

Aleda sat down at her computer, ready to begin her sermon. War, wiith many of its victims innocent and young, was something that most people wanted to ignore. But how could anyone in North America ignore the impact of hostility when both Canada and the United States were so heavily involved in war activity? Was it easy to pretend that it simply wasn't happening because it was far away and out of sight?

Ultimately, Aleda concluded, it comes down to one ponderous, perplexing question, a theological question of great importance: Why does God allow suffering? Why do bad things happen? Why are innocent people, even babies, killed? And where is God in all of this?

In seminary, she and her classmates had struggled through a course called Recent Theodicy. It was a fancy term for the study of how contemporary theologians attempt to explain why evil exists and where God is in the midst of suffering. Their study had taken them through many painful twists and turns with a major focus on the events of the Holocaust. At the time, perhaps because she and her classmates had been unsettled by this course of study, they be-gan to make jokes about theodicy. When there was not enough hot water for showers in their ancient dormitory, they would call out, "It's that old theodicy question. Why does God allow suffering?" Or when the meal in the great hall cafeteria was soggy, grey, and unappetizing, someone would say, with a laugh, "It's that theodicy question. Where is God when we suffer?"

But then, as now, Aleda understood that this was not a laugh-ing matter. Poised in front of her computer, Aleda recognized that her parishioners wondered about this question in a similar way. Why was one of the McNally twins born with cerebral palsy and not the other? Why is it that the Weyburn family just seems to have one tragedy after another? How do we make sense of evil and suffering and God's care in the midst of hardship?

That Sunday Aleda read out the scriptures and then began her sermon in a tender and ponderous voice.

"These scriptures today point to one of the most difficult questions that human beings have to face. Why is there suffering in the world, and where is God in the midst of suffering?"

Although Aleda herself loved to grapple with these grand questions, she realized that it was important to express hope – not a naive and simple hope, although for some people that seemed to work too, but a deep, strong hope that comes from believing in the creative expanding love of God, from believing in a God whose love triumphs over hate and war and torture, in having confidence in a God whose very nature is acceptance and forgiveness. It was in this manner that Aleda concluded her sermon. She could see her quiet congregation deep in thought in front of her and for perhaps the hundredth time in her ministry she felt humbled and awed by the responsibility she had been given to prepare and deliver sermons. She paused, waiting a moment before announcing a hymn.

Suddenly there was a stir in the back pew where the teenagers sat together when they were not playing music. Dwayne stood up, his face flushed, the plump flesh above his belt shaking. He stood very tall and erect and at the top of his lungs, his voice quivering, sounding as if he might burst into tears, he shouted out, "That's a piece of crap! What do you know about suffering? This is all a pile of shit!"

Before anyone could respond, Dwayne turned and rushed out, leaving a startled congregation looking back at the empty swinging doors.

5

Strawberries

N THE AFTERNOON OF THAT upsetting Sunday when Dwayne had erupted in anger during worship, Aleda drove to Owen Sound to see Robert.

Robert's wife, Patrice, answered the door. As usual, Patrice looked elegant and stunning in a style that was unique to her. Her thick silver hair was swept back into a coiled bun, and she wore a full-length silver lamé dress and black high heels with open toes that revealed scarlet nails. Patrice embraced Aleda and ushered her toward the living room where Robert was reading.

"I'll make some tea for the two of you."

"Oh, tea would be lovely, but I would like you to join us. This is not a confidential matter by any means, and I feel the need for all the guidance and support I can get."

A flush crept into Aleda's cheeks as she heard in her own words how needy she sounded. "I'm so grateful to have the two of you in my life," she added, attempting to cover up her unease.

Aleda started at the beginning – her brooding and concern about escalating terrorism and war, her desire to address the complicated issues of suffering and God's care in the middle of hardship. She talked about her close but complex relationship with the teens in her church and her ongoing work to bridge the gap between the generations. Mostly she talked about Dwayne; his sullen way of managing his life, his obvious struggle of which she knew and understood little. She told Patrice and Robert about Savannah's friendly persistence in keeping Dwayne interested in life and engaged with the other youth in the village.

Aleda described how she had gone around to the little house where Dwayne lived with his grandmother. The old woman, wearing a faded cotton housecoat and carpet slippers, met Aleda at the door but said, "He don't want to see nobody. Don't know what's got into him, but when he come from church, he just went straight to his room and won't come out. Won't even come out for tomato soup, his favourite."

Aleda described how she had left a note telling Dwayne that she was sorry he had been upset by her sermon and that she would like to talk to him about it. She added that Savannah would see him at the bus stop the next morning.

Aleda's words spilled out and Robert nodded and listened. They began to discuss the theology of suffering and Aleda asked Robert if she should have expressed her ideas and beliefs differently, and if that might have avoided the upsetting outburst from Dwayne. Patrice sat without speaking, sipping tea from a rose-patterned bone china cup. Suddenly Aleda burst out, "I just don't know where I went wrong!"

Patrice set down her cup and saucer and reached out to take Aleda's hand between her own. "But my dear, you did everything just right, absolutely right. When someone is hurting they don't care about advice and ideas and theology. They just want you to be there for them. And you were. And you are."

Aleda's eyes filled with tears. She looked at Robert and he nodded, smiling a little. "As usual, my dear wise and beautiful Patrice, you are dead right."

On the Tuesday following the long weekend, as she lay steeling herself to get up and moving, Aleda thought back on that day, and the memory still brought pain. To distract herself, she began to mentally list her responsibilities for the day ahead. In the morning, prepare for a worship service at the retirement home in Owen

Sound. Drive into Owen Sound by 2 p.m. Visit two elderly parishioners who live in the nursing home. Would she have time to slip into her favourite book shop on Second Avenue? Evening ... At that moment, Aleda bolted upright from her warm sheets and remembered that this was the evening of the Ladies Guild meeting and she had promised the youth that she would present their proposal about the strawberries. Aleda sighed and said aloud, "Okay, God. I'm gonna need all the help I can get today."

She crawled from her bed, walked to the window, and stretched. She had lain in bed much later than usual and as she stood there she saw children from the village making their way to school. Aleda recognized Callum as he rounded the corner by the store. He was swinging a plastic grocery bag and wearing the same large red shorts. It's strange that I've never noticed him before, Aleda mused. The child had no jacket to protect him from the drizzle that had continued overnight, but if he was cold and wet he showed no signs of being unhappy.

Aleda was surprised to see movement at the side door of Grace's house. Coming down the driveway, her flowered bib apron already wrapped around her cotton dress, a beige sweater coat around her shoulders, Grace was holding out a foil-wrapped package. Callum grinned up at her and whisked the package into his plastic bag.

How often did this happen? Aleda wondered. And what was in the package? Cookies? Muffins? Butter tarts filled with pecans and raisins? Aleda stood watching until the boy had passed her house, then she turned and padded in her bare feet toward the shower.

When she had dressed, Aleda headed across the backyard to give Tracker his oats. Part way across the lawn, she stopped and sniffed. What was that dreadful smell?

As Aleda arrived in the church basement that evening, she heard the familiar buzz of women's conversation. She took a deep breath and mentally quoted a phrase from her favourite medieval mystic,

Julian of Norwich: "All shall be well, and all shall be well, and all manner of thing shall be well".

The meeting started on time with Aleda leading in prayer. The roll call followed, although why it was necessary was a mystery to Aleda when it was evident that certain people were either there or absent. Sally called for the gathering of the offering and said a prayer over the coins and small bills in the offering plate. It was a source of great pride to the Ladies Guild that they donated all their money – their offerings and their profits from the strawberry social and the Christmas bazaar – to the Board of the church. They wanted no greater reward than to hear the chairman of the Board say at the annual meeting, "Our ladies, bless them, have made a generous donation again to keep our church afloat and pay our minister's salary." Aleda cringed when she heard this. It made her feel as if she were a drain on the church instead of what she longed to be: a beloved pastor, a respected leader, and a spiritual guide.

After the roll call and offering, the Ladies Guild had a program, a time to broaden their perspective and help them experience something beyond the village of Milburn Corners. Murta, who sincerely believed that idle hands are the work of the devil, pulled out her needles and yarn and cast on stitches as she waited for the program to begin. Today's presentation was a story and discussion about one of the most obscure countries in Africa, Burkina Faso. How these women love stories of Africa, Aleda thought a little mercilessly. Perhaps it helped them feel more in control of their own lives to think that others, with their dark skin and primitive ways, were "less fortunate" but, as someone also pointed out – yes, Aleda could count on someone saying it – "they seem happy."

"Now to the business of the meeting," Sally announced. "I suppose we should start with working out the details of the strawberry social. Grace, will you lead the discussion please?"

Everything went as planned. Doris, who had made the potato salad for several years, would make it again, while two women offered to boil eggs, chop the celery and onions, and cook the homemade mayonnaise that, Doris declared, was essential to a proper potato salad. Margaret, who always made the coleslaw, declared that she did not need help chopping the cabbage this year as she had a new food processor and her husband enjoyed using it. Bessie volunteered her husband to pick up the ham, and while he was at it he could swing by the bakery in Owen Sound and pick up the dinner rolls.

There was a small debate about the cooked peas and carrots.

"Surely," someone protested, "we don't need to offer a hot vegetable at a cold plate meal." A discussion followed, some women favouring the idea of hot peas and carrots, some women opposed to it. Grace, who had been silent through the dispute, declared, "The men will expect something hot. So we will have hot peas and carrots as usual."

So I guess that is that, Aleda thought. She sensed that the discussion on peas and carrots took place every year.

"Now the strawberries," Grace said. "We'll get Spence's Berry Farm to deliver them as usual. Who can come early on Saturday morning and help wash and stem the berries?" Grace paused, staring around at the women who had not yet offered to do anything.

Aleda recognized that this was her moment. It was now or never. "Um…I am wondering…that is, the youth group has been wondering…"

The women were all looking at her and Aleda smiled a little as if what she was about to suggest was simply a friendly amendment.

"You see, most of our youth are involved in the high school band and they need to raise money for their school trip to the music festival in Ottawa next month. They are wondering if *they* could pick the berries on Saturday morning at Spence's farm. Then they would sell them to you."

Aleda paused, letting this information sink in. "They are also offering to wash and stem the berries as part of their contribution to the strawberry social."

No one spoke. Aleda waited.

"It would be a win-win situation," she continued into the silence. "The youth group could earn a little money for their school trip and you would not have the bother and work of picking up the berries or getting them ready for the supper."

Sally cleared her throat. "Well," she said, turning from Aleda to the women, "what do you girls think?" Margaret was the first to speak.

"But what would happen if it was to rain on that Saturday?" she asked.

"Rain?" Aleda repeated. "Well, I suppose if it rains, it rains. How did you get your strawberries picked in the past if it rained on the Saturday of the strawberry social?"

She looked around, and no one answered until someone muttered quietly, "Don't remember that happening."

"What if the young people pick too many of them small seedy berries, the ones with the hard green knobs on the end?" Murta asked, setting down her knitting.

"I imagine that they will know a good strawberry when they see one," Aleda responded, hoping that her tone of voice was not sarcastic.

Grace asked the final question that closed the discussion. "But this is the *ladies* strawberry social. How can we let the teenagers take over?"

Aleda felt a tremulous shaking in her knees, but before she could say anything, Grace said, "Ladies, I move that we get Spence's Berry Farm to deliver the strawberries to the church on Saturday morning of the supper as usual."

Before waiting for someone to second the motion or call for the vote, all the women raised their hands. Aleda took a deep breath, feeling a slow flush rise in her cheeks. This is a small matter, she reminded herself; but nonetheless she felt hurt and discouraged. Things had not gone as she had hoped. The other women avoided her eyes. Two women rose and went into the kitchen to put on the kettle for tea.

Just when she thought that things could not get worse, Aleda heard Grace's voice.

"I have one more item for new business," Grace said, turning to Sally. "I came in the back door of the church because I had the muffins and cheese for our refreshments tonight. I couldn't help but notice that there is a terrible smell at the back of the church. Something needs to be done!"

6

Sourdough

Y WEDNESDAY THE MISTY RAIN had stopped. The sun rose hot and bright, creating a warm humidity that was unusual for the end of May. Aleda stepped out onto the veranda and stood leaning on the railing, assessing the day. A vapour seemed to be rising from the edges of her back lawn. As she stared, it slowly dawned on her that the steam and the strange odour were rising from the piles of horse manure she had shovelled onto the perennial beds on Saturday. Roy. I have to call Roy. What was the time? She glanced at her watch. Yes, Roy will be up.

Moments later Roy tapped on her front door and Aleda led him through to the backyard, explaining what she had done. Roy looked thoughtful, then nodded, walked toward a pile of fresh manure, and kicked it with the toe of his work boot.

"Well you see, you can't put fresh manure directly on flower beds because it will burn your plants."

"Oh! How could I be so stupid! But what do I know about gardening, or horse manure either for that matter?"

Roy nodded. "I'll be back later. What you need here is a good composter. I'll see if I have some lumber lying around the shed." With that, he turned and headed back toward his own tidy perennial gardens and his shed where lumber, tools, and nails were arranged in meticulous order. Grateful that he had not laughed, Aleda raised an imaginary wine glass in a toast to the best neighbour a woman could have.

After breakfast, Aleda settled into her office and opened the book that she had come to call "the big red binder." It was her turn to attend her church's General Assembly in Winnipeg in June. It was both an honour and a responsibility, as each attendee was expected to have read and understood pages of reports. Aleda sighed and bent her head to read. There were reports on ecumenical partnerships, charitable gift annuities, experiential learning, and development projects in Africa, among others. It was hard reading. Perhaps she would distract herself and have a look at the list of delegates to see if she recognized anyone. Perhaps some of her classmates from seminary days would be attending? She ran her finger down the list and then stopped. Her finger had come to rest on the name of someone she tried never to think about: Ben Snell.

For a moment, it felt as though her heart had stopped beating. Ben Snell. Funny, charming, outgoing Ben who had been her confidante and lover in 1982. She remembered with stabbing clarity how stunned and hurt she was when Ben announced that he was engaged to her best friend, and then became proud father of a little girl five months later. It had broken her heart. Even all these years later, Aleda felt a flush creep up her neck and her pulse quicken. The possibility of seeing Ben again filled her with excitement and dread.

The telephone rang and it was Martin's mother, Rose Hart. "Aleda, I want to talk to you about the meeting of the Ladies Guild last night. Do you have a moment?"

"Yes, yes of course."

"You may know that I've lived in this village most of my life, and I raised my boys here. I don't always agree with the decisions that the women make at our meetings, and I often don't care for the things they talk about at the meetings either, but these women are my long-time friends. They check in on me every day, and I check in on them."

Aleda massaged the bridge of her nose. Where was this heading?

"Those young people," Rose said. "I want to ask you about those young people."

"Yes."

"What can you tell me about them?" Rose asked again.

Aleda told her about Savannah and her enormous capacity to help others, and Dwayne with his struggle to accept friendship and embrace life. She told Rose about Victoria's sweet and gentle nature, about Ashley, the flamboyant red head, and about Jacob's excellence at sports. Michael was the brainy popular kid, the one most likely to be valedictorian for his class.

"They're a great bunch of kids," Aleda said, her voice rising.

There was a moment of silence on the telephone line.

"Just as I thought," Rose said. "You see, I admire that the youth are so enterprising and want to pick and sell the strawberries for our social. I know that the Ladies Guild finds this offer hard to accept, so I would like to donate five hundred dollars toward the school band trip."

There was silence as Aleda took in the news.

"Mrs. Hart," she said, her voice breathless, "that is so amazing. I just can't tell you how thrilled the kids will be to hear this news. Are you quite sure?"

"Quite sure, Aleda. Absolutely sure. You see, my younger son, James, is the band teacher at Owen Sound Collegiate. I know that he would want me to help in this small way. Are you able to come by this afternoon and pick up a cheque?"

It was 2 p.m. when Aleda arrived at Rose Hart's neat stone house, built in the Ontario cottage style with a dormer over a centre door and a window on either side of the door. In the front garden, a white picket fence supported blooming red and pink rugosa roses. Aleda walked through a trellis and up the front walk, pausing for a moment before knocking to enjoy the perfume of the roses.

Rose led Aleda past the living room with its wingback chairs and fireplace to the back of the house and into the kitchen. Aleda could see that this room, with its bouquet of cinnamon, sage, and coconut, was the heart of the home, the operations centre for Rose's life.

"Have you ever baked with sourdough?" Rose asked, turning to Aleda. Surprised, Aleda shook her head.

"Please. Sit down."

Rose reached up into a cupboard over the stove and lifted down a large brown ceramic bowl full of frothy bubbles.

"Sourdough," Rose said. "I learned to make it when I lived in the Yukon, in Whitehorse. I was a nurse there before I got married, and the women in the Yukon introduced me to sourdough. I've been using it ever since. I'll give you a container to take home. It makes wonderful bread and biscuits and muffins and lemon scones and, our favourite, cinnamon rolls. I'll give you some recipes to try."

Rose reached for her chequebook among the clutter on the kitchen table. Aleda noticed a book lying open on the table. She lifted the cover and glanced at the title.

"Nietzsche?" she said, looking up. "You're reading Nietzsche?" Aleda stared at the book cover: *Beyond Good and Evil.*

"Well, yes, I read those things," Rose said, writing the cheque.

Although she hadn't read Nietzsche herself, Aleda did remember from her seminary days that Nietzsche was credited with inventing the phrase "God is dead." She was about to ask Rose if she concurred with Nietzsche's opinion when she heard someone at the back door.

"Oh, that will be my son," Rose said as Martin walked into the room.

Martin, dressed in jeans, a red plaid shirt and now in stocking feet, turned a kitchen chair around and straddled it, his arms resting on the chair back. "I see you've been introduced to my mother's famous sourdough," he said, grinning. "Welcome to the world of fantastic baked goods. Your waistline will never be the same again."

As if she had been waiting for this cue, Rose reached into a cupboard and brought out a square tray of cinnamon rolls, redolent of cinnamon, the raisins shining with caramelized brown sugar.

"Mother, really. You shouldn't have," Martin joked as he broke off a roll. "Dig in," he said to Aleda, his mouth full. "They really are very good. I grew up on them, and look how well I turned out!"

As Aleda was leaving the house, full of cinnamon rolls and heady new ideas about Nietzsche, she thanked Rose again for what she had done for the youth. Rose shook her head, smiling a little, and then clasped Aleda's hand. She looked into Aleda's eyes.

"You know, Aleda," she said in a somber voice, "I've never had the experience of having a female minister before and I have to say that I quite like it. It makes me feel as if I might be able to really talk over some things with you."

"Thanks for the vote of confidence," Aleda grinned. "And thanks, too, for the sourdough. I'll see you again soon."

By the time Aleda returned home with her tub of sourdough and Rose's handwritten instructions, it was late afternoon. She walked into the backyard, where she could hear the sound of hammering. Roy was constructing what seemed to be a large, three-sided wooden box with sturdy corner posts in the back corner of the yard.

"Ta-da!" he called as Aleda approached. "Your new composter, ready in an afternoon. Just don't use it until tomorrow. Gotta let the posts settle into their cement pads." Aleda and Roy stood admiring the composter as if it were a genuine piece of art.

"Put a few day lilies around the edge there, maybe a border of cone flowers, it'll be a sight fit for a gardening magazine."

"Roy, honestly, I don't know what I would do without you," Aleda gushed. "But..." She flung out her arms, gesturing to the heaps of manure smothering the perennial beds.

"I'll be back tomorrow to saw off the tops of the posts," Roy said. "I'll be carrying two of my best shovels, too. You and me, Aleda, we're going have the time of our lives shovelling horse shit into the new composter. Git out them red rubber boots, Aleda."

7

Laura

LTHOUGH SHE HADN'T ADMITTED IT to herself for several days after, Laura Browning felt sorry about her encounter with Aleda on the previous Sunday. Why had she been so chilly? After all, Aleda seemed to be a nice person and just dropped by to be friendly. No need to have been so discourteous. She knew that she couldn't continue to blame everything on a broken ankle, but the truth was she was lonely, bored, and unhappy cooped up in the old house she had grown up in. She felt trapped in memories and monotony.

She wondered again if it had been wise to come back to Milburn Corners while her ankle healed. Her life in Toronto was busy with teaching and coaching her high school students, and she was as engaged as she chose to be in her social life with her friends. And at the moment, she was nostalgic about that lifestyle.

By the time she had washed and dressed with the painstaking slowness of someone who must hobble around on crutches, she felt cranky and out of sorts. She leaned against the kitchen counter, washed her plate and knife from breakfast, and then swung into the living room where she lowered herself into the old easy chair that had been her father's place. Most nights, she recalled, he sat in this chair – sometimes reading, sometimes smoking a cigar and sipping Scotch.

Laura glanced around the room, thinking again that she must get in touch with her brother in Edmonton and ask what they should do with this old house and its contents. We can't just let it sit unoccupied like this, she thought, folding her arms and wondering how others in a similar situation went about disposing of the contents of a family house from a past era: the heavy mahogany dining room suite that had been a wedding gift to her parents, the rocking chair that had belonged to her grandmother and in which Laura's mother had nursed both Laura and her brother, the little drop-leaf tea wagon with its glass top and scalloped edges, the spool beds and heavy oak armoires in the upstairs rooms.

Laura stared at the entrance to her father's office across the hall. The glass-panelled doors, windows covered in a shirred gold-striped maroon fabric, defined the mystifying site that had embraced a stream of pregnant women, children with bleeding foreheads, and worried old men with pains in their bellies. Day after day, people had disappeared into the antiseptic smells of the room behind the covered doors of the doctor's office.

To the young Laura it was simply a reality of her life that this parade of sick and injured people came through the front door of their home. She and her brother barely noticed. They ate their meals, did their homework, and played games together in the kitchen and large den by the back door. That part of the house was the domain of the children and their mother. The living room though, with its book-lined shelves and later, an ancient television set, was the evening resting place of Dr. Browning. He was not to be disturbed after his evening meal except when Laura's mother took her by the hand and she stood on tiptoe to kiss her father goodnight. Sometimes he smiled and said, "Sweet dreams, favourite daughter." Sometimes though, he was distracted and appeared startled when she came to give him a kiss.

In her memory, Laura could see him sitting in the same chair in which she now sprawled, his long lean legs stretched out, a hand pressed against his head, his dark blond hair touched with silver and falling across his forehead, an open book lying on his lap, a smouldering cigar in his right hand. Laura had grown up hearing wonder and respect in the voices of the village people when they spoke of her father. To the people in the village and surrounding area, Dr. Browning was one of the last of an incredible but vanishing breed: the independent, old-time, caring local doctor.

But as she grew older, Laura began to understand that something was awry, and with the ruthless judging attitude that sometimes comes with adolescence, Laura began to see the flaws in her father's life. She could see that her mother was protective of her husband in a quiet and complicit way. She seemed often on edge, ready to protect the children from the doctor's lapses into bad temper, his unpredictable evening eruptions, his times of morose withdrawal when he stayed up late into the night smoking and drinking and staring out the living room window down into the village.

By the time Laura and David had gone off to university, their father was often without patients throughout the day. Many of the villagers now used the new medical clinic in Owen Sound where the young doctors used different methods and where there was a lab that tested blood and gave flu shots. Dr. Browning found his consolation in Scotch and in his conviction that, old-fashioned though he might be, he was still right in many ways. What did these young doctors, still wet behind the ears, know about things?

Laura speculated on what it might have been like for her father, a man committed to healing and wellness, but a man who didn't seem able to offer comfort and contentment to either himself or his family. Laura pressed her hands together and rested her fingers against her mouth. Why was she unable to let go of this grand old house with all its melancholy? Why could she find no peace in her memories of her father?

Lost in thought, Laura picked up a magazine and flipped through the pages. Another day stretched before her, and she was overwhelmed with languor, weighed down by the tedium of unfilled time. She set down the magazine and, reaching for her crutches, swung herself out to the kitchen. When she caught sight of the pink phone on the kitchen counter – one of the last pretty things her mother had purchased for herself – Laura knew what she would do.

When Aleda picked up the phone, Laura began, "Rev. Vastag, Aleda, I'm calling to apologize for my rudeness on Sunday."

"Rude? No. Really…"

Laura hesitated. "I don't feel like myself these days, but I was wondering if you would be free to come over for dinner tomorrow night."

"Oh!" Aleda responded. "Oh, that would be wonderful. There's just one small snag. I meet with the village young people every Friday evening until eight. Is it too late if I arrive after that?"

"Not at all," Laura assured her. "I have to warn you, though, that I'm not much of a cook. I just order in from the village store, so don't expect a home-cooked gourmet meal."

"Then let's make it potluck!" Aleda exclaimed.

"Potluck?"

"Yes, you know. We each provide something." Her mind was already sorting through possibilities.

"Sounds wonderful," Laura said. "See you then. And oh, by the way, I've invited an old high school friend as well. We were good friends as teens even though I was a couple of years older than him, but we drifted apart. You know how that happens. I heard that he's back in the area for the summer so I called and invited him too. His name is Martin Hart."

Pleased that she had taken the right step toward mending a social *faux pas*, Laura smiled and was grabbing her crutches when she heard a soft rap on the kitchen door. Through the screen, she saw Rose Hart holding a pan and a book.

"Come in. Come in," Laura called out, and in a few minutes the two women were seated at the kitchen table eating cinnamon rolls and talking about recent novels.

"I read this one yesterday," Rose said. She leaned forward as if imparting a small secret. "I try to read all the novels on the *New York Times* bestseller list, even if they aren't particularly appealing to me."

Laura glanced down, setting her hand on the book that lay between them. "This one?"

Rose nodded. "Not due at the library until next week, so you are welcome to read it."

Laura picked up the book and read the title aloud: *The Perfect Girl.*

"Is there such a thing? I'm not sure that my father would have thought so."

"Oh come now dear. Your father was very fond of you, and very proud. He loved his children and wanted only the best for them."

"Do you really think so?" Laura pulled her sweater around her shoulders.

"Oh I'm absolutely positive about that," Rose said, rising to get ready to go home. "If you like, I'm happy to lend you more books, and I'm always happy to share some baked goods."

"That would be wonderful," Laura said. "It's been rather…well, quite frankly, I've been a bit unhappy here this week, and what else do I have to do but read and think?"

Laura heard the bitterness in her own voice, and feeling a flush of shame, she quickly added, "I would look forward to you dropping in. Maybe you could bring me the news from the corner store."

Rose smiled, and as she watched Laura struggle with her crutches she picked up the book and said, "Where do you sit to read? Let me take the book to your reading spot."

"Most of the time in Dad's favourite chair in the living room."

Laura watched as Rose walked into the living room, hesitated for a moment, then dropped briefly into the old easy chair before setting the novel on the side table. It was only later when Rose had gone and Laura was sitting in the chair that Laura realized that from this vantage point she could see Rose walking down the hill, crossing the main street, and walking up her front path, pausing to inhale the fragrance from her roses. Laura watched as Rose stopped on the doorstep, dug in her pocket for her house key, and let herself in the front door. How many times had her father, sipping Scotch and smoking a cigar in this old chair, seen this same thing? she wondered.

Maybe I'll make *lecsó* with sausage and paprika potatoes for tonight, Aleda mused. It had been one of her favourite dishes as a child. She would need fresh tomatoes, peppers, cooking onions, smoked sausage, and small new potatoes. Glancing at her watch, Aleda saw that she had time to drive into Owen Sound to the supermarket. A little time and space in the van would also help her mull over what to do with the youth that evening, she decided.

Remembering that she had not checked her email that morning, she turned back to her computer and clicked on the email box. There, seeming to jump out from the computer screen, making her inhale in a soft gasp, was the name that took her breath away. Ben Snell. After all these years, she had received a message from Ben Snell. Aleda's hand trembled as she clicked to open the email.

My dear Aleda,

I was so excited to open my GA binder and find that you'll be attending the Assembly in Winnipeg too. I'm really looking forward to reconnecting with you. I've missed you a lot over the years.

Best ever, Ben.

She shivered. Then she re-read the email. What would it be like to see Ben again?

After lunch, Aleda's kitchen was filled with the pungent fragrance of frying onion, green and yellow peppers, and tomatoes, cooked with mild sweet paprika and smoked meat. She ladled the contents of the skillet into a deep casserole, set it in the refrigerator, and then sank onto a chair to think about the youth group meeting.

First we'll have to talk about strawberries, she considered. She would explain, with care, that the Ladies Guild had a system from previous years and they preferred to follow it. Then she would tell them the thrilling news of the generous donation from Mrs. Hart. But what should she do for the program? Nothing came to mind. Aleda chewed the end of her pen. It's that issue of Dwayne, she thought. It's worrying all of us. What is it that Dwayne is struggling with?

Aleda set down her pen with a clatter. The meaning of life, she thought. Dwayne is wondering about the meaning of life. What is the *point* of life? Does my life matter? I do believe that's what Dwayne is wrestling with, and it's painful for the rest of us to watch him go through this. Even Savannah with her persistently upbeat attitude is powerless to help him, yet we all want to.

There was a deeper worry for Aleda too. If they met this challenge head on by talking about the point of life, would this help or hurt Dwayne?

Feeling uncertain and restless, Aleda stood up and paced back and forth in the kitchen. She wandered down the hall and into her office and stood scanning the shelf where she stacked youth program books. She pulled out a book entitled *Dynamic Youth Programs* and flipped through it before slapping it shut and choosing another. Here's one that might work, she thought, picking up a book called *When Youth are Hurting*. She read through program suggestions for exploring the meaning of life.

The advice given was good, Aleda thought, but most of the suggestions were focused on parents engaging and encouraging their teens, and parents were something that Dwayne simply didn't have in his daily life. However, the last suggestion had possibilities: Give a teen plenty of opportunity to care about others, to develop empathy. This helps the teen evolve into a better person and also helps young people to be less self-focused and worried.

Aleda sank into her office chair. Was it possible that Dwayne might become more settled and find more meaning in life if he were given opportunities to show care for others, to assume responsibility for someone besides himself? An idea formed in Aleda's mind. I'll propose it tonight and see what happens, she thought.

Aleda rushed home after the youth meeting to feed Tracker and pack the casserole and bottle of Merlot into her oversized tote bag. When she pulled into the driveway of Laura's house she parked behind Martin's truck and moved tentatively toward the back door. Laura limped to the door to meet her. Martin was perched on a stool by the kitchen counter drinking what appeared to be Scotch on ice.

"Please," Laura said, indicating to Aleda that she should come in and set the casserole on the stovetop. "May I pour you a glass of wine?"

If Aleda had been uneasy about having dinner with two people she had just met, her worries vanished as the dinner progressed. Laura had insisted that they have a kitchen party as she disliked the dreary formality of the dining room. The evening was filled with good food: the smoky, pungent *lecsó*; an artisan herb bread to dip in flavoured oil; hot pepper olives stuffed with garlic; and roast chicken flecked with buttered sage, which Martin claimed he had made himself although it had arrived in a supermarket container. They finished their meal with a mocha cheesecake, straight from the freezer of the village store. It was a true potluck meal.

As Martin pushed back from the kitchen table, he raised his glass and toasted, "To reconnecting with my long-time-ago friend Laura, and to my new friend Aleda. Wonderful food. Wonderful conversation. Wonderful women."

"Flattery may not get you a return invitation," Laura said, smiling. "Bring your glasses into the living room. We'll find some comfy chairs and have coffee later."

As the evening progressed and Aleda learned a little more about Laura, she believed they might become good friends. About Martin, she learned little more than what she already knew: he had a soft spot for a seemingly neglected little boy and an equally tender heart for the child's injured dog. And, despite the fact that he drove a rusty truck, she knew that he had enough money to pay a substantial veterinary bill.

"So," Aleda said to Martin cautiously, with a small shrug of her shoulders. "How long have you lived on the farm?"

"Oh, I don't live there. Just camp out there in the summer."

"Where do you live for the rest of the year?"

Martin shifted in his chair. "Guelph. We live in Guelph. My wife and daughter don't much care for farm life, so they go to the Muskoka lakes for the summer." Martin shrugged. "We all get what suits us."

"Guelph." Aleda repeated, her tone neutral.

Laura set her wine glass down on a side table and shifted her crutches to one side of her chair.

"Good luck finding out anything about this guy. When we were in high school, we met at the corner store and took the same school bus day after day and I tried for four years to find out his middle name. It became such a joke."

Aleda smiled. "Okay, mystery man. What do you do for a living in Guelph?"

"Oh, a bit of this and a bit of that," he said, adopting a teasing tone of voice.

Laura twisted in her chair toward Aleda. "You know, Aleda, I've been wondering what it's like to be the minister in a small village where everyone knows everyone else's business, and to be a woman, and single on top of that."

Perhaps it was the wine, but perhaps it was also the permission-giving atmosphere of the evening that led Aleda to tell humorous stories about adopting a cranky old horse, of forming a praise band with the teenagers, of giving her perennial flowers a burial in horse manure. She even made the Ladies Guild and their angst about strawberries a tale that resulted in hearty laughter.

Martin told Aleda and Laura about the steady progress of the pregnant dog thriving in his back kitchen. The dog seemed to delight in two meals a day in the peace and quiet of the farm house. When Aleda asked about Callum, Martin shrugged and said, "Far as I can tell, he seems more or less to look out for himself. The father – I've met him a few times – isn't abusive, and doesn't seem to drink too much. Far as I can make out, Callum's father just hasn't been the same since his wife died. But that doesn't seem to affect the boy. You know yourself what he's like."

When they were ready to part for the evening, Laura felt hopeful and content. She was sated with good food, wine, laughter, and companionship. The old house had come to life for an evening, and it had lifted her spirits.

"This may be a bit of a crazy idea," she said to Aleda and Martin, "but here we are, three middle-aged people alone in a sleepy village for the summer. If we're all free, why don't we get together every Friday for dinner and wine?"

Aleda looked at Martin, then back at Laura. "Great idea," she responded with enthusiasm. Martin nodded in agreement and said, "It would be a break from work."

Aleda looked at him but before she could ask *what work?* he had turned toward his truck.

"See you next Friday, same time, same place," he called out as he turned the key in the ignition.

Content and sleepy, Aleda tugged off her clothes and tossed them onto the old chair in the corner of her bedroom. She pulled on her big loose T-shirt, raised the window to hear the swamp frogs, and climbed into bed. She sighed as she stretched out under the sheets, and thought that it had been a good day, even though the youth group meeting had been a little rocky.

She revisited her conversation with the youth about the strawberries. She had downplayed the real reason why the Ladies Guild women had wanted to stay with their traditional way of obtaining the berries. Then she had pulled out the cheque and waved it with a smile in front of their faces.

"Wow! Five hundred bucks!" they exclaimed. "That's awesome."

Dwayne, too, seemed happy with this unexpected and big-hearted gift, even though he was not involved in the school music program and would not be travelling to the music festival in Ottawa.

"I have an idea!" Savannah said, bouncing in her seat. "Why don't we keep going with our fundraising? We can't just stop because someone gives us a big cheque. Why don't we ask Spence's Berry Farm if we can pick strawberries every Saturday during June and sell them at the village store? The Spences have all kinds of berries ya know, early ones, ever-bearing ones…"

Savannah, breathless, looked around at her friends. Jacob nodded, but Michael said nothing. Dwayne sat looking down at his unlaced running shoes with their separated soles. He could use a new pair of sneakers, Aleda thought, before turning to look at Victoria and Ashley.

"Well," Victoria murmured and Aleda could hear the hesitation in her voice. Ashley, too, remained silent. It was evident that a month of picking strawberries on Saturdays was not what anyone but Savannah would enjoy.

It's now or never, Aleda thought.

"I've been thinking," she started, "that there are a lot of young children in the area. Would it be possible to run a Saturday camp for kids during June? You would be the leaders and you could coach the kids in drama, sports, and music. You could take them on nature hikes and have recreation breaks at the school playground. You could have a cook-out and make doughboys and s'mores. You could find a great story book and read it when the kids need a rest. You could charge enough to help with your school trip fundraising but not so much that parents would worry about the cost. And think of how wonderful this would look on your résumés!"

Aleda paused, letting the teenagers consider this possibility. Her mind was already racing ahead, thinking up a catchy name for this new June Saturday camp. She was imagining designs for bright appealing posters. But mainly, Aleda was making one secret connection. She would pair the grubby, forthright Callum with Dwayne. Dwayne with his quiet reserve; Dwayne, the youth of few words. It was her hope – she could feel this hope forming like a prayer inside her – that pairing Dwayne with Callum would help both of them in immeasurable ways. Callum would have a calm older friend, and Dwayne would have an opportunity to think beyond himself, to develop empathy as he cared for a little ragamuffin who was, in his own way, as alone in the world as Dwayne was. It was a win-win situation. Aleda felt quite sure about that.

8

Chocolate

T WAS THE TASK THAT ALEDA hated most, but she knew she could no longer put it off. She had to clean her house. It had been – how long? – at least two weeks since she had pulled out the vacuum cleaner, scrubbed the bathroom, or washed the kitchen floor. She groaned. Would it perhaps be overlooked in the village if she were to engage a cleaning woman? Stupid question, she told herself irritably. People would say, "She doesn't have a husband or kids to look after. She doesn't need to hoe a vegetable garden or feed the chickens. Surely she can do her own housework." Aleda groaned again.

Sitting at her kitchen table on this bright Saturday morning, trying to remember where she last left the scrub pail, she came to a decision. She would set her kitchen timer for one hour in which to do housework, then she would offer herself a reward. An hour in the sunshine with her new library book? A brisk walk down to the swamp to see if the marsh marigolds were still blooming? A fresh muffin from the village store?

It was the thought of the muffin that made her jump to her feet. The sourdough! She had been given strict instructions by Rose about what to do with it.

"The thing you need to remember is that the starter needs to be refreshed every two or three days. Just add a little bit of flour and water and stir with a wooden spoon. This keeps the sourdough fresh. It should have a clean sour milk smell."

Rose had explained that in the Yukon, sourdough was the title given to Yukon old-timers, the rugged, tough, determined men searching for gold. Over time, the term *sourdough* also became the name of the starter used for baking.

"No one had yeast, so this method of creating a rise with carbon dioxide bubbles proved quite adequate. As it turned out, sourdough starter was as hardy as the old-timers who lived there. They used to say that when the men were out in the wilderness they carried a little package of sourdough inside their shirts to keep it alive."

Listening to this, Aleda had shuddered, thinking of sweaty men protecting a packet of sourdough against some mysterious part of their unwashed bodies.

Now Aleda's eyes rolled upward to look at a cupboard high over the kitchen sink where she had stored her sourdough starter. What day had she visited Rose to pick up the cheque? Tuesday? No, it was Wednesday. Wednesday, Thursday, Friday, Saturday. Aleda climbed onto a chair and eased open the door as one might do if there had been a mouse trap set there overnight.

Aleda let out a scream, slammed shut the cupboard door, and jumped off the chair. But it was too late. A slow-moving molten rivulet of foaming, frothy sourdough poured over the ledge of the cupboard and, with a heavy sucking noise sank with a great slow plop into the kitchen sink.

It all happened in a few seconds, but it seemed to Aleda as if she were watching a slow motion movie clip of herself watching the errant sourdough ooze from the cupboard in a slow molten rivulet and gather until it accumulated enough weight to drop into the sink. Aleda laughed until her sides were sore, reached under the sink for a cleaning cloth, and laughed some more.

She had just finished cleaning up when the doorbell rang. Savannah was on the step, holding a flat gold box. "I have something to show you," she said, dancing from one foot to the other.

"You are a sight for sore eyes."

"Am I interrupting something important?"

"Yes, you are," Aleda said with mock severity, then smiled. "My Saturday morning mop-up-the-house routine. Come in. I'm grateful for the interruption."

When they had settled at the kitchen table, Savannah said, "See, I had this idea. You know how we decided to do the Saturday camp, and you know how the women wanted to look after their own strawberries…"

Aleda nodded.

"Well, I had an idea. On our first day of camp it would be fun to make chocolate-coated strawberries. So last night me and Ashley and Victoria got together to experiment."

Savannah leaned forward as if she were about to impart a great secret. "We thought that we could work with the kids on the day before the strawberry social and make chocolate-coated strawberries so that everyone could have one on their plate of strawberry shortcake!

"A wonderful idea, Savannah! Totally brilliant!" Aleda exclaimed, gesturing with her hand toward the gold box that sat between them. Savannah squared the box and with exaggerated slowness removed the lid, using only her thumbs and forefingers, her little fingers sticking out as if she were a Victorian duchess. There was a thin sheet of pink tissue paper on top of the berries. Savannah lifted it and set it aside.

Aleda gasped. "Savannah! I don't know what to say! They are absolutely beautiful. They are Picassos! They are Rembrandts! They are extraordinary!"

For a moment they gazed down at crimson berries partially coated in rich brown chocolate and decorated with white chocolate. Some had tiny white rose buds, some had swirls, and some had been rolled sideways in brown chocolate and had tiny dots down the middle, making the strawberries look as if they were wearing tuxedos.

In an excited tone, Savannah told Aleda how she and her friends had used toothpicks to create the designs; how they had used spoons and forks to create swirls and patterns.

"Simply amazing," Aleda said, then paused. "I have one question, though."

"Don't you think that the kids will have so much fun making these?" Savannah rushed on. "It seemed quite a bit like finger painting to us."

"I have one serious question to ask," Aleda repeated.

Savannah looked up, an anxious expression on her face. "What?"

"Do they taste good?"

9

Knife

UNDAY MORNING HAD ROLLED around again. Aleda was unlocking the church doors when Savannah arrived, carrying a vase of bleeding heart flowers. She shrugged and said, "From my mom. Where shall I put them?"

It perplexed Aleda that while the youth regularly attended their Friday meetings and the Sunday morning services, their parents were absent from church life. If they cared at all for the life and work of the village church, Aleda didn't know about it; yet every now and then, along came a gift: flowers from Savannah's mother's garden, or a plate of cookies from Jacob's mother. It seemed to be some little suggestion that while they themselves didn't associate with the church, it was something they appreciated for their kids.

"It's hard to believe," Savannah said, "that it was just a little over a week ago that we were all in a flap about that dog that was hit by the car."

Aleda agreed. "It seems that a lot has gone on this week, that's for sure."

"How's the dog doing?"

"Quite well from what I hear. I haven't seen it, but I did talk with Martin Hart – he's the man who drove you to the veterinary clinic. Martin is looking after the dog and Callum – you know, that little boy who wears the red shorts – he and his dad are the dog's owners – Callum goes to Martin's house twice a day to feed it. Callum and the dog seem to have quite a bond."

Aleda stood in the vestibule of the church gazing at the vase of bleeding hearts and thinking that Martin and Callum also seemed to have created a strong bond. "We'll put them on this flower stand," she said, finally. "Did you deliver the invitations for the first day of June camp? It's such short notice. I've been a bit worried about that since Friday."

With a wave of her hand, Savannah said, "Oh! Don't worry. We already have eight kids signed up. By the way, Callum signed up. I was kinda surprised about that."

"I'm surprised too. I'm glad to hear that his dad signed him up."

"Oh, it wasn't him. It was Martin Hart. He wrote a note on the bottom of the form to say that he would drop Callum off and pick him up."

Aleda, preparing her sermon notes on the pulpit, raised her eyebrows.

"Well, this is ready," Savannah said, setting the last music stand in front of the guitar amplifier. "I'm off now to get Dwayne."

When Savannah and Dwayne returned, Aleda gave Dwayne a thumbs-up, the signal that he could ring the bell before settling in behind the sound booth. Then, in the lull before the service began, as people were settling into their pews, Aleda strolled to the back of the church where Dwayne was adjusting the sliding bars on the sound panel.

"How are you today, Dwayne?" Aleda asked, smiling but noting with concern that Dwayne seemed even more dishevelled than usual.

"Okay."

"How's school going?"

"Okay."

"Any big assignments coming up?"

"Nope."

"You have an order of service for today?"

Dwayne nodded.

Toward the end of the worship service, Aleda looked up and was startled to see that Dwayne had disappeared from the sound booth.

"Did you notice Dwayne leave part way through worship?" she asked Savannah when worship was over.

Savannah shook her head. "I have no idea where he went. I didn't see him leave at all."

"I'm worried about Dwayne. He seems so depressed and unhappy. Does he worry you?"

Savannah hesitated for a moment. "Well, if you had asked me yesterday, I might have said yes, but today, no. Today he seemed almost cheerful. When we were on our way to church this morning he gave me a gift. Dwayne's never given me anything in all the time I've known him. I've given him lots of things, but he has never given me anything. He gave me his Swiss Army knife."

Savannah snapped shut the box that stored the praise band music and, reaching into her pocket, pulled out the knife. "I can't believe he gave me his Swiss Army knife. He's so proud of it. He would show it to us at the bus stop. It has about eight or nine things on one little knife: blades of different sizes, a nail file, a toothpick of all things, a corkscrew, and even a tiny fork and spoon. Dwayne used to say that he could get lost in a swamp for a week and he would have everything he needed to survive. He was so proud of it."

Aleda stood frowning, her arms folded. "Then why would he give it away?"

"Beats me. He just said that he wanted me to have it." Savannah stood staring at the knife lying flat in her hand, her face grave. "Dwayne told me that it's the only gift his father ever gave him."

After lunch, Aleda stretched out on the couch in the living room for a Sunday afternoon nap, but once again sleep eluded her. She was thinking of the moment after worship when she and Savannah had stood looking down at the many blades and attachments on Dwayne's Swiss Army knife. Aleda sighed and sat up. "I've got to do it," she said, and in a few minutes she was strolling along Main Street, past Roy's late spring tulips dancing in the afternoon breeze, past Grace's brick bungalow where the smell of apple pie drifted through the open kitchen window, past the village store locked up for Sunday. She walked straight to the edge of the village and up the gravel path of a small house covered in maroon insulbrick. Aleda stopped in front of the house, realizing that there was no step up onto the sagging covered porch. She stood staring at the exposed wooden doorframe where the insulbrick had lifted and saw it was crawling with carpenter ants. Before Aleda could decide what to do, the front door opened and Dwayne's grandmother called out, "Hello Reverend. Come on in."

There seemed to be no other choice. Aleda took a large ungraceful step up onto the porch, glad that she had chosen to wear jeans.

"Oh, gracious, there's a step over here," Dwayne's grandmother said, pointing to the side of the porch where a cement block lay on its side.

As the old woman shuffled down the hall in her fur-lined carpet slippers, Aleda was grateful for the slow passage as it gave her eyes time to adjust to the dark interior. There were no curtains or blinds on the windows, but someone had thumbtacked old bed sheets over the windows. In the kitchen, Dwayne's grandmother motioned Aleda to a wooden chair and Aleda sat down carefully, noting that several rungs were missing from the back of it.

"Will you be taking a cup of tea, Reverend?"

"Yes, thank you. That would be grand." Grand, Aleda thought, disgusted with herself. Where do these words come from?

"I ain't got no baking today," the old woman said, as she filled the kettle from the kitchen tap. "That boy eats me out of house and home."

Aleda glanced at the woman's face to see if she was smiling, but her face was stoic. She set two stained mugs on the table. When the tea was poured, Aleda picked up a spoon, added a half spoonful of sugar, and stirred slowly. Dwayne's grandmother sat waiting. The house was quiet.

"Is Dwayne home?" Aleda asked.

"Nope. Went out when that Savannah girl got him for church. Not sure where he is. Sometimes he goes down to the swamp."

Aleda set down her spoon. "You see, we've been concerned about Dwayne lately. He just doesn't seem happy."

"Happy?" Dwayne's grandmother picked up her mug. "Oh, that boy ain't never been what you might call happy."

"Maybe this is none of my business, but Dwayne gave away his Swiss Army knife to Savannah this morning. He has never talked much about his parents, but he said that the knife had been a gift from his father, and he seemed to value it a great deal."

Aleda looked in the old woman's face, trying to catch some clue as to what might be happening in Dwayne's life, but the woman's expression remained the same.

"Oh, that boy's always doing some darn senseless thing."

"Dwayne's parents, are they dead?"

The old woman's laughter came out like a rasp, and Aleda wondered for a moment if the old woman was unwell.

"Them two. They might as well be dead. Last I heard they was in Calgary getting ready to work the Stampede. My daughter got mixed up in the wrong crowd and ran away from here when she was 17. Then a couple of years later, she comes back with some pothead guy and a baby. They stuck around for a few weeks and then one night they just took off. Left the baby behind."

"Dwayne?" Aleda exclaimed, setting down her mug. "But that's terrible!"

"Well, them kind are no good I say, even if she is my own daughter. I done my best to raise Dwayne, but you know what kids are like. They ask questions. Where are my mom and dad? Why don't they take me with them? When're they coming back? And it don't help that they come back sometimes, just enough to raise the boy's hopes. Then they tell him that goin' around from rodeo to rodeo ain't no way for a boy to grow up and that he needs to be in school and stay in one place."

"I suppose that Dwayne wouldn't have understood that as a kid, or even as a teenager."

"Oh no. No, he don't. He don't understand still. He thinks it would be an exciting life, full of adventure and fun."

"His dad did give him a Swiss Army knife though?"

"Oh yeah. They showed up here last October on their way to Kentucky for a rodeo there. Dwayne's dad spent a lot of time showin' him that knife. But they only stayed a day or two. You could just see 'em gittin' restless. Then they's off again in some old beat-up vehicle."

"I was wondering," Aleda said slowly. "Is there any way we could help Dwayne?"

The old woman sat staring down into her empty mug. "Ain't no way to help somebody who don't want helping," she said.

"Well, thank you for the tea," Aleda said, sighing a little, standing up. "Please call me if there is anything you think of."

Aleda stepped off the front porch into the bright afternoon, and although the day was clear and warm she shivered as she headed back up Main Street.

10

Steeples

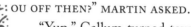

"YOU OFF THEN?" MARTIN ASKED.

"Yup." Callum turned toward the back door of Martin's farmhouse and stooped to pet Buddy on his way out.

"Your lunch?" Martin asked. "Where's your school lunch?"

Callum shrugged. "Oh, the teacher will give me crackers from the cupboard."

"Crackers from the cupboard? Hey, wait a minute. You can't go all day on some crackers. That brain of yours needs to be fed so you can do that complicated math. Come into the kitchen. We're going make you some peanut butter sandwiches."

"Don't allow peanut butter in school," Callum muttered, but Martin could see that the boy didn't move from the doorway.

"Then how about ham?" Martin asked.

The boy nodded.

Martin buttered four slices of bread, removed a ham from the refrigerator, cut two thick slices, and looked toward the boy. "Mustard?"

Callum shook his head, but his eyes never left the table. Martin wrapped the sandwiches, put them into a plastic grocery bag, and added a can of cola and an apple. He twirled the bag to form a knot and handed it to Callum.

"See you after school," Martin called out as the boy ran down the back steps. Martin stood watching him tear down the gravel laneway but noticed that as soon as Callum reached the end of the laneway he retrieved a ham sandwich from the bag. Those sandwiches aren't going to make it to lunch time, Martin thought, shaking his head. He may need crackers after all.

Callum was faithful about visiting Buddy before setting off for school, and when school was over for the day he dropped into Martin's house again. Sometimes he came back to pet the dog and "put her to bed," as he said to Martin. The dog thrived on the attention. Her body filled out from having regular meals and she even submitted to Martin and Callum brushing out her matted fur. Martin noticed that he had begun to structure his day around the boy, making sure that he was home by four in the afternoon for Callum's visit.

Martin turned back into his house and began to gather up file folders lying on the kitchen table. He set them in alphabetical order into a brown metal file case, his mind on the boy. I have a daughter of my own, he thought. What is it that makes me feel so protective of this kid? Maybe it's because the boy seems neglected. Maybe he brings out the helper in me. But really, what he loved most about Callum was his fierce independence and his fiery self-confidence. You have to admire a boy like that, he mused.

Martin sat down at the table and made a shopping list: dog food, bread, oatmeal cookies, and given the events of the morning, another piece of ham. Then as he stood up and tucked the list into the side pocket of his jeans, he resolved to face the inevitable. He had to go across the road and talk to Callum's father, find out what was going on over there. The man must wonder about some stranger befriending his boy.

Martin stooped and patted the dog and left the farm house carrying his file box. He climbed into the cab of his truck and settled the box so that it was easy to reach. Martin hesitated at the end of his laneway before turning toward the village, thinking that he should drive across the road to Callum's house to see the boy's father.

Later. I'll do that later, he thought.

As often as he could, Martin shopped at the village store. It was Martin's opinion that people should patronize local businesses because they were often the heart of the community. The village store was the place you went to talk to someone when you were lonely, and where you could hear the local news. Besides, shopping in the village gave him an excuse to pop in to visit his mother, and the chances were always good that there would be warm cinnamon rolls and a cup of hot coffee ready for him.

As Martin was passing the doctor's house, he noticed Laura sitting in the shady arbour, reading a book. On an impulse, he eased the truck into the driveway.

"Mornin' Laura. That a good book?"

Laura smiled and laid down her book.

"You're reading a book called *What Is It Like to Be a Bat?*"

"It's an essay, really," she said, leaning forward. "Your mother's been to visit."

"Ah. That explains everything."

"She wanted to know if she could pick up some interesting reading for me from the Owen Sound library, and what else do I have to do with my days? I never thought that I would be reading a book called *What Is It Like to Be a Bat?*"

"You interested in bats? Or vampires?"

"Not a bit. Your mother explained that it's written by Thomas Nagel, a contemporary philosopher. She said that most of us believe that profound philosophy started and ended with Plato and Aristotle and that we postmoderns should expand our minds and read some contemporary philosophy."

"It's an interest for the select few, I'm afraid," Martin mumbled, shuffling his feet. "If only that woman would stick to the construction of sourdough cinnamon rolls."

As they laughed together, Martin stood up and said, "I'm off, then, to shop and ...I don't suppose...you wouldn't like to..."

He stopped and looked so self-conscious and embarrassed that Laura laughed again. "Hey, spit it out, Martin. What are you asking?"

"I have a hobby of exploring old buildings. Been at it for a number of years and it's rather an obsession with me in the summer because I've got the time for it. Today I'm off to explore some old churches. Would you be interested in coming along for the ride?"

To Martin's surprise, Laura smiled eagerly, her face animated. "I'd love to, as long as you can be patient with my slowness."

When Laura had settled into the cab of the truck, Martin eased down the hill to the store. He nodded to two old men on the benches, warming themselves in the morning sunshine.

"Great day," he called out. "Anything new?"

"Not much," one man replied. "You still up to that crazy business on your farm?"

"I'll keep you posted," Martin said with a grin. "You'll be the first to know." He bounded up the stairs two at a time.

He was putting his groceries into a cooler in the back of his truck when he spotted Roy and Aleda standing at the end of Roy's driveway. Both were leaning on shovels and looking down at a tangled mess spread out on newspapers on the driveway. With a wave to Laura sitting in the cab of his truck and putting up his fingers to indicate two minutes, Martin walked the short distance to Roy's house.

"What are you two up to?" he inquired.

"Trying to make sense of my day lilies," Roy answered. "Aleda here thinks she might like to plant some around her new composter, but she can't make up her mind which ones."

Aleda smiled and shrugged. "Maybe I'll take a couple of each."

"You're welcome to them," Roy responded. "Tell you the truth, I don't pick day lilies for their colour. I grow day lilies 'cause they're so easy to grow. They don't need special attention, not like those fussy prima donna delphiniums over there. Nope, day lily flowers last only one day, but the whole plant just keeps on blooming. Especially this one. It's *Stella D'Oro*, one of my favourites. Did you know there are thousands of varieties of daylilies? I go all over the countryside lookin' for new varieties."

"Thousands!" Martin and Aleda exclaimed together. "How do you choose which ones to bring home?"

"Oh, easy. I pick them for their names."

"Their names?"

"Yup. This one here, as I said, is *Stella D'Oro*, gold Stella. Don't that just make you think of a dark-haired Spanish beauty, all sassy and decked out in a red dress and a gold shawl and a fan, maybe swirling around with some castanets?"

Martin glanced at Aleda, who was staring at Roy.

"And this one," Roy continued, moving some of the muddy tubers with the end of his shovel, "this one is called *Rosy Returns*. Now, don't you just imagine sittin' in your garden longing for a little company and then in through the garden gate strolls Rosy, the girl of your dreams, all decked out in pink and lace and ribbons. I always put *Rosy Returns* right next to this one in my garden. It's called *When My Sweetheart Returns*. A beauty she is, too. All pink and cream."

Roy, Aleda, and Martin stood staring down at the muddy jumble of roots spread on the driveway.

"Why, Roy," Aleda said, "I never realized that you're so romantic."

Since it was Monday and officially her day off, Aleda had intended to spend her time filling her new composter and planting day lilies. But after Aleda, Roy, and Martin had finished scrutinizing the pile of bulbous roots in Roy's driveway, Martin turned to Aleda and said, "Laura and I are off around the countryside on a wild goose chase. Roy may search for day lilies, but I'm on a mission to find unique old buildings. It's a bit of a hobby with me. I focus on buildings built in the 1800s. Last month I did barns. This month I'm doing churches. I want to take some photos of steeples. Are you interested in coming along for the ride?"

"Old churches and steeples," Aleda repeated flatly. "Um, sure." The idea of spending a day rattling around the countryside with Martin and Laura had a certain appeal.

"I have to be back by four so it won't be a long day. You'll still have time to get your planting done before the sun goes down."

"Why not!" Aleda exclaimed.

Laura shuffled into the centre of the cab bench and Martin stowed the file box and Laura's crutches in the back of the pickup. "Off we go then," he called out. He shifted gears and headed west. "First stop is Tara, Christ Church Anglican."

Speaking in a loud voice over the whine of the engine and the wind whistling through the driver's-side window that would not close to the top, Martin began to explain why some churches had intricate soaring steeples while others were stumpy and squat.

"I suppose it had to do with the resources of the people who were building the church. Everybody wanted a grand tall steeple, of course. I've heard, too, that there was a bit of competition about steeple size. If the Anglicans put up a church steeple, then the Presbyterians or Roman Catholics tried to build their steeple higher."

"Are you kidding me?" Aleda exclaimed.

Martin shrugged. "There was a spiritual aspect to the steeple too. The vertical line was to draw the eye up, to remind people of the heavens. God was presumably up there somewhere, and the steeple was to point people to God. And most of the steeples had a belfry, like yours. Before telephones and clocks, the bell would ring to call people to worship or announce a birth or a wedding or a funeral. Sometimes it rang for emergencies, too. If people heard the bell ringing midweek, they would drop everything and run to the church. Most steeples in the churches in small rural communities were built in the middle of the church over the front door, but the builder of your church, Aleda, set the front door and steeple to the right of the worship space. It gives your church a bit of an off-set look that is distinctive."

"I've often wondered why the door to the steeple is located between the church and the parsonage. Is that normal?"

Martin laughed. "I wouldn't presume to know the first thing about normal when it comes to churches, but it is unusual. Perhaps it means nothing more than the fact that the builder had a bit of a creative streak."

Martin slowed in front of a farm lane lined with maple trees.

"See that house on the right?" Both Laura and Aleda bent their heads sideways, peering out the dusty window. "That is the most characteristic house style in rural southern Ontario. They're everywhere.

"Oh. I hadn't noticed before." Laura turned her head to get a better look.

"Some people call them the 'Ontario cottage' or the 'Ontario farmhouse'. Architects and historians refer to the style as Gothic Revival but since I'm neither architect nor historian, I call them Ontario cottages. They're a solid little house, quite functional really, and rather beautiful in their symmetry, don't you think? Those two balanced side windows, the door in the middle, the single gable in the centre, just like the house I grew up in."

Martin drove on, glancing sideways at the two women and wondering if they were really all that interested in old buildings. He knew that his wife and daughter hadn't shared this interest. He had taken them along on a couple of his rambles, but after a few excursions they had politely made excuses. He told himself that sometimes, despite his best intentions, he got too excited about this particular amateur interest.

After they had crossed the county line, Aleda turned to Martin and said, "This may be a stupid question, but I've been wondering how there got to be so many Ontario cottages. Did they all buy the same pattern from the Eaton's catalogue?"

Martin laughed. "The reason was more practical. In the early 1800s the tax rate was based on the style and size of your house. If you lived in a grand two storey Georgian house with lots of windows at the front like yours, Laura, your taxes would be about 60 pounds, but if you had an Ontario cottage that had one and a half storeys and only two windows at the front, the taxes were only 35 pounds. Those early settlers were sly. They knew that the tax man assessed their house by looking at it from the roadway. They tried to make their houses look as small as possible in order to deceive the tax-man. Some things never change! That tax system was abandoned in 1853, but by then people were used to the style, so it remained. Of course, there's hardly one today that hasn't been added to."

Martin slowed to enter the village of Tara.

After Martin and Aleda had walked the perimeter and grave-yard of Christ Church Anglican and returned to the truck, Laura asked Martin, "Do you never go inside these old churches?"

"Oh, I'm not one for the inside. To me, they all look the same and smell the same – dusty, stale, airless. They all reek of old hym-nals to me."

Martin noticed that Aleda jerked her head sideways to look at him and he wondered if he had offended her, but when he glanced over she had turned back toward the windshield and was staring straight ahead. Because he hadn't meant to hurt her feelings, and hoping to make up for his remark, Martin said, "There's a church I want to see in Wiarton. So why don't I take the two of you for a hamburger and fries at Dockside Willies? Then, if you're well be-haved," he said, adopting a British accent, "we'll go next door and see if the famous Wiarton Willie groundhog will deign to receive us this afternoon."

"I may not know my rural Ontario architecture," Aleda said, pretending to be indignant, "but I do know about this famous ro-dent who has an uncanny ability to predict whether spring will come early or late. Or is it that Wiarton Willie has an uncanny ability to put new commercial life into a sleepy little Georgian Bay town in February?"

At 3 p.m. Martin announced that it wass time to head home. "Gotta get those day lilies planted," he said.

Aleda sighed. Somehow it all sounded like a lot of work, but she couldn't disappoint Roy. After the truck rolled to a stop in front of her house, she thanked Martin rather too profusely and jumped out of the truck.

"Be honest with me, Aleda. Did you enjoy it?"

"I did. I didn't expect to, but I do love the unexpected, and I learned a lot about old buildings, especially church steeples."

"Sometime I'll give you a rundown on this house you live in," he said, gesturing to the parsonage.

With a wave of her hand, Aleda turned into the alleyway between the church and the house and stood for a moment looking up at the steeple, wishing that she could see into the minds and hearts of the pioneers who had erected it. She opened the back door of the parsonage and saw the blinking red light on her answering machine. She punched play and was surprised to hear Savannah's voice.

"Aleda, I'm sorry to bother you on your day off. A couple of things… Mrs. Hart said her son, James, he's our music teacher, is coming for dinner at her house tomorrow night, and I could give him the cheque if I want. Could you come with me to drop it off? At six? And the second thing…this may be nothing to worry about, but Dwayne didn't go to school today. Wasn't at the bus stop, and when I went round to his Grandma's after school she said she hadn't seen him since Sunday morning. I just thought that's kinda weird you know. Well, bye."

Aleda stood staring down at the tangled coil of telephone wire, thinking that she had to do something. But what?

II

Eadie

HE NEXT MORNING ALEDA WENT outside and looked at the steeple. It was tall and grand; indications, Aleda hoped, that the early settlers in Milburn Corners had had a burning desire to express their strong belief in God and wanted to convey the importance of looking up to God.

Her eyes stopped at the small doorway built into the base of the steeple, the doorway through which Dwayne ducked each Sunday morning in order to ring the bell. On the ground in front of the door was a large flat stone worn smooth and concave from years of footsteps. When Aleda walked forward onto the stone, she could see that the door to the steeple hung slightly open. Puzzled by this, she eased open the door and peered into the dark space. A light bulb had been mounted on the side of the door frame and when Aleda pulled the string to turn it on she could see that there was nothing in the small room except a small pile of dried leaves swept up against one wall, spider webs in the corner, and the long thick rope hanging from the bell. When an image of bats and mice swept through her mind, Aleda slammed shut the door and latched it securely.

Aleda settled herself in her office for the morning, studying the scriptures for the following Sunday's worship and preparing for a baptism. It had been some months since there had been an infant baptism in Milburn Corners Community Church, so Aleda and the church leaders had planned carefully. The baby girl, Eden, would be presented by her grandfather, one of the elders of the church, and Aleda had purchased some gifts for the baby and her family on behalf of the members: a picture Bible, a baptismal candle, a silver cross on a chain. It will be encouraging for all of us to have a baptism this week, she thought.

Earlier that morning Aleda had bumped into Rose on her way to the mailbox. No point in avoiding this, Aleda thought. When Rose asks about the sourdough I will just be honest. But Rose was not thinking about cinnamon rolls and sourdough. Rather, she was worrying over Eadie.

"I hear that my dear, dear friend Eadie is in hospital and is not expected to live long."

"That's correct," Aleda replied softly. "I'm on my way to visit her this afternoon."

"Eadie and I go back a long way. We have many parallels in our lives, really. Our memories and experiences of the war – she came here as a young war bride, you know."

Aleda nodded.

"And you may have heard that my husband came back from the war with severe injuries. No one was better to me than Eadie in those years when we were all adjusting to new realities."

Aleda nodded again and touched Rose lightly on the arm.

"Is it possible that I might go along with you to see Eadie this afternoon?" Rose asked.

"Of course. I would be delighted with the company and I'm sure Eadie would be very happy to see you."

Aleda and Rose quietly entered the room where Eadie lay, her thin hands folded on top of a patch-work quilt brought from her bed at home. The room was warm and quiet, the blinds pulled down. They stood by the door for a moment, letting their eyes adjust to the dim light. Rose gestured Aleda to an empty chair beside the bed and they waited, listening to the rhythmic clicking of a monitor.

Sensing a presence in the room, Eadie opened her eyes. She smiled when she saw Aleda sitting beside her and Rose standing close by on the other side of the bed. They both smiled back and Aleda placed a hand gently over the thin folded hands, noticing that the skin was so transparent that they could see Eadie's pulse throbbing in the raised blue arteries.

"I'm so glad you both came," Eadie said. "Have you been here long?"

They shook their heads.

"I sleep so much that sometimes I miss my visitors."

"Do you mind if they waken you?"

"No no, not at all. I wish they would. I feel bad when I find out that they've been here and I've slept through their visit. While I was sleeping just now, I was sure I could smell cinnamon. That's what wakened me." She smiled up at Rose.

Rose squeezed Eadie's hand gently and Aleda could see tears shining in both pairs of eyes.

Turning to Aleda, Eadie said, "Aleda…the baptism…my granddaughter is having her baby baptized on Sunday. It's my first great-grandchild, a little girl, Eden. They brought the baby to see me yesterday."

"Yes." Aleda smiled, nodding. "Wonderful, isn't it? We're all looking forward to it so much."

"There's something I've been wondering," Eadie said. Aleda waited. "I've been wondering if I could go to church on Sunday to see the baptism. It would mean the world to me."

Aleda nodded slowly. "Have you talked to your daughter and granddaughter about this?"

With difficulty, as if she were very weary, Eadie turned her head on the pillow. "I mentioned it to my daughter yesterday and I mentioned it to the doctor when he was in, but neither of them thought that it would be a good idea. Aleda, you will try to help me, won't you?" Aleda nodded and glanced up at Rose. Eadie sighed and, looking directly at Aleda, said, "I know I'm not long for this world."

Aleda dipped her head and then, realizing that Eadie wanted to talk about dying, Aleda said softly, "Do you have hope, Eadie?"

"Oh, yes," Eadie smiled. "I know that I will be with the Lord, and will see my dear husband again, and our little son who only lived three days. You remember that time, don't you Rose?"

"Oh, I do. I do."

"I know I will see them soon," she said. But then she added, whispering, "The hardest part is leaving behind the ones I love. I can't tell you how happy it would make me to see my great-grand-daughter baptized."

"I think we can manage that, Eadie. Yes, I think we can make that happen."

Rose had been quiet on the journey home, but as they pulled up in front of her house she said, "You know, Aleda, this afternoon reminded me again that life is fragile and that we should try to tidy up some of our loose ends before we go to meet our Maker. There's something that has been a worry and concern to me and I feel that it might help a great deal if I just told you about it."

When she returned home Aleda slumped into the wicker porch chair, sobered by her conversation with Rose. It would take some time to make sense of the story that Rose had just confided.

She also thought back to her conversation with Eadie. Why on earth, she demanded of herself, had she made an impossible promise to a dying old woman who can barely turn her head on a pillow? How would Eadie get to church on Sunday? Even if we could get her into a wheelchair, and even if four strong men carried her up the steps into the church, we wouldn't be able to get the wheelchair into the sanctuary. The aisles in our old church are just too narrow. What was I thinking? At that very moment she had an idea. But before she phoned Eadie's daughter to see what she thought she would have to talk to Michael and see if it was even possible.

From the porch window, Aleda glanced every few minutes toward the corner store. When she spotted the teens getting off the school bus, she hurried out and stood waiting as the five friends ambled up the road. Aleda frowned, noticing that Dwayne had not been on the bus. As the group of teens approached, she called out, "Dwayne not at school today?"

"Nope. None of us has seen or heard from him since Sunday," Savannah responded, shaking her head.

They stood in silence for a moment, wondering what on earth had happened to Dwayne.

Aleda remembered her conversation earlier that day with Eadie and turned to Michael. "Michael, I'm sorry to bother you with this, and I don't want this to interfere with your homework tonight, but I have a problem and wonder if you could give me some advice."

Michael looked up in surprise.

Aleda's words tumbled out. "We have an elderly member of our church who is dying in the hospital, but this Sunday her great-granddaughter will be baptized here at the church. It's her dying wish to come and see the baptism but the problem is neither her daughter nor the doctor thinks that this is possible or wise. She's just too ill. So I was wondering if we might videotape the baptism and show it to her in the hospital. If her daughter is there to watch it with her, Eadie might feel as if she had been there. You're the most tech-savvy kid I know. Do you think you could do this?"

"Sure!" Michael answered. "Easy. Gravy train. You guys go on," Michael waved to his friends and turned back to Aleda. "If you have the key, we could go into the church for a sec and figure out the best way to do it and where we could set up for Sunday."

When they had switched on the lights, Michael wandered to the front of the church. "All we'll need is a small table here to sit at, and an extension cord."

Aleda nodded and turned toward the narrow vestry by the side of the chancel. She opened the door, turned on the light, and slid back the bolt on the cupboard that held the extension cords. Then she stopped, frozen. Beside the cupboard was a metal trash can overflowing with empty pizza boxes and drained cola bottles.

"Michael," she called out in a voice that sounded too high to her own ears. "Michael, come here."

Michael hurried to the door. "Something wrong?"

"Look!" Aleda said pointing to the trash can. "These weren't here Sunday, and there have been no meetings this week. You don't suppose that Dwayne has been living in the church, do you?"

"Beats me," Michael replied, shrugging. "He's been so badass lately. Oh, excuse the language, Rev, but honestly, the guy can be such a jerk sometimes. I just can't figure him out."

Aleda nodded and pulled an extension cord from the cupboard. "Yes. Well. Let's get this thing set up."

At six o'clock, Savannah rolled into Aleda's driveway on her bike. "Ready to go to Mrs. Hart's to deliver the cheque?" she called through the screen door.

"Were you afraid to go by yourself?" Aleda asked in a teasing tone of voice.

"No not really. I just thought that since you helped us get the money you should be there to help us hand it over to the band teacher. It all seems a bit weird though, don't you think? The band teacher's mother gives us a cheque and we hand it over to the band teacher who is her son."

"Try not to over-analyze," Aleda smiled, patting Savannah on the shoulder. "It's just one wonderful woman helping some wonderful kids who have a wonderful band teacher."

12

Ordinary Day

ROBERT HAD ONCE GIVEN ALEDA some advice.

"Aleda, my dear," he had said, smiling and leaning toward her, "you tend to overthink things."

"Overthink? What are you saying? I always believe that I don't use my brain enough! I just jump right in and try to get out of trouble later."

Robert nodded. "May I suggest one little thing to you? At the end of the day – don't do this in the morning when everything seems possible – ask yourself, 'What did this ordinary day bring to me?' I've found it a helpful little question myself, for I find that I berate myself for not getting a task done or for neglecting a parishioner. So at the end of day when I ask myself what the day brought, I'm often surprised by the opportunities I had for a small gesture of hope, or a word of comfort to someone, or a moment of being just plain good to myself. I'm often amazed that an ordinary day can result in such extraordinary things."

"Hmm …" Aleda had murmured, for at the time she had been disappointed with Robert's advice.

Sometimes, though, at the end of the day her conversation with Robert came back to her and she found herself asking, "What did this ordinary day bring to me?"

Aleda opened the refrigerator door to reach for cream for her breakfast coffee. She lifted the empty carton and shook it. Now why would I put an empty carton back into the fridge? She slipped on her shoes, grabbed a five dollar bill and started down the street toward the store.

The two old men who enjoyed the morning sun outside the store on the green steel benches called out good morning.

"Lovely country air today!" Aleda answered. "Somebody must be cleaning out his pig barn."

"Humph," one old man snorted. "Either that or that Martin Hart is up to that business of his on his farm again."

"Business?" But the man stopped talking as he spotted Rose Hart coming down the street toward the store.

"Good morning, Aleda! How wonderful to see you this morning," Rose called out. She shifted the net shopping bag onto her left arm. "I forgot to ask you last night how the sourdough recipes turned out."

"And I've been meaning to ask how you are getting along with your Nietzsche book," Aleda countered, hoping to steer the conversation away from the failed sourdough that had overflowed its bowl and escaped from her cupboard.

"Oh that Martin," Rose laughed. "Now he has me reading Simone de Beauvoir."

At that moment, by the grace of God, or so Aleda thought, they were interrupted by Grace, who had crossed the street on a mission, no doubt, for more baking powder or a box of salt. Aleda turned to run up the store steps while Rose was distracted with talking to Grace.

On her way home, cream clutched in one hand, Aleda noticed Roy, watering can in hand, at the end of his driveway.

"Fertilizing the roses," he called out. "Ya got those day lilies in the ground all right, Aleda?"

Aleda's mind flashed to the tangled mess of muddy roots lying in the washtub by her back door. Monday, Tuesday, Wednesday, she counted. How long do unplanted day lily roots live? To her relief, she spotted Grace returning from the store, carrying a box of baking soda. When Grace saw Aleda and Roy together, she marched toward them.

"I've been wondering if you've given more thought to the strawberry social?" She peered at Aleda, frowning.

"More thought? Well, um, I thought things were all organized."

"Well, that's what everyone thinks," Grace responded in a testy, complaining voice. "People think these events just happen. They take a lot of organization, you know."

"I know, I know," Aleda said quickly, turning away from Roy and Grace. She gained a distraction as a car slowed down beside them and the driver rolled down the window.

"I'm finally able to drive again! I picked up a rental car in Owen Sound just now. I got the cast off and now have a walking boot," Laura called out through the car window. "Freedom!" She pumped her fist in the air and Aleda looked into the car and pursed her lips in mock admiration of the pristine white walking boot on Laura's left foot.

"Wonderful!" Aleda called out.

"I'm off to shop," Laura called. "See you Friday night?"

"Sure thing," Aleda called back, waving and smiling.

Both Grace and Roy were staring at Aleda. "You've become friends? You've become friends with the Doctor's daughter?" Aleda nodded.

"Maybe you could bring her to church sometime," Roy suggested.

"Maybe."

"Maybe she would like to join our Ladies Guild," Grace proposed.

"Maybe, but I did hear her say that she would like to bring two pounds of butter to the strawberry social. Gotta run," Aleda said, turning to hurry up the street.

Later that afternoon, after two hours of reading reports for the upcoming General Assembly, trying not to let her mind linger on her dread and excitement about meeting Ben again, Aleda stood up, stretched, and was standing by the kitchen window, her mind vacant and her body tense, when the telephone rang. It was Eadie's daughter.

"I'm sorry to tell you, but mother passed away quietly this afternoon."

"Oh, I am so sorry," Aleda said. "So terribly sorry."

There was silence on the phone for a moment, and Aleda could hear quiet sobs. "Your mother was so looking forward to seeing the video recording of the baptism."

Eadie's daughter blew her nose. "I know, and now we have a sad funeral and a happy baptism all in one week."

"Yes."

"But that's life, isn't it? You never know what life will bring, do you?"

Aleda was on the verge of saying what she often said in situations like this because she was convinced of it – but we know that God is with us in both the good times and the bad times of life – but Eadie's daughter was asking her if the funeral could be on Friday at 11 a.m.

Aleda had just hung up the phone when it rang again. Savannah.

"Aleda I have good news!"

"I could use some of that."

"It's Dwayne! He's back. He's home. He just walked into his grandmother's house today as if he'd never been away. We met him after school and he didn't say a word about where he's been and we didn't ask. We just talked about the kid's camp on Saturday and he seems happy to help."

"That's wonderful, Savannah! I'm very relieved and happy to hear this. Very relieved." Aleda raised her shoulders, shrugging out the tension. She was extremely thankful to hear that Dwayne was safe.

Okay Robert, she thought as she prepared for bed. What did this ordinary day bring to me? She thought back over her narrow escapes from having to explain why the sourdough hadn't produced delectable cinnamon rolls and why the day lily roots were still mouldering in the washtub. She thought about Rose struggling to read Simone de Beauvoir while she herself struggled to read weighty church reports. She thought about her delight in seeing Laura so happy to be mobile again. She remembered her heavy heart after hearing of Eadie's death and her sadness at not being able to grant an old woman her dying wish. She thought of the leap in her heart when she heard from Savannah that Dwayne was safe at home. It's like Eadie's daughter said: life has many ups and downs.

What did this ordinary day bring to me? It brought me a day where I felt humbled to be pastor to these people in their ups and downs. In that instant, Aleda recognized that this was where she was meant to be, and that she *was* making a difference in the lives of people. Could she hold on to this belief?

13

Desk

AURA'S DECISION TO RETURN to her parents' former home in the quiet village of Milburn Corners while her broken ankle healed had seemed sensible at the time. She would finally have an opportunity to sort things out in the grand old Georgian house that had been vacant for four years.

But shortly after arriving, she repeatedly questioned her decision to spend time in a house that was full of memories, mementos, and dust. So far, her stay there had been full of empty hours, tedium, and loneliness. The house was even more dated and stuffy than Laura remembered, and each small task was arduous as she hoisted herself from place to place on crutches, bumping into things, annoyed that every ordinary activity was so difficult to accomplish. After a week, she had been on the verge of calling her friend for a ride back to her condo on St. Clair Avenue in Toronto.

Yet she hadn't made the phone call. When and how had it happened that she began to enjoy being in Milburn Corners? Was it when she initiated friendships with Martin and Aleda? Was it Rose dropping in with cinnamon rolls and books? Was it when she began to watch for the little boy in red shorts making his way down the hill past her house on his way to school? Was it her new walking boot that gave her a sense of independence and freedom? Probably a bit of all these things, she thought as she stood in the living room.

Laura looked out over the village. Where was everyone? There were no men sitting in front of the store. Roy's garage door was shut and there seemed to be less traffic than usual on Main Street. What she didn't know was that most people were busy preparing for Eadie's funeral. Aleda was in her office writing a funeral meditation, Roy was tidying up the perennial beds on the west side of the church, Grace was rolling out pastry for raisin and walnut butter tarts, Rose was shaping two loaves of sourdough cinnamon bread, and Margaret was boiling eggs to make egg salad sandwiches.

Stratus clouds had moved in to cover the sky like a gray blanket, and a light drizzle had begun to fall. Laura stood in the window with her arms crossed and her sweater pulled tightly around her shoulders, wondering if the day had at last arrived when she could begin to sort out her father's office. She turned toward the curtained doors of the clinic; a visual block between what happened in the doctor's private life and the secrecy, as it seemed to Laura, of his professional practice. Odd that her mother had not entered the room after the doctor's death, not even to clear off the desk. She had shut the doors the day after the funeral, as if pretending that section of the house did not exist.

When their mother had died, Laura and David had not come back to sort out the house and prepare it for sale. Instead, they had asked Roy to look in from time to time to check that no water pipes had burst during the icy months of winter. After she broke her ankle though, Laura had phoned David in Edmonton.

"Hey, Dave, I'm thinking I'll go up to Milburn Corners for a bit while this ankle heals. We've got to do something with the old house."

"I hear you, sis. Totally agree. How would it be if I take a week of vacation in July and come to Milburn Corners? In the meantime, if you could maybe get a start on Dad's office, that would be helpful. Maybe rent a dumpster? You can check with some medical libraries, but his medical books are so old I doubt they'll want any, unless there is some historical value, of course."

Laura hadn't made a start yet. Something had been holding her back. But perhaps this was the day.

After Laura had graduated from university she had gone into therapy for a time. When the therapist asked her what had brought her to the office, Laura had responded, "It's my father. I wish I could talk with him. It's like we have things to resolve and I don't know what the issues are. I feel as if I'm never enough. Neither is my brother, or my mother. My father isn't abusive, but we're all so afraid of him; yet at the same time we're always trying to please him. He doesn't seem happy and that makes all of us unhappy. I'd like to be able to enjoy the company of my father and not be afraid."

Laura flung open the doors to her father's office, removed the drapes and dumped them in the corner of the hall. She turned on all the lights – the crystal chandelier in the front hallway, the thin yellowed bulb in the tiny waiting room, the dusty green lamp on her father's desk, and the glaring fluorescent tubes in the adjoining examining room. Then she hobbled back out into the hall and flung open the door to the living room and turned on every lamp in that room. She walked over to the out-of-date audio centre that her mother had installed years ago to play her favourite recordings of Brahms and Beethoven. Shuffling through her mother's collection she was surprised to find a Rolling Stones record. She put it on and raised the volume high enough to make her ears buzz, returned to the office.

Air. What this room needs is fresh air, she thought, hobbling over to the window. She unlatched the bottom sash, raised the window a few inches, and propped it open with a medical dictionary. If there had ever been a screen, it had long ago disappeared.

Laura returned to the desk and sank down into the leather chair that was inclined to tip backward as if worn out by years of use. She listened to the rain that had begun to drip off the roof overhang. Through the open window came the musky root cellar smell of last fall's dampened leaves blown up against the side of the house. The Stones belted out "Brown Sugar" as she sat. What is wrong with me? she demanded of herself. Why can't I get started? The task felt overwhelming, colossal in its demands. Not only did her body feel weary but a somnolence fell over her spirit and left her drained. Why did I think I could do this? There must be companies that come in and clear out old houses. Laura stared around the room and recalled the discreet hush of the old house. She felt the old silence seeping into her as surely as the misty rain was seeping into the untilled flower beds under the eaves of the house. They had all been tiptoeing through life, waiting for the Doctor's roar.

Laura was about to abandon any thoughts of sorting when she realized that she could do a little piece at a time. Today she would just clean the top of the desk. Tomorrow she could do the drawers on the right hand side. Just a little bit at a time. It would be a start.

She fetched an empty clothes basket and a plastic garbage bag. Keepers go in here, she thought, setting the clothes basket to her left, and everything else goes in the garbage bag. She folded back the top of the bag and set it to her right.

Her father's rolltop desk was vintage dark oak, and as she sat at it she felt amazed that she had never been on this side of the desk. Centred on the desktop was a large blotter that served both as a calendar and an appointment book. To the right of the blotter were a yellowed prescription pad and a leather cup holding pens and blunt pencils. To the left was a coaster. The rest of the desktop was bare, dull, and dusty.

It was the back of the desk that intrigued Laura. Across the top was a bank of eight small drawers with tiny wooden knobs. A square metal label holder fronted each drawer, but her father had not labelled any of them. In the centre were five small shelves where her father had stored pamphlets of one kind or another. Laura picked them up and shuffled through the yellowed brittle papers: breast feeding problems in infants, how to care for a loved one after surgery, how to treat gout. Laura tossed them into the garbage bag. Situated on either side of the back of the desktop were two long drawers in which she found samples of medications. She pulled out both drawers and dropped the contents into the garbage bag. She cleaned out the eight small drawers on the top – old thermometers, a pearl-handled mirror, two old stethoscopes, a package of suppositories, and a pair of forceps. "Top of the desk all cleaned out," she said aloud. She squeezed the old desk pad in two and dumped it, along with the prescriptions pads and old pens and pencils, into the garbage bag. Laura held the leather pen holder up to the light and then set it into the laundry basket.

Still sitting in her father's chair, she picked up the garbage bag and smiled, proud that she had made a start on what had seemed a gargantuan task. I'll go to the kitchen and bring back some furniture polish for this desktop, she decided, and this old coaster — well, I'll keep it until I'm through with sorting the desk. I may need many cups of coffee and may even graduate to wine if the going gets tough.

Laura set the coaster to the right side of the desk, rose to gather up the garbage bag, and then glanced back. Lying on the desk where the coaster had been was a small silver key. Laura sat back down and began opening all the desk drawers. More pens and paper clips, envelopes, prescription pads, a stapler; but nothing requiring a key. Why had this key been close to her father's fingertips during his lifetime? And what did it open?

14

Sawdust

S ALEDA SAT AT HER DESK preparing to write a meditation for Eadie's funeral, she posed the question that she always asked as she settled into this task. What story do I most remember from Eadie's life, and what biblical story seems to best connect with Eadie's life?

Aleda remembered the first time she had visited the old woman. Eadie had told her about coming to Canada to marry her husband who had been posted in England during the war.

"I was so lonely and homesick," Eadie had said. "If it hadn't been for my mother-in-law, I think I would have died. She was so good to me, always checking in and making sure that I had everything I needed.

"I only had the one daughter, you know, but I vowed I would try to be the best possible mother, and if she ever married, a good mother-in-law too."

Aleda had noticed that Eadie and her daughter were close. She knew that Eadie was also very proud of her only granddaughter and had been delighted to see her newborn great-granddaughter, Eden. Aleda recognized that there was a fierce and tender loyalty among the women in Eadie's family and knew that the tears shed at the funeral would be genuine and copious. Ah! There can be no other Bible story that expresses a deep and abiding connection and affection between women than that of Ruth and Naomi. Aleda hunched over her computer, ready to write.

After the funeral was over, Aleda stood looking into the church hall. Roy, wearing a white chef's apron, was steeping tea in the kitchen – steaming hot and strong as only Roy can make it, the women always said. Rose, Grace, and the others from the Ladies Guild were carrying out platters of egg salad and red salmon sandwiches; pink salmon would not do, they had told Aleda many times. The tables were covered with linen and decorated with flowers. Crystal plates held sweet pickles, olives, and celery. A side table was covered with trays of butter tarts, chocolate chip cookies, marshmallow squares, and buttered sourdough cinnamon bread. Tears had turned to hugs and even laughter. Friends shared stories of Eadie with Eadie's family, and all the stories were told with tenderness and care. These are some of our finest moments together as a community, Aleda thought. Give me a good old funeral, where there is genuine emotion and compassion, any day. Aleda, feeling a little foolish and sentimental, smiled through tears as she watched her parishioners settle into the bounty of their funeral luncheon.

At home later, when Aleda thought ahead to the youth group meeting that night, she remembered that she would not need to prepare a thing. The time would be consumed with planning for the day camp the following day. Aleda sighed in relief, anticipating her Friday night dinner with Laura and Martin. She hadn't prepared any food to take! As if Laura had read her mind, the telephone rang.

"Aleda, are you still able to come to dinner tonight? I hear you had a funeral today."

"Oh, of course, it's just that…"

"I was wondering, well, I've been busy sorting out my father's study, and Martin's just called to say that he picked up a package of fresh sausages, so why don't we just have sausages and eggs for dinner? That goes well with wine, doesn't it?" Laura laughed.

"Wonderful idea!" Aleda responded. "I'll bring some eggs. You have any stale bread for toast?"

"Oh, you can count on that."

"I'll see you after eight, then. First I have to help the young people think through their day camp plans for tomorrow."

Aleda rushed around her kitchen, stuffed food items into her tote bag, grabbed her notebook and pen, hurried out to feed Tracker, and dashed over to the church to unlock the front door. The six friends were waiting for her, the girls sitting on the steep cement steps leading up to the front door and the boys standing around the iron railings.

"So sorry I'm late," Aleda panted. "Busy day. Let's get in and get started."

Things fell into place quickly. Jacob would take the lead with sports, Victoria would lead the songs. Ashley loved crafts so she agreed to plan them, Michael said he would do a nature walk, and Savannah offered to help the kids prepare their own snack. She also wanted them to try making and decorating chocolate-dipped strawberries.

It was quiet for a moment and Aleda sat looking down at her notepad. As if both Aleda and Savannah had the same thought, Aleda looked up quickly and met Savannah's gaze: We didn't assign anything to Dwayne. What on earth is Dwayne good at? Savannah looked down at her hands, her thumbs twisting together.

Aleda sat up tall and spoke in a slow and thoughtful voice. "There's something I've been wondering, something I've been really worried about. We have one special little boy who will be coming to camp. I think this child could benefit from some personal attention because one-on-one care is lacking in his home life. His name is Callum and you may have seen him wandering home from school, picking up frogs and sticks along the way. He's always collecting stuff. He's a most interesting boy and is very fond of his dog, Buddy. Buddy is the dog that got hit by the car a week ago. I know Callum is coming to the camp because his neighbour has offered to drive him."

Aleda stopped, then squared herself to look at Dwayne, trying to meet his eyes. "I was wondering, Dwayne, if you might take on the task of being a special mentor to Callum, a sort of older brother. What do you think?"

For a moment, Dwayne didn't say anything. Then, in a slow motion, he raised his head and said, "I guess I could do that."

Aleda smiled, closed her notepad and said, "Well, then, let's take a half hour to think through what each of us has to prepare for our segment of the camp tomorrow, then I suggest you all go out and have fun. I brought along some potato chips and soft drinks. That should help the planning process."

"Oh, one more thing, Rev," Jacob said. "This may be a crazy thought, but I was wondering if we could take the kids to meet your horse. Maybe even feed him or something."

Aleda hesitated. "Hmm. I'll think about that. He can be bad-tempered at times. I would want to make sure that the children stand well back so they are safe. Let me think about it."

"Awesome," Jacob said, ripping open a bag of potato chips.

When Aleda arrived at the doctor's house, Laura met her at the door saying, "Come in! I can't tell you how much happier I am now that I have this adorable walking boot. I feel like a new person! Come and see what I've been up to!" Laura led her down the hall to the office. Six large garbage bags stood in the hallway, stuffed full.

"I have a long way to go, but I've made a start and I'm so proud of myself. These are next," she said, gesturing to the shelves over-flowing with old medical books. Aleda ran her hand across the top of the desk.

"Absolutely gorgeous piece of furniture," she said.

"You want it? It's yours."

"Oh no, no, no. Really, I was just admiring it. I do love old furniture and this is so well cared for. Not a dent or a scratch."

Laura nodded. "My brother, David, is coming from Edmonton in a few weeks. There will have to be lots of decisions to be made, no doubt. Come on. Let's take our wine into the arbour until Martin gets here."

"Don't you want to know why I'm late?" asked Martin when he finally arrived and was sitting in the arbour. Aleda and Laura sat looking at him as he moved with exaggerated slowness to take a deliberate sip of beer.

Martin laughed when he saw the curiosity on their faces. "I finally did it. I've been putting off having a good conversation with Callum's father for days. I can be such a coward at times, or maybe a procrastinator. I'd promised to pick up Callum for camp tomorrow and I couldn't very well do that without touching base with his father."

"And?" Aleda asked, leaning forward.

"Not much to tell, really," Martin shrugged. "His father is...I dunno...depressed? Not very enthused about life, that's for sure. It was hard to get a read on things, but from what I could tell he gives the boy lots of permission to explore and do whatever he likes. The father doesn't much care what they eat and doesn't seem to pay much attention to the boy's clothes, but he didn't seem unkind or abusive in any way." Martin paused, lost in thought. "The whole time I was there talking with his father, Callum was in the back shed building a park for grasshoppers."

"Grasshoppers!" Aleda and Laura exclaimed in unison.

Martin laughed. "Oh, that boy has interesting ideas. He told me that he's making a grasshopper park and that the best time to catch grasshoppers is in the morning when it's cool, because then they don't jump as high. He said that it's a little early in the season to catch grasshoppers, but there will be plenty around in August, and he wants to have his park ready."

"No kidding."

"When he gets them all collected, he's going to give them names. Then he's going to measure how far each grasshopper can jump. Not sure why he wants to do that, but I think he would just find that interesting. On the way home from school, he found a lid from a plastic margarine tub. He told me that it will be the feeding station. The dining room table for insects, if you like."

"Really." Laura nodded in mock sincerity.

"And what, pray tell, do grasshoppers eat?" Aleda inquired.

"Ah, my dear, dear friends. I thought you would never ask." Martin sat back, folded his arms, and said gravely in a deep voice, "According to a recently interviewed seven-year-old expert, grasshoppers are herbivores, and they are particularly fond of…" Martin leaned forward and whispered, "fresh clover."

The three friends settled into their lawn chairs laughing, content to let the conversation lead them one way and another. Laura inquired about Eadie's funeral, and Aleda found herself telling her new friends about the camp happening the following day. Laura talked about how pleased she was to be more mobile and independent with her new walking boot. She told Martin and Aleda about her start at clearing her father's office, and when she pulled the small silver key from the pocket of her slacks, they both inspected it, rolling it over in the palms of their hands as if expecting to see something different on the other side. They agreed that Laura would, without a doubt, come across a locked metal box during the rest of her sorting.

Martin said that he had spent the afternoon waiting for the dump truck to arrive with a load of sawdust.

"Sawdust?" Aleda tilted her head sideways, frowning. "Why on earth do you need a truckload of sawdust?"

"Oh, you know," Martin said with a dismissive wave of his hand. "As they say from the benches at the corner store, it's that business I'm up to on my farm."

"Hey, Aleda," Laura said, "even I know the local gossip. Martin, here, is experimenting with composting dead farm animals."

Aleda stared at Martin, her mouth open, a look of incredulity on her face. Martin glanced at her and shrugged. "Well, I didn't want to mention it to you because I thought you might wonder if I was after Tracker."

"Tracker!" Aleda could hear that her voice was too loud. "Are you serious?" Looking at Martin, she couldn't tell if he was teasing her.

"Hey, hey, hey," he said in a soothing way. "It's a harmless enough thing you know. And someone has to take the lead. Death happens all the time on farms. Farmers aren't happy when it occurs, but animals do die. And what do you do with the carcasses?"

Aleda shook her head slowly.

"You have some options," Martin continued. "You can bury them or call in someone from a dead stock plant and get them to remove the dead animal and incinerate it. Farmers around here do sometimes just leave the animal on a stone fence and let scavengers slowly dispose of the body. Then there is often the stink factor, as you can imagine. Or there may be pathogens."

"Pathogens," Aleda said flatly.

"Sure. Disease-causing spores. And then there's the issue of social annoyance too. Imagine going for a lovely stroll through a hardwood forest and coming across a decaying horse. That would put you off hiking for a lifetime," Martin laughed. "Composting dead animals is a good option if I could just convince the farmers in these parts to try it, and the compost can be used back on the land. So it's a good environmental option too."

Aleda sat in silence, lost for words.

Laura reached out and touched her arm. "Hey, it's okay Aleda. What Martin is doing is very useful." She glanced over at Martin, who shrugged.

The three friends sat without speaking for a minute until Aleda turned and stared at Martin. "But why? Why are you doing this?"

Martin looked surprised, and before he could answer Laura turned to Aleda and said, "But didn't you know that Martin is an agricultural researcher at the University of Guelph?"

Aleda looked into her empty wine glass.

"Nobody tells me anything," she muttered morosely, and when Martin and Laura began to laugh, Aleda stared at her friends until finally she began to laugh too.

"We either need to pour a second glass of wine or start grilling up those sausages," Laura said.

Aleda jumped up. "I vote for more wine. I've completely gone off the idea of eating meat tonight."

15

Camp

N SATURDAY MORNING, Aleda rose early, showered and dressed quickly, and rushed to the barn to feed Tracker. She opened the shed door to let in fresh air and sunshine, but left him in his stall.

She felt that it would be safe to let the children come in to visit him if she gave them careful instructions.

Aleda set a red apple on top of the feed bin and hurried to open the doors of the church. She could see Savannah and Victoria heading down from the subdivision. Behind them came Jacob with a soccer ball tucked under his arm. Ashley was carrying a wicker basket piled with raffia and twigs. Michael was missing, but Aleda knew he would be along shortly. Wonderful kids, so full of life and fun and energy, she thought with pride as they approached the church. She glanced to the east end of the village. There was no sign of Dwayne.

The young people began setting up work and play stations. Savannah pulled out pots and chocolate and set out the strawberries on clean tea towels. Ashley began to place supplies on the craft table. Jacob was searching the craft cupboard for bean bags and Michael, who had just rushed in, was photocopying the nature scavenger hunt that he had developed. Upstairs, Victoria was setting out the sound equipment. Why didn't I think to make Dwayne responsible for that? Aleda scolded herself. Where is Dwayne?

Aleda hurried up the basement steps and out the front door. To her relief she caught sight of Dwayne shuffling, head down, toward the church. He wore a pair of baggy jeans that hung low on his hips, an oversized football jersey that hadn't been washed in some time and, as usual, the now familiar beat-up running shoes, the laces untied. Aleda busied herself, pretending to tidy something by the doorway.

"Dwayne! Lovely morning isn't it?" Aleda called out, smiling. "And it's great to see you."

Dwayne didn't answer for a minute and then said, "I thought it would be sunny today."

Aleda nodded. "You ready for this?" she asked.

Dwayne shrugged.

A little boy in baggy red shorts wandered up and down the ditch along Main Street, swinging a plastic grocery bag. From time to time, he stooped to pick something up and put it in the bag.

"Poor little bugger," Dwayne said, staring down the road at Callum. "Poor little bugger."

Aleda glanced sideways at Dwayne, then glanced away quickly when she saw the look of desolation on his face.

Martin approached in his truck and pulled up alongside Callum, who continued to rove around in the ditch, not looking up. The truck crawled forward toward the church, and when Martin saw Aleda and Dwayne, he parked and walked toward the church steps.

"I told Callum and his father that I would drive him, but I guess he prefers to walk," Martin shrugged. "I'll pick him up at two if that's okay. And I brought him a lunch. Somehow, I figured that his dad might forget."

"Good idea. Could you leave the lunch with Dwayne? Dwayne is going to be Callum's mentor for the camp. We thought that Callum might benefit from some one-on-one attention, so we've assigned Dwayne that important role."

Martin glanced at the slouching teenager and gave him a gentle punch on the top of his arm.

"Good luck, son. You're in for an interesting day." Then he turned, waved, climbed into the truck and did a U-turn in front of the church.

In the opinion of Aleda and the teens, the camp was a great success. The dipped strawberries were a huge hit and Aleda snapped photographs of smiling faces smudged with chocolate that didn't make its way on to the fruit. Jacob's enthusiasm for games was contagious. With Ashley's help each child had a nature collage to take home. Victoria taught the children action songs, rounds, and dance moves. At the end of the camp, she set up a make-believe campfire with three blocks of wood, and as the children sat cross-legged she taught them "Fire's Burning" and "Kum Ba Yah".

After exploring in the swamp for their nature scavenger hunt, Michael led the children up through the village, their bags full of boggy treasures. Callum and Dwayne lagged behind, but Dwayne seemed to be helping Callum find valuables to put into his plastic bag. They made their way to the parsonage backyard shed, and Tracker, as it turned out, seemed oblivious to the fact that his living space was in an instant full of small bodies swinging plastic bags full of swamp treasures. Aleda showed them that Tracker liked to have his forehead scratched; she showed them how she combed his coat and mane, and, to the delight of the children, she let Tracker chomp the apple that she held out on a flat palm. When it was time to leave the shed, Aleda led the way to the front lawn of the church.

After they reached the front lawn, Jacob called out, "Who's for a game of dodge ball before lunch?"

As Aleda turned back toward her house, intending to grab her own packed lunch so she could join the children and youth for a picnic, she noticed that the side door into the bell tower was ajar. Through the open door Aleda saw that Dwayne had taken Callum into the small dusty room and both were looking up at the stout rope that was used to pull the heavy bell. Aleda stood looking at the two boys. I guess there's no harm in it, she thought, turning toward the house.

When the children had gone home and the teens had tidied up the church basement, Aleda concluded that it had been a wonderful day. She was proud of the way the youth had conducted themselves as leaders. She smiled and sighed. They are a real tribute to our church and community, and I'm so lucky to have them in my life.

But there was a nagging worry in her mind. When Martin had come to pick up Callum, Aleda had chatted with them for a minute. When she turned back toward her house, there was Dwayne, standing in front of the grass alley. He was just standing, standing and staring into the space between the house and the church.

16

Rope

June 2002

ALEDA WAKENED WITH A START, damp with perspiration. Gasping, she sat up in bed and said aloud, "What was that?"

I could have sworn that I heard the church bell ring, she thought, and as she bent her head sideways she knew that she could hear a faint metallic echo. She glanced at the alarm clock: 2:26 a.m. Hooligans. Young punks drinking at Sauble Beach then sneaking through villages to see what trouble they could make. Well, she thought, pulling up the bed sheet, I shall deal with that in the morning. She rolled over and went back to sleep.

Aleda wakened earlier than usual and lay in bed thinking of the day ahead. Sermon to look over. Worship. Maybe a long walk down to the swamp. She stretched, swung her legs over the edge of the bed, and sat hunched over for a minute.

With a start, she remembered the sound of the church bell in the middle of the night. "Oh, shit, I've gotta deal with that before worship," she said, thinking that she would have to gather up beer bottles from the alleyway. She pulled on some sweat pants and an old sweat shirt and was unlocking the front door when she was startled to see Roy come running from the grass alley shouting, "Aleda! Aleda!"

Roy's face was drained of colour. Aleda stood frozen, her hand on the screen door knob.

"911! Call 911!" he gasped, bending over to catch his breath. "Quick! Quick!"

But Aleda, thinking that perhaps Roy was having a heart attack, ran down the front stairs toward Roy. "What?" Aleda shouted. "Roy! What?"

Down the alley she saw that the door into the steeple was ajar. She stopped abruptly. Through the door, straight ahead of her at eye level, she saw a pair of beat-up running shoes that she could never mistake for anyone else's. A step ladder had fallen over against the back wall.

Somewhere in the distance she heard Roy shouting, but Aleda could not stop herself. She put her head inside the small room and looked up.

There was Dwayne, hanging motionless from the bell rope. His head was bent at a peculiar angle, his eyes were open and bulging, and his tongue protruded from a face streaked with purple and red.

Aleda took a step back out of the room; she heard a whoosh and then her ears began to buzz. Her chest felt heavy and as her knees went soft, she began to sag forward and drop down onto the cold wet grass.

"Aleda, Aleda," she heard Roy shouting as if he were calling from a canyon where echoes bounced this way and that. "Aleda, don't faint. We have to call for help."

Seeing that Aleda had already crumbled to the ground, Roy ran for the back door. Locked. He raced toward the front of the house and ran up the steps. Frantically, he searched for the telephone and with trembling fingers punched in 911.

By the time Roy got back to Aleda, she was sitting up and staring at Dwayne's dangling shoes, her eyes glassy and uncomprehending.

"Oh, Aleda! Thank goodness you're okay." Roy put his hands under her forearms and raised her slowly to her feet. "Come," he said, gently leading her toward the front porch. "Come. I've called for help."

Aleda allowed herself to be led like a child up the front stairs of the house, but when they got inside she began to shake, her teeth chattering. She began to moan softly, "Why? Why?"

"Sit here. Sit here. It's a terrible shock," Roy said, urging her into the porch chair. He grabbed the pink afghan and tucked it around her. Aleda looked up at Roy. His face was ashen and drawn, but before either of them had time to say anything, they heard sirens.

"Stay here, stay here," Roy said, and hurried down the steps to meet the police officer and the paramedics. Aleda shivered under the blanket, teeth chattering, fist pressed against her mouth, until she caught sight of the paramedics wheeling away Dwayne's body covered in a blanket. Villagers had begun to gather on the church lawn, awakened by the sirens.

Aleda rose from her chair and walked down the stairs, holding the rail to steady her knees. I must be strong, I must be strong, she repeated like a mantra. A police officer was attaching yellow caution tape to the entrance of the alley. Then the officer turned to Roy. Roy motioned to where Aleda stood immobile, caught between whether she should talk to the villagers huddled together on the church lawn or move toward the police officer. She stood undecided, then turned to the police officer.

"We meet again, but sadly under terrible circumstances," he said, and Aleda recognized the trace of Irish accent before she looked into his face.

"Constable Brennan. I'm happy to talk to you and tell you what I know."

Just then a car sped up the street into the village, slowed, and stopped in front of the church. Robert and Patrice jumped out and hurried across the lawn. Aleda began to sob. She fell against Robert's comforting big shoulders; Patrice put her arms around Aleda and murmured, "There, there. We're here."

Robert and Patrice led Aleda into the front porch of the parsonage as Aleda broke down. Roy and the police officer watched, bewildered, worried, and hesitant to interfere. Aleda sobbed and wailed as Patrice put her arms around her and Robert stood beside them, an arm around the shoulder of each woman, solid as a rock. Roy looked over at his friends and neighbours gathered in a huddle on the church lawn, their faces a combination of worry, horror, and concern.

After a time, Patrice reached into her handbag and pulled out a rose scented embroidered handkerchief. "Aleda, here," she said, offering the handkerchief.

"Oh, Patrice," Aleda said, holding the handkerchief between her thumb and first finger at arm's length, "I couldn't possibly deposit snot in that."

Patrice stared at Aleda. Aleda stared at Patrice, then, still hiccupping and sobbing, Aleda began to laugh. Patrice, now smiling, led Aleda into the kitchen, handed her a box of tissues and said in a strong voice, "Sit down, and I will make us a cup of tea."

Patrice busied herself filling the kettle, opening cupboard doors to find the teapot, and Robert sat at the kitchen table stroking Aleda's hand. Then Patrice glanced up and saw Constable Brennan at the door.

"I am so sorry," she said. "It's all such a muddle."

"No problem. When you're ready…"

"Come into the kitchen," she said, waving him toward the back of the house in time to hear Robert murmuring to Aleda, "Now my dear, we need to hear what has gone on, in order that we can figure out what we must do."

Aleda nodded. She glanced toward Constable Brennan who stood at the end of the table.

"Please," she said. "Sit down. I'm not used to an armed guard."

She smiled a little, blinking her swollen eyelids in order to hold back a fresh flood of tears. She took a deep breath, and the police officer, looking much too large for the small kitchen, lowered himself onto a chair.

"And now my dear," Robert urged Aleda, "you must tell us what you know."

Aleda nodded and then looked up, startled. "Roy! Where's Roy?" They all glanced in the direction of the church, although none of them could see it through the barrier of the kitchen walls.

"Shall I get this Roy?" the officer asked, and rose to go outside.

Aleda took a sip of tea, shook her head, blew her nose, and took a long deep breath.

When Roy and the officer returned and had settled in at the kitchen table, all four people turned toward Aleda, waiting.

"Dwayne," she said, sighing. "Where do I begin?"

The people of the congregation and the others in the village all said – yes, this they agreed on – that this was the only time in the history of the village that the worship service had been cancelled. Not in the great ice storm of 1957, not even the time when the minister of the church came down with stomach flu; no, an elder had taken over. No, everyone agreed that the morning of Dwayne's death was the only time worship had been cancelled. The pastor was too upset they said, but the truth was the entire village was upset. Bad enough that it was a young person, but then to commit suicide by hanging himself from the church bell, they said over and over. It was too much to comprehend. Like Aleda, the villagers found themselves repeatedly asking, "Why? But why?"

By mid-morning, Robert and Patrice were confident that Aleda was calm enough to be on her own.

"You're sure you don't want me to go with you to visit Dwayne's grandmother?" Robert asked for the third time.

"No, no. I'm fine now. It was the shock. I need to go alone to see the grandmother. I'll be fine, I promise." She hugged both of them fiercely. "Thank you so much for being here for me. I don't know what I would have done without you."

But as they were turning to walk toward their car, Aleda called out, "Wait! There's something I forgot to ask. How on earth did you hear about this so quickly?"

"Oh, my dear, it was Grace," Robert said, turning back to touch her arm. "She was letting out her dog when she noticed you and Roy racing about in the grass alley. She knew something was terribly wrong so she phoned us immediately."

Aleda changed into dress pants, a cotton shirt, and sandals. As she headed toward Dwayne's house, she saw Grace moving from the side door of her house. Oh, please God, I just can't deal with Grace just now. Aleda took a deep breath.

"Oh, Aleda!" Grace said, hurrying down the driveway. "I suppose you're on your way to see Dwayne's grandmother."

Aleda bobbed her head up and down, impatient to get past Grace.

"We're all in shock. None of us can understand why this happened."

Aleda nodded again.

"But the thing is, it's one thing for a young lad to be troubled and unhappy and to think about ending it all, but...he was one of our own!" Grace's voice rose at the end of her sentence, making her statement sound like a wail.

Aleda stood staring at Grace. "Yes," she said, putting her arm around Grace's shoulders. "Yes Grace, you're absolutely right. Dwayne *was* one of our own, and that is why we are all so shocked and devastated."

Aleda gave Grace's hand a squeeze and started on down the road. When she reached the old cottage she remembered to use the cement block to step up onto the porch. She tapped on the door. Dwayne's grandmother opened it and stood leaning against the doorframe, looking small and frail.

"I thought maybe you was the police come back," she said.

"May I come in?"

Dwayne's grandmother turned toward the kitchen at the back of the house. There was no offer to sit, no offer of tea, but on the kitchen counter Aleda spotted a fresh apple pie in what she recognized was Grace's pie pan. After a moment of standing together in the kitchen, Aleda touched the old woman's arm and gestured to the kitchen chairs.

"Shall we sit?" she asked, as if she were the hostess and Dwayne's grandmother the guest. The woman sank onto a chair, looking down at a worn spot on the oil cloth that covered the table top. Finally she said, "This is where he always sat. To eat, I mean."

Aleda began to talk about what Dwayne had contributed to the church and how his friends in the youth group had looked out for him and what a gap it would leave in their lives. *I'm rambling. I'm rambling, but I can't stop,* Aleda scolded herself. She stopped talking and took a deep breath. She glanced over at the old woman and witnessed a look of such deep anguish on her face that Aleda had to swallow hard and blink to hold back tears.

"There's two things," Dwayne's grandmother said. "How can I tell his folks that I let the boy kill his self? And how will I pay for a funeral?"

As Aleda walked home she heard someone calling her name. Laura was hurrying as fast as she could toward her.

"Aleda, Aleda, I'm so very sorry," Laura said, reaching out to hug Aleda. "I just heard the news. Grace called me to tell me what happened. Are you okay?"

Aleda's eyes filled with tears and she stood gulping and shaking her head. "I've just been to see Dwayne's grandmother," she said, reaching into a pocket to retrieve a tissue.

"Come on, I'll walk you home." Laura took Aleda's hand as if the two of them were five-year-olds returning from an excursion to the village store to buy candy.

When they got to the parsonage Aleda realized she was suddenly very hungry. She had forgotten to feed Tracker too. While she went to the shed to give Tracker some ground oats, Laura prepared some toasted tomato and mayonnaise sandwiches.

The women were sitting together on the back porch eating their sandwiches, saying little, when the telephone rang.

"This is Constable Brennan calling."

"Oh, yes, yes. Thank you so much for your help and patience this morning."

"Not a problem. I just thought I'd let you know that we won't have a completed death certificate until tomorrow or Tuesday, but it's likely that the coroner's report will state that the sudden unexpected death was self-inflicted and there is no evidence of foul play. The coroner will consult a forensic pathologist, but it seems that an autopsy won't be necessary."

"That's all good I assume?" Aleda massaged the bridge of her nose.

"Yes, all good. There is one thing, though, that we could use your help with."

Aleda's words rushed out. "Anything. Anything at all."

"The grandmother. We're having trouble getting some idea of where she would like the body to be sent. She doesn't seem to be able to decide anything."

"I've been to see her. Perhaps she is waiting until she can be in touch with Dwayne's parents. They were working in a rodeo in Calgary." Aleda paused. She sensed the real reason why Dwayne's grandmother could not make up her mind. For at least the second time recently, she wondered just how far could she stretch the criteria of the benevolent fund.

"May I get back to you tomorrow about this?" Aleda asked in a plaintive voice.

Aleda was grateful for Laura's quiet presence during the afternoon and evening and, as nightfall came Laura again offered her a sleeping pill. Aleda knew her refusal was false bravado. She knew she would have trouble falling asleep and staying asleep, but she resigned herself to a night of tossing and turning, the bedside light on.

She hugged her friend, thanked her, and walked with Laura to the front door. She stood watching as Laura limped down the street toward the corner store. The village was quiet, but just as Laura turned up the hill toward her house, Aleda noticed some movement at the east edge of the village. Rose Hart was stepping down off the front porch of Dwayne's house, holding what appeared to be an empty square pan in her hand. Aleda pressed her finger against her lip to hold back a fresh flood of tears.

17

Ghosts

S ALEDA HAD PREDICTED, it had been the night that seemed never-ending. Somewhere around midnight she jerked awake, crying out. An image of battered running shoes dangling in front of her face haunted her dreams. She sat up, wet with perspiration, and took a sip of water. Breathing in long slow gulps to calm herself, she shook her head, trying to chase out unwanted images. After, she lay staring at the alarm clock as the numbers flipped over, waiting fruitlessly for sleep to reclaim her.

She remembered how her father had had what her mother called "night terrors" and how he could not tolerate Halloween. Once, when she was seven or eight, she begged her father to accompany her down St. Mary Street and into Barton Street. Reluctantly, her father walked with her through the rainy night, but when they came to the third house and rounded the corner to walk up to the front door, Aleda's father gasped and grabbed her small hand. He raced with her back to their house, but not before Aleda witnessed a look of horror on his face.

When they had arrived home, Aleda's mother hurried them into the kitchen where she poured her husband something from a green bottle, then dumped into Aleda's bag all the Halloween candies she had planned to pass out to the neighbourhood children. She rushed back to the front door to turn out the outside lights and lock the door, and then drew the heavy curtains in the tiny front room.

"We just went around the corner and there was a ghost hanging from the tree," Aleda said to her mother in a bewildered and frightened voice.

"Hush, child. Come along. Papa needs some time to rest," and she led Aleda into her bedroom at the back of the house. "Why don't you count your candies?" she suggested.

As she lay awake in her bed, Aleda realized that it was only much later in life that she had come to understand the full story. As university students in Budapest during the 1956 revolution, her parents had attempted, with thousands of other students, to rebel peacefully but forcefully against the tyranny of Soviet occupation. With a passionate desire to reclaim their homeland, the students had printed brochures, organized rallies, shouted out the national anthem, and met with Hungarian nationals.

On October 25, 1956 – a fateful day – thousands of women, children, students, and workers flooded into Budapest's Liberty Square for a peaceful demonstration. Soviet troops, seemingly friendly, stood guard in front of the British and American embassies. It was a day of national pride, a day for people to revel in their Magyar heritage, a day to take back their country from fear, brutality, and corruption. Then came that disastrous, terrifying moment when the Russian troops suddenly turned their guns on the people and opened fire.

Amidst the screaming and the chaos, her parents and other students fled; but some students were recognized by Russian troops as rebel leaders and did not manage to twist and turn out of the mess. The following day the surviving students crept through the silent streets until they stood staring into Liberty Square, where they saw the bodies of their co-students – friends with whom they had studied, friends with whom they had drunk beer, friends who were the pride and joy of their parents, friends now dead – hanging from lampposts. When Aleda understood this history, she also comprehended the real cause of her father's Halloween terror.

When the sky began to lighten, Aleda got out of bed, feeling as if she had never slept. She stood in the shower and let the hot water pour over her head and roll over her back like a liquid benediction.

After breakfast she sat at the kitchen table and reached for her worn Bible. She sat for a moment with her hand on the soft leather cover. Although she possessed many versions of the Bible, this was her favourite. She often thought of it as her working Bible. It was the one she used for preparing her Sunday sermons, and when she looked up obscure things in her reference books it was into this Bible that she recorded her findings, using a fine-tip red felt pen. She had used this Bible since her seminary days.

As she sat staring at the Bible, her mind wandered. How can I be a spiritual leader in this community when I can't think of one thing to say or do that makes any sense of Dwayne's life or death? What good is the Bible? How is it that I have read this book from cover to cover and made notes in it and reflected on so many passages and now all of a sudden it seems a worthless collection of old-fashioned, useless, out-of-date and out-of-touch writings? How can I possibly imagine that I know how to be a spiritual leader in this situation? She laid her head down on her arms and sobbed.

It was mid-morning when Aleda walked into the backyard to open the door for Tracker. She scratched his head for a moment before giving him an apple.

"Sorry, old boy." she said to the horse. "You are going to have to stay in for another day." She left the shed door open, consoling herself that at least he could look out from his stall, and went back into the house. She grabbed her purse and keys and let herself out the front porch, locking the door behind her.

There was an unusual silence in Milburn Corners, as if the whole village was holding its breath. Perhaps the school had been closed for the day, Aleda thought, turning toward her van. She hadn't seen any children walking to school.

She suddenly noticed the sign on the church lawn. Always the church sign read *Sunday Worship 10:30 a.m. Everyone welcome.* But someone had replaced that with *Church is open for prayer.*

Aleda slipped her car keys into a pocket and crept up the front steps of the church. The door opened easily and she stepped inside. Someone had hooked back the swinging inner doors into the sanctuary and raised the side windows to let in the morning breeze.

Three people sat in the church, far apart from each other. Roy was near the side wall, his head bent and solemn. Grace sat in her usual place under the clock, staring straight ahead. Although the day was warm, she clutched a beige sweater coat around her shoulders. Near the back of the church was one of the younger women from the subdivision. Aleda inched forward, then stopped and slipped into a pew. She had a sudden urge to kneel but there were no kneelers in the church, so she bowed her head low on her chest and closed her eyes. She heard footsteps behind her and sensed someone slide into a pew across the aisle. Everyone sat in silence for what seemed a long time. When Aleda rose to leave the church, she saw that someone had hooked back the wooden front doors on the outside of the church so that they too were flung open, solid and welcoming like a grandmother at the kitchen door waiting to hug.

Later in the day as she walked through the village on her way to visit Dwayne's grandmother, Aleda berated herself. She was on her way to offer to pay for Dwayne's funeral service, but she had not consulted the elders, or at the very least, Roy. She couldn't go spending money out of the benevolent fund without consultation.

As it turned out, it was a needless worry. As Aleda and Dwayne's grandmother sat at the kitchen table, the old woman said directly, "It's all settled then, Reverend."

Aleda shook her head, puzzled.

"The police. It was them that helped."

Aleda nodded, not understanding.

"They found Dwayne's folks, my daughter and her guy. They's at the rodeo, out there in Calgary, and they can't git home before the weekend. They can't help with the funeral, they've got no money, but the police can."

"The police?"

"It was that nice Constable Brennan. He said since Dwayne's folks can't git home for a bit, why don't we have Dwayne cremated. They found me one of them cremation places and they told me that the Police Association has a benevolent fund to help out in situations like this. All I have to take care of is paying to send," Dwayne's grandmother paused, "the remains to the crematorium."

The old woman sat back, looking down at her hands folded in her lap, and Aleda could see that much of the worry and stress from the previous day had vanished from her face.

"That's good," Aleda murmured, while a sharp inner voice complained about how the police benevolent fund beat the church benevolent fund to the punch. Something bitter rose in Aleda's throat. Dwayne was one of our own and we look after our own, she thought with a stubborn fierceness. She took a deep breath and sighed.

"Well. That's that, then," she said, and patting the old woman on the forearm, she rose to go.

After her visit, Aleda was overcome with weariness. She went home and lay down on the sofa in the living room. A swath of sunshine from the west window warmed her legs. She watched mites of dust dance in a golden patch of air as she sank into a heavy sleep.

When Aleda awakened, the sun had disappeared behind the church. She felt refreshed and rested until she suddenly remembered the terrible reality of Dwayne's death. She jumped to her feet and stretched as the doorbell rang. She was relieved to see Martin at the front door, holding a black insulated bag. He gave her a quick hug, then walked ahead of her into the kitchen and opened the fridge.

"Got a cold beer in here?" he grinned, crouching down to peer inside.

"Never drink the stuff."

"Then it's about time you learned." Martin shut the refrigerator and unzipped the black bag. He pulled out two frosty bottles, twisted off the caps, and set them down on the kitchen table.

"Sit down, why don't you?" he said, pointing to a kitchen chair.

For a moment, surprised by Martin's forthright manner, Aleda forgot about the trauma of Dwayne's death. She laughed and pulled out a chair.

"Oh," Martin said, jumping up. "I forgot that women drink beer out of a glass," and he began banging kitchen cupboards open and shut until he found a large water glass. He set it down beside Aleda's beer bottle and, clinking his bottle against the empty glass said, "Drink up."

He had come, he said, to look in on Aleda and see that she was okay, but he had also come because he had something on his mind.

"It's Callum," he said. "In just one short morning at the day camp he got very attached to Dwayne. It's all he could talk about on Saturday afternoon. My friend Dwayne said this, my friend Dwayne is going to take me to the swamp to hunt for frogs, my friend Dwayne showed me where he rings the church bell."

"Yes. It was uncanny really, how they bonded. Which makes Dwayne's death all the more tragic." Tears blurred Aleda's eyes and pooled under her reddened eyelids, ready to roll down her cheeks. Martin stared down into his beer.

"The thing is," Martin said, "I don't think Callum has heard about Dwayne's death. I'd like to be the one to tell him tonight when he comes over to my house to visit the dog. I think it would be better for me to break the news to him, rather than have him learn the awful truth on the schoolyard tomorrow when school reopens. Don't you think so?"

Aleda, her eyes now dry, gazed at Martin, who in that moment looked like a sad and uncertain young boy himself.

"Yes. Yes, I do think it would be better for you to tell him."

"This is what I thought I might say. Can you let me know if you think this is okay?"

Aleda nodded, and Martin turned toward the empty chair at the end of the table, staring at it as if the small boy with the tousled hair and too-large red shorts was sitting there.

"Callum, I'm afraid I have some bad news to tell you. I want to tell you myself because I think it is better for me to tell you, rather than you hearing it in the schoolyard tomorrow. You remember yesterday how you told me that sad story about the grasshoppers you caught last summer, how you kept them in a cardboard box and tried so hard to look after them, but they all died? You remember telling me that?"

Martin paused, glancing at Aleda. He shrugged and said, "He told me that he had figured out that the grasshoppers had died because he had captured them and they didn't want to be captured, and that they couldn't find a way out of the cardboard box so they just died, and that is why he is building them a more natural habitat this year."

"Oh. Oh, I see."

"So, I thought that I might say to the boy," Martin hesitated, then looked back again at the empty chair, speaking slowly, "I'm sorry to tell you that your new friend Dwayne has died. He died on Sunday – yesterday – and that is why school was cancelled today. I'm so sorry to tell you this, because I know you really liked Dwayne. But you see, son," Martin took a deep breath, "maybe Dwayne was like the grasshoppers, in a way. He felt trapped and he couldn't see any way out, and that is why he died."

Martin took a long gulp of beer. He glanced over at Aleda.

"What do you think? Is that a good way to explain things to a seven-year-old?"

"I think so," she replied, her voice thoughtful. "I think that's a very fine way to explain a most difficult thing."

"There's one huge problem." Martin's voice was full of distress. "I know that kid well enough to know with certainty what he will ask next."

"Which is?"

"*How* did he die? Have you any idea how I am to explain suicide to a seven-year-old?"

After Martin left, Aleda picked up the phone

"Robert," she said, her words pouring out, "I'm sorry to bother
you, but I could use your advice about something. And it's important that I have it tonight. Can I pop into Owen Sound for a few
minutes to see you?"

"Of course my dear! We've finished dinner. Come anytime."

Within twenty minutes Aleda was sitting with Robert and
Patrice at their dining room table. They cradled mugs of hot tea as
Aleda described Martin's explanation of Dwayne's death to Callum.

"I think it's a very good idea to relate the death to something
Callum can understand – the deaths of his beloved grasshoppers – but
where I'm stuck, as is Martin, is on the *how*. We just can't figure out
how to explain suicide to a seven-year-old boy who adored Dwayne."

Robert nodded and folded his hands together, wiggling his
forefingers. "It is a problem," he answered slowly, "because, of course,
no one wants a small child to feel in some way responsible for the
death. Not that he would, necessarily, of course, but you did say
that they had a wonderful time together on Saturday morning, so
it might be that the boy would feel somehow responsible for
Dwayne's decision. These things are not all that rational, of course,
but the boy might have thought that Dwayne didn't really like him
or care about him; if he had, he wouldn't have killed himself.

"I think the less the boy knows about the circumstances, the
better it will be. I think you should advise Martin to say to the boy,
'We're not at all sure how Dwayne died, but we do know that he is
now in the loving care of God.' He should keep it as short and as
simple as that."

Aleda looked down into her rose-painted mug. After a few
minutes she gave Robert and Patrice a hug and headed to the door.

"It's been a long day," she said. "Thank you both so much for
your care and support. I don't know what I'd do without you."

As Aleda sped along toward Milburn Corners, she realized that she didn't care at all for Robert's advice. First of all, Robert didn't know Callum. That child will never settle for being told no one is sure how Dwayne died. Secondly, she was not at all sure that Callum had the word *God* in his vocabulary; nor was she sure that Martin would feel comfortable saying what Robert had suggested. She imagined Martin exclaiming, "God! You expect me to imply to the boy that God took his new best friend?"

No. It simply wouldn't do. And for the first time since she had adopted Robert as her sage older friend and mentor, she thought, Robert didn't get this one right.

And yet she had no better idea. Maybe seven-year-olds needed more protection than she knew. But she had to pass on Robert's suggestion to Martin in any case.

In the kitchen, she pulled open a drawer and began rummaging for the phonebook. Running her finger through the directory she found there was no Martin Hart listed. I shall have to call Rose and get Martin's number, she thought.

"Oh hello Aleda," Rose answered. "It's wonderful to hear from you, but what a terrible business this has been. It must be a harrowing time for you."

"Oh, beyond harrowing," Aleda sighed, then explained to Rose that she needed to call Martin about a rather urgent matter but couldn't find his phone number in the telephone directory. She added that she needed to speak with Martin before the sun went down, as she remembered that Callum left Martin's house to amble home before dark.

"Martin has an unlisted number, probably because he is at the farm for only three or four months of the year and he doesn't want to be bothered with all the telemarketing messages. But may I ask what is so urgent? It's not Tracker I hope?"

"Oh, no, no," Aleda exclaimed. She explained what Martin intended to say to the boy about Dwayne's death. She told Rose about the advice that Robert had given her. Then, with hesitancy in her voice, she confessed that she hadn't been very comfortable with Robert's advice, but she couldn't think of anything better to say.

Rose was silent on the other end of the line for what seemed a long time. "I've heard Martin say that the boy is precocious, so I share your reservation about your friend's advice, although I'm sure your friend means well."

Aleda waited while Rose fell silent again. When she spoke, her voice was thoughtful and measured, as if she were putting together her ideas as she spoke.

"I believe that children can deal with difficult situations as long as they can talk about them openly with a trusted adult. I think that even a seven-year-old needs to know what suicide means — that it is an incredibly sad happening when someone does something to himself to cause his own death. I don't think that's too harsh for a child to hear, do you? It's rather like learning about sex. It's better to have the facts than just hear bits and pieces of misinformation on the school yard. I think it's okay to say that suicide is a way that some people stop the life in their body because they are so very sad, or so angry, or so mixed up. They feel as if they are trapped and they don't see any way to keep on living, and that is why Dwayne put a rope around his neck until his breath stopped. Nobody can live without air."

Rose paused again. "It's so, so sad, really, because, of course, we all know that everyone around Dwayne was willing and able to help. Even Callum."

"Exactly. Precisely. Rose, I can't tell you how grateful I am to have had this talk with you. It has truly been God-sent. But I'm wondering if you could do me one more favour?"

"Of course. I'm glad to help."

"It's been a long day and I feel so tired. Would you mind calling Martin and telling him what you just said to me? And could you please do it right away, before the sun goes down?"

147

18

Pulpit

LEDA STOOD FOR A MOMENT in the open porch doorway on Tuesday morning. The sun shone with clarity, washing the village with a golden hue and burning off the morning fog from the swamp. The sign on the church lawn still read *Church open for prayer*. Someone – Roy perhaps? – had already hooked back the front doors.

Aleda spotted Roy coming around the corner of the church, a hoe in his hand. He waved and walked toward her.

"You okay, then, Aleda? We've all been a bit worried about you."

Before she could answer, a black and white police cruiser pulled up in front of the parsonage. They watched as Constable Brennan swung his long legs out of the vehicle then reached back inside to retrieve something from the passenger seat. "Thought you might enjoy a morning coffee," he said, looking a little bashful. "Oh hello. Roy, isn't it? I should have brought three coffees."

"Come in, come in," Aleda gestured, flustered. "You too, Roy. I'll share my coffee with you." Then, sensing the shyness of the police officer, she gestured to his gun and grinned. "But I wish you'd take off that gun. You know it unnerves me!"

Constable Brennan laughed. "Sorry," he said. "Never know if there's a dangerous felon hiding out in the rectory."

After they had settled at the kitchen table, the policeman asked how people were taking the news of Dwayne's death. Aleda's words tumbled out as she told him about Martin and Callum, about Rose and her advice, about people gathering to pray.

Then Aleda remembered the issue of the police benevolent fund donating the cost of Dwayne's cremation. She was grateful that the Police Association had helped – thanks to Constable Brennan, she assumed – but, at the same time, she felt annoyance welling up inside her knowing that she and her church community had not been able to respond as quickly.

"I want to sincerely thank you," she began, in a subdued voice "for what you have done for Dwayne and his grandmother. You have no idea what a burden it lifted."

The Constable shifted his large boots under the table and shrugged. "It's the suicides that get me," he said, looking down. "Some officers say that it's the accidents that get to them, especially if there are children killed. But it's always the suicides that get to me. Being raised Catholic, I think it was more drummed into me that life is sacred and that suicide is such a failure. A failure on our part, I mean. I don't blame the poor tormented souls who can't see any other way out of their trouble. Sometimes I think that suicides must make God cry."

Lifting his head and looking at Aleda, Constable Brennan said, "And what about you? I think that this must be very hard on you."

Tears filled Aleda's eyes, and Roy and the officer looked at her with concern.

"It's just like you said! I did fail Dwayne. I tried, but it wasn't enough, and now I have to live with that horrible awareness. I should have done more and this wouldn't have happened. I keep asking myself, what if I'd done this or that." Aleda's voice ended in a wail and tears poured down her cheeks.

Roy and Constable Brennan sat staring at her, then glanced uneasily at each other. The police officer shrugged one shoulder slightly, nodding toward Roy as if to ask *May I?* When Roy nodded, the officer rose, pushing the chair back. Startled, Aleda stood up too. Constable Brennan took a step forward and put his arms around her.

"There, there. I didn't mean it like that. I didn't mean it like that at all. My words were clumsy. I didn't mean to upset you. It is not your fault. You are not to blame. This is just some sad thing that happened. You mustn't go blaming yourself. That won't help anyone. You can't control what another person will do. You did your best and that is all that could be done. I apologize if I've caused you more trouble."

Roy sat waiting, a grave look on his face. When Aleda was calm again, she turned and reached for a tissue.

"Was that a professional moment?" she asked, looking up at Constable Brennan, her laughter coming out with a gurgling sound.

"It was a human moment."

After the men had gone – he had come to take down the yellow tape, Constable Brennan said – Aleda went out the front door, backed her van across the end of the driveway. She walked back into the house and out the back door to avoid walking through the grass alley, crossed the dew-moistened lawn, and released a grateful horse into the morning sunshine.

Aleda settled again at the kitchen table. Somehow she had to formulate a sermon for the coming Sunday morning and write a meditation for Dwayne's funeral. She opened the Bible and flipped to some scriptures that might be appropriate. Maybe the story of Jesus healing the man with the troubled spirit? No, that wouldn't do. Why does the Bible call it an evil spirit? Too harsh. Besides, Dwayne *hadn't* been healed, and that was part of the dilemma. She pushed aside her Bible.

As she was thinking about scripture, the telephone rang. Aleda sighed and stood up. She knew that the people of the community meant well and that they, too, were trying to make sense of the tragedy, but the morning had been full of interruptions. Would it be appropriate to take a casserole to Dwayne's grandmother? Had there been a decision as to when the funeral would be? Wouldn't it be nice to invite the young people to honour Dwayne by playing and singing at the funeral? Could Aleda use some early lettuce?

Tucking her Bible under her arm, Aleda walked across the lawn to the church. Two or three people sat in silence in the pews as she slipped into a seat. No sooner had she settled when she felt a gentle tap on her shoulder. "I'm sorry to bother you Aleda, but the Ladies Guild is wondering if we might bring in some flowers for the funeral."

"Of course. Of course," Aleda whispered back.

It was almost lunchtime when Aleda next looked up from her Bible. She could see that the church was empty. Sighing, she rose from her pew, flexed her stiff legs, and walked to the front of the church, pacing back and forth. She needed time. She needed time alone to think and ponder and pray. But where could she go? Her instinct was to go to the cemetery, to sit on the bench under the oak tree, but even there someone was sure to spot her. She walked up the steps toward the pulpit, stopping behind it for a moment. She remembered her first week in Milburn Corners. Roy had unlocked the church and guided her in to see the sanctuary. When they walked around the pulpit, Aleda stopped in amazement.

"Mr. Gregory!" she had exclaimed.

"Roy," he said patiently.

"Roy," she continued, "this is the largest pulpit I've ever seen. Why, if it were lined with concrete, it could be a bomb shelter!"

Aleda caught a hurt look on Roy's face. Careful there Aleda, she silently scolded herself, and, hoping to repair the damage, she ran her hand over the polished wood. "Beautiful, just beautiful."

"My grandfather made this pulpit," Roy said. "I've never been able to figure out if he used a plane to make this front piece and carved out the cross from the raised wood, or whether he carved the cross separately and somehow glued it on the front. Anyway, it's a piece of art. My grandfather was known far and wide for his woodworking. This pulpit is his finest piece I think."

Now, a year later, Aleda tried out the space. She crouched and folded herself into the cross-legged sitting position she had learned at yoga, and then shifted around until she was comfortable. Perfect hiding place for a five foot four inch minister.

As soon as she had settled she realized that she had forgotten her Bible, which remained in the centre pew. Glancing at her watch, she also noticed that it was noon and she was hungry. She stood up cautiously. The building was still empty. She hurried back to the parsonage, made herself a soft, non-smelly cheese and mayonnaise sandwich, grabbed a pillow from the living room and returned to the church, pausing at the front door to make sure that she was alone. She reached for her Bible in the centre pew and tiptoed to the pulpit. Glancing around again, she folded herself into the space, sitting on the pillow and pulling her Bible and noiseless lunch toward her. Perfect.

From time to time she heard stirrings in the church, but by the time she next glanced at her watch she was restored and calm. She knew what she wanted to do for Dwayne's funeral, and she had a sermon outline. She eased herself into a standing position and gathered up her pillow and her Bible. She was heading out the front door when she noticed Roy rushing up the sidewalk.

"Oh Aleda! Thank goodness. We've been worried about you."

"Really?"

"No one could find you. People were asking me if I'd seen you. Nobody knew where you were. They were ringing the doorbell and phoning."

"I needed a little time to myself to think things through," Aleda said in a vague manner. When she saw the look of concern on Roy's face, she touched his sleeve and added, "Sorry to worry you."

Roy nodded. "We just want to make sure that you're okay."

"Oh, Roy! You are the sweetest man."

Although he looked embarrassed, Roy laughed and said, "Not many people can get away with calling me sweet."

Back in her kitchen, Aleda began to make herself some dinner – something her mother called *Jókai bableves* – a thick soup with sausage and beans. As she chopped onions, she glanced at the blinking light on the telephone. She promised herself that she would check the messages after she got the soup cooking.

There were eight. Sighing, Aleda listened to them one by one. Two were of special interest. One of those was from Roy.

"Aleda, since the lad is to be cremated I was wondering if I might have the honour of making a special box to hold his ashes. My grandfather taught me a thing or two about woodworking and I would be honoured to do that." There was a pause, then Roy added, "If you think this is appropriate, could you let me know if the boy had something that was special to him – something I could carve on the box? Well, that's all for now." There was a soft click.

The other was from Constable Brennan.

"Just letting you know that Dwayne's ashes will be back from the crematorium tomorrow. Could you let Dwayne's grandmother know, please? Oh, and one more thing, I'd like to arrange to be off duty and attend the funeral if that's okay with you, so if you could let me know the day and time…"

There was a pause on the line until he continued, "I know that folks will give you lots of suggestions for the funeral, but, as for me, I've always considered Chopin's Prelude in E minor a great choice…Chopin asked for it to be played at his own funeral, did you know? Or maybe Dietrich Buxtehude's 'We Pray Now to the Holy Spirit.' Well, that's all for now."

Smiling, Aleda turned to the stove, removed the lid of the soup pot, and inhaled deeply.

19

Arrangements

LEDA HAD THREE VISITS to make as she strode east on Main Street.

First she needed to call on Dwayne's grandmother to arrange a time for the funeral. As it turned out, that was an easy call. Dwayne's parents were arriving on Friday and the funeral could be Saturday morning.

Her second call was on Roy. That, too, was easy. Roy was in his front garden planting zinnia seeds. "Roy," she said, "I spoke to Dwayne's grandmother about the box and we both agree that this is a most generous and welcome gift."

"Good," Roy said, setting down the seed packet, "because I've already got it made. Only thing I need is some symbol to put on the front."

Aleda folded her arms. "Hmm. I'm not sure how you could use this, but Savannah told me that what Dwayne most treasured in his life was a Swiss Army knife his father had given him."

"Swiss Army knife," Roy said in a flat voice. "Possibilities. Real possibilities." Aleda glanced inquiringly at Roy. "The cross. Don't you remember that the Swiss Army knife has a cross on the top? It's a great symbol."

The third visit was easy too. As she and Roy stood talking, Aleda spotted Grace coming out of her house.

"Grace," she called out, "We've just been discussing Dwayne's funeral. It's been arranged for 11 a.m. Saturday. Would you be able to organize the Ladies Guild to prepare a luncheon for after the funeral?"

"Of course. Of course."

"But Grace, you do know that, this being a tragedy, it will be a big luncheon." Aleda shook her head. "With a sudden and tragic death, especially the death of a young person, there are always more people at the funeral."

"It's not a problem. We can manage it."

"But, well, you know that Dwayne's grandmother isn't well off…"

To Aleda's surprise, Grace waved her hand and said, "Oh, we wouldn't expect to receive a donation for the funeral luncheon. After all, we're happy to do this for him. Dwayne was one of our own."

The remainder of the day sped by for Aleda. By late afternoon she had written the meditation and the sermon. She took down her *Not Available* sign and put the telephone back in its cradle. As usual, the red message light began to flash.

"Aleda, Savannah here. All of us in the youth group were wondering if we could hold a candlelight vigil for Dwayne at the church. We could invite his friends from school. Maybe Thursday or Friday night? You wouldn't have to do a thing, honestly. We could look after it all. Call me back when you have a sec."

After Aleda and Savannah had agreed on a vigil at 8 p.m. Thursday, Aleda phoned Laura.

"I'm calling to ask a favour."

"Anything. Anything at all."

"Would you be able to come to a vigil at the church on Thursday night?" Aleda explained the teens' idea. "They said that I wouldn't have to do anything but I would feel so much better if we had a few adults here. I'll ask Roy too, of course."

"Oh, of course," Laura said quickly. "I'm glad to come. When I was teaching, we had a suicide at the high school. It was terribly upsetting to the kids, I remember that. It seemed to stir up a pri-

mal fear. Even though it's not rational, it's as if the kids are wondering if it could happen to them. I'll ask Martin to come, too. His
daughter is 17. I think he would empathize with what the kids are
going through, and it might help him feel more comfortable about
talking to Callum about Dwayne's death."

20

Vigil

ONE MORE DAY AND I'LL have cleaned out all the old medical books from the south wall, Laura thought. She had discovered that her father's books were neither up-to-date enough for current use nor old enough to classify as history, so, with some reluctance she had carried box after box to the blue metal dumpster that sat on the driveway.

She now surveyed the room that had once been her father's office. The imposing oak desk had been emptied and polished. The oak shelves also gleamed with polish. This will never be a cheerful room, Laura thought. Too much shade, too much northern exposure, too few windows; but having cleaned and polished the wooden bones of the room, she felt a serenity and stillness that made the space almost appealing.

Her self-assigned chore on Thursday morning was to clean out the cupboards under the bookshelves. More medical journals, boxes of gauze, packets of surgical tape, and, surprisingly, unopened packages of cloth diapers and old-fashioned smocks for babies. Why had her father stockpiled new baby clothes? Laura wondered if he had assisted at the birth of babies where the parents were too impoverished to buy clothing for a newborn. Or had he simply taken along a gift as a gesture of goodwill? The telephone rang.

"Laura? It's David."

"Dave! What a surprise! You must be a mind reader. I've been cleaning out Dad's study all week and I have been thinking that I wish that we had known him a little better. Do you ever think about that?"

"Not a lot," David said, "but you've had some time to jump back into the past. How's it going?"

"Not bad. Not bad. The first day was rough, but each day I make some progress and every day I come across something that surprises me. Guess what I found today? A cupboard full of baby clothes. All new. Never out of the package."

"That *is* odd. He gave them away as needed?"

"That's what I figure. It's hard for me to put together that image of Dad saving up baby clothes for poor families when my main memory of him is of a volatile, stern man. Don't you think that's hard to reconcile?"

"It is."

"And I've become friends with Rose Hart from the village. Remember her? She brings me library books and cinnamon buns, and once, when I mentioned to her that I remembered Dad as stern and volatile, she said, 'Oh, no, no, my dear Laura. Your father was anything but stern and volatile. He was a gentle, kind man and a great deal of fun too.'"

"Are we talking about the same man here?"

"Exactly what I thought."

"Laura, I have to fly to Toronto tomorrow for business. I could rent a car and come up to Milburn Corners on Saturday if you like. I need to return to Edmonton on Sunday, so it would be a flying visit."

"That would be totally wonderful! I can't wait to see you again."

"Do you have plans?"

"Let's see, what day is this? It's so easy to lose track of the days here. Thursday. Well, tonight I promised my friend Aleda that I would be an adult presence at a vigil at the village church for a teenager who committed suicide. Very sad. Tragic, in fact. He hung himself in the middle of the night in the church steeple. The whole village is in shock. Then, on Friday night, Martin, Aleda, and I have been getting together for dinner, and I will need to shop in the morning for that and for the funeral luncheon. I offered to provide some squares and cookies. And Saturday morning we have the funeral, of course."

"Whoa, Laura," David laughed. "Are you sure you can squeeze me into your schedule? I can't believe that you are so involved in the life of our little village."

"Sometimes I can't believe it either." Laura paused. "There's something I'd like to discuss with you. When I was cleaning out Dad's desk, I came across a little key that he kept on his desktop. I couldn't figure out what it was for, but yesterday when I was cleaning a cupboard I discovered a metal box. The key fits perfectly."

"Really."

"You'll never guess what was in it."

"I give up. Tell me."

"It seems that our father was a member of a secret society, something that he didn't want us to know about."

"A secret society? You've got to be joking."

"I haven't had time to read all of the files, but it seems that our father was a member of a eugenics society."

"Eugenics."

"But there is something more," Laura said, pausing. "I just can't make sense of it. Something I found in the box. I need to show it to you on Saturday. Maybe *you'll* understand."

Aleda rummaged in the storage cupboard in the church hall until she found the cardboard box that held the candles for the Christmas Eve candlelight service. Rooting around in the box, she found the paper holders that people could push into the base of a candle to protect their hands from melting wax. Aleda walked into the back of the church and set the box down, ready for the vigil.

Aleda and Roy were sitting on the front steps of the church when Martin and Laura pulled up in Martin's truck. Laura lowered herself out of the passenger side.

"No kids yet?" Martin asked, coming up the steps. Aleda shook her head and glanced at her watch. She began to worry that no one would come. After all, Dwayne wouldn't have won a popularity contest.

Five minutes before the vigil was scheduled to begin, Aleda spotted the five youth walking toward the church. Michael carried his guitar and Ashley had her tambourine. They came up to where the adults stood waiting.

"I invited along a few adult friends. I hope that's okay," Aleda said.

"Oh, that's fine," Savannah replied. "Did you find the candles?"

"Yes. They're in a box at the back of the church."

"Then I'll get them," Savannah announced, running up the steps.

When Savannah returned, the other youth followed her around the corner. At that moment, there was a rumble on Main Street as car after car, each full of teenagers, streamed into the village. Young people began to file into the alleyway between the parsonage and the church. One after another they laid bouquets around the entrance to the bell tower and in turn received a candle from Savannah.

The air in the grass alley was still, dark, and soft. The young people, subdued and grave, began to drop to the grass that had not yet dampened with dew. Michael walked among the crowd and lit some candles, but it was not necessary for him to continue as teenager after teenager turned to one another in a sombre ritual of sharing the light.

When it looked as though everyone had arrived, Aleda, Martin, Laura, and Roy accepted candles from Savannah and waited as a boy in sweat pants gave them each a light. They stood together with their backs pressed into the warm bricks on the side of the house.

Savannah said in a loud and clear voice, "Thank you all for

coming tonight. It may be hard for you guys from Owen Sound to understand this because there are so many of you in the city, but here in Milburn Corners there are only six of us. For the last three years, the six of us waited for the school bus together." Her voice caught. "We compared homework. We lent each other CDs, sometimes even clothes. Now there are only five of us, and that makes us so sad."

Aleda heard soft crying from a circle of girls close to Savannah.

"Dwayne was our friend. Not always easy to get to know. We had to work at that sometimes. But he was always in our circle of friends, and tonight we thank you for coming to cry with us and remember him."

Savannah paused and looked down at her candle. Aleda, her eyes filling with tears, longed to move over to Savannah, but it was Victoria – my sweet, sweet Victoria, Aleda thought – who stepped over and put her arm around Savannah's shoulders.

Victoria stood looking out over the sea of youth sitting on the grass and said in a strong, firm voice that Aleda had never heard before, "Dwayne was the sound system guy at our church. Music was important to him. Sometimes he even forgot to return the CDs we lent him."

Some of the youth laughed quietly.

"So we are going to honour him by singing. At our kid's camp last week, Dwayne helped me lead the singing, and tonight we're gonna sing to honour Dwayne."

Jacob pulled out his flute, Ashley stepped forward with a tambourine, Michael strapped on his acoustic guitar, and Victoria's clear soprano soared like the voice of an angel: *Kum ba yah, my lord, come by here.*

21

Mysteries

T HAD BEEN OVER THREE WEEKS since she had arrived in Milburn Corners. Looking back, Laura was amazed at how quickly the time had sped by after that first lonely week, and at how soon she had felt herself to be part of a village she had not even thought about in almost a decade.

Sorting out the office had been a focus, and befriending Martin and Aleda – or had they befriended her? – had helped her feel grounded. Yes, Laura thought, I can't imagine a day now without wondering about the teens at Aleda's church, or how Aleda is getting on with Tracker. I can't conceive of a day passing without watching out for Callum making his way toward school.

A day would not pass without looking down the hill to Grace's house and wondering what Grace had baking. It was also impossible to ignore Roy – she had a clear view of his open garage – busy at his table saw and lathe. And then there was Rose. Rose dropped in frequently to see Laura and bring fresh supplies of cinnamon buns and library books; but even more importantly, she had taken a keen interest in helping Laura sift through memories and mementos of her father.

It seemed to Laura that her focus had shifted away from her life in Toronto and toward the people that she shared life with in a village that was small enough to be called a hamlet. Of course she had been involved with people in the city – friends, colleagues, students, and her basketball team. But somehow, since becoming part of a village that teemed with secrets and activity and tragedy and change, she had come to see her former life as a bit sterile. It feels to me as if this is the real thing, she thought. Life here is engaged, gossipy, annoying at times, but connected. For the first time in a long while it seemed to Laura that someone would care a great deal if she lived or died. She shook her head, thinking that perhaps she was just overly sentimental today because she had been so deeply moved by the teen vigil the previous evening.

Laura turned from the living room window and hobbled down the hall toward the office. She switched on as many lights as possible. She now kept the kitchen and living room doors wide open, something that had never happened in her childhood. She was introducing the separated rooms to one another, giving the grand house a new sense of welcome, of unity, of connection.

Laura was determined to continue her sorting, so she opened the metal filing box and pulled out the manila file folders. Starting at the bottom of the pile – her father had been meticulous in filing these papers in chronological order – she began to read: Minutes of Southern Ontario Eugenics Society, September 1994. Laura recognized with a start that this was two weeks before her father had died. Had he stopped going to the meetings? Where were the meetings? Why did it never say in the minutes where the meetings were held or who attended?

She opened the next file: Minutes of Southern Ontario Eugenics Society, March 1994. Perhaps the society met infrequently, or her father had not attended all the meetings.

The next folder contained a brittle, yellowed news clipping. Someone – her father? – had put a star beside the headline *Resolution Passed by Canadian Medical Association.* Laura skimmed the article entitled *Family Planning Has Beneficial Effects on Health and Well-Being of Families.* The article described how most Canadians practise family planning in a manner consistent with their personal, religious, moral, and ethical standards and that many families of the lower socio-economic group, who would benefit most from such planning, lack information or the means to obtain information. It was, therefore, resolved that the Canadian Medical Association endorse, in accordance with the law, the development and provision of family planning programs for all those who need them. Laura noted that her father had added a note, in pencil, "especially those of low intelligence."

As Laura continued to read, turning the papers over after perusing each one, one phrase jumped out at her: "Many families of the lower socio-economic group would benefit most from such planning". An idea was forming in her mind. She began to wonder if her father might have been motivated to alleviate what he saw as the suffering of women who endured pregnancy after pregnancy until their worn bodies succumbed to fatigue, exhaustion, poverty, and, in a few cases, even death. Did her father's eugenic beliefs motivate him to advocate birth control especially for women who were poor or less intelligent? Laura wondered. It would seem that her father believed that the stronger, "more desirable" people of civilization should increase; the weaker, "less desirable" people should not have children.

Laura read stories about Barbara and George Cadbury, church leaders and prominent doctors, who set up the first chapter of Planned Parenthood Association in Canada in 1962. Church leaders. Laura smiled. *Something to tell Aleda tonight. I wonder if she knows that church leaders were among the early proponents of birth control.*

Another article was about pharmacist Harold Fine, who was charged, convicted, and fined for selling condoms in his drugstore in Toronto in April 1961. *Hard to believe,* Laura mused, *that something as common as a condom could have set off such a furor, and 1961 doesn't seem so long ago.*

She pulled out an April 1960 article about a birth control pill available in Canada – but only for therapeutic reasons. *Oh, how people now take the birth control pill and condoms for granted,* Laura mused.

The next article was dated 1936. It described the work of a

nurse by the name of Dorothea Palmer who was charged with giv-
ing out information about contraceptives in a poor area of Ottawa.
Someone by the name of A.R. Kaufman welcomed the opportu-
nity to defend his employee and to test Canada's law in court. A.R.
Kaufman. Why was that name familiar? Then she remembered
that Kaufman had owned and operated a large rubber factory in
Kitchener. Made boots, if she remembered correctly. Perhaps
Kaufman also had the means and motivation to make condoms.
But why?

The next article partially answered her question. It was dated
1935 and described Alvin Ratz Kaufman, an industrialist, philan-
thropist, and early pioneer of the birth control movement in Canada.
From his office in Kitchener he founded a Parents' Information
Bureau that distributed information and sent nurses out to call door-
to-door and provide families with condoms and contraceptive jelly.
But why? Her father's belief in eugenics genuinely puzzled and
confused her.

Perhaps, she thought, not all of these early birth control proponents were motivated by eugenics. Laura now pulled out a folder
containing a 1932 article on Dr. Elizabeth Bagshaw, one of Canada's early female doctors, who expounded the idea that women
should have the right to prevent pregnancy. Dr. Bagshaw had opened
the first family planning clinic in Hamilton, Ontario. But surely,
Laura reflected, that was illegal. What a brave woman she must
have been. Hamilton. Aleda had grown up in Hamilton. Another
thing to tell her tonight. Laura looked at the neat stack of news
clippings and articles, interspersed with the minutes of the Southern Ontario Eugenic Society meetings. She had no idea what she
would do with this information – probably nothing – but she did
have a sense of *why* she was doing it. Her father had been a fright-
ening mystery to her as she grew up, and now that his death made
his influence more benign, she wanted – maybe even needed – to
come to some understanding of what motivated her father. Maybe
if she understood who he was she could, at last, let him go.

"Rest in peace, Father," she said, raising her empty mug.

She picked up the last folder. This folder confounded her. This was the folder that she needed to discuss with David. This folder contained a mystery that did not make any sense to her.

There was nothing in it except for two birth certificates, one dated 1952 and the other 1954. The first was issued from Guelph General Hospital and the second from Hamilton General Hospital. The mother's name on both was Rose Hart, and the father was Arthur Hart. Laura remembered that Arthur had come back from World War II with severe injuries that he had lived with for the rest of his life. The first certificate was for Martin Arthur Hart; the second certificate read James Andrew Hart.

Still as stunned and puzzled as she had been when she discovered the birth certificates a few days ago, Laura set down the file and leaned back. Why were these Hart family birth certificates in her father's locked files? And, given that almost all the babies in the region were born in the Owen Sound hospital, why were the Hart boys born in Guelph and Hamilton? What did this mean?

Aleda wondered if the youth would want to hold their usual meeting on Friday; they had held the vigil on the previous evening and they would all be coming to the funeral on Saturday morning.

Later in the afternoon, Savannah telephoned. "You still okay for youth group tonight, Aleda? We thought you might have things to do for the funeral."

"No, no. Everything's ready. I'm happy to be there. Is that what you want?"

When she had hung up the phone, she wondered if there was anything she should prepare, but then understood that the meeting would have its own agenda. The teens needed to be together and they needed to be together with her. They needed to find some way to make sense of Dwayne's death.

Just before the meeting, some instinct told Aleda not to load up her big tote bag with potato chips and soft drinks as she often did. Instead she set out a large pitcher filled with water and ice.

"I want to say a sincere thank you for organizing the vigil last night," she began. "I was so proud of all of you."

Despite herself, Aleda's eyes were shining with tears. Victoria and Savannah nodded gravely, but Ashley, Michael, and Jacob stared at the ice cubes floating in their paper cups.

"You okay for the funeral tomorrow, Michael?"

Michael looked up and nodded. "My mom looked over my speech. She said it was pretty good." He didn't add, because it would have been just too embarrassing, that his mother had cried after she finished reading it. She had said, "Michael, I've never been more proud of you, not in my whole life."

"Then is there anything else you want to talk about?"

"Well," Jacob began tentatively, "there's something that I've been wondering." The others looked at Jacob and waited. "I mean," Jacob's voice had a plaintive quality that Aleda had never heard before, "exactly where is Dwayne now? I know that his body was cremated, but is he in heaven? Or where?"

A moment of panic flashed through Aleda, making it hard for her to breathe. What do I say? These kids are new to the church, new to the Christian faith. They're not going to stand for a pat answer. She took a deep breath.

"I do believe, without any doubt, that Dwayne is with God. Do I believe that there is a life after death? Yes, I do."

Aleda looked around at the five young faces gazing at her. "Something – someone – God, we say in the church – planted in all people a great desire to be whole and perfect. But we're all human so we goof up a lot of the time and we never seem to be able to get whole and perfect during our lifetime, but I do believe that God plants in us the thought that we become whole and perfect after we die. God would not have placed a hope for heaven in our hearts unless there *is* a heaven."

Victoria looked up, and Aleda noticed a small smile on her

lips. "I like that," she said, shrugging. "I like the idea that God puts a hope for heaven in our hearts."

All was quiet, although Aleda could see Savannah nodding slowly. Were all the youth thinking like she was, trying to imagine Dwayne singing with the angels, completely whole and perfect?

"There are many mysteries expressed in all religions," Aleda said, remembering her old seminary professor saying that Christian faith asks questions and seeks understanding because God is always greater than our ideas of God. "We don't know what will happen after death, but in the Bible it says that when we can no longer live in our physical bodies we are given new spiritual bodies."

There were more questions. Will we recognize each other after death? What about my step-dad? Jacob asked. He's divorced and remarried to my mom. Will he have two wives in heaven? And Victoria wanted to know if there was really a hell. And who goes there? But the questions that were most difficult were the last ones posed by Savannah. Why did Dwayne die? Why does anyone need to die? Why would God let someone die when he is only 17?

Afterward, Aleda was not sure she had handled all the questions well enough for the teens to understand. "It's such a temptation," she explained to Martin and Laura later, "to fall back into clichés − well, I shouldn't call them clichés. They are the traditional truths of the church. But I just felt that I couldn't do that with these young people. I struggled to find the right words, to use a language they could understand."

Aleda and her friends had finished dinner and the second bottle of red wine when Aleda swirled in her chair and faced Martin and Laura. "I'm sick and tired of worrying about death and suffering and looking after everybody. Let's talk about something more uplifting. What did you do today, Laura?"

When Laura had finished telling Aleda and Martin about the discoveries − but not the birth certificates − Martin said, "That's fascinating stuff, Laura."

"I have to admit," Aleda added, "that this is all new to me. I don't really understand what *eugenics* means."

"From a Greek word meaning *well born*, Laura responded. "As of this morning I'm an expert."

"Oh, that is dangerous," Martin replied.

"I know. I know. I found some references to the science of eugenics beginning in England in the late 1800s. It caught on quickly after that in both Canada and the United States. It seems that there was lots of appeal in thinking that people and groups with desirable characteristics and genes should produce lots of children, while those who were considered inferior were discouraged from reproduction." Laura paused, shook her head, and added, "It's hard for us to grasp the popularity of this belief now, but you have to understand that it was held by nearly all the leaders of society."

"I'm already imagining some terrible outcomes resulting from that way of thinking," Aleda said slowly. "Could the state forcibly sterilize people, prohibit certain marriages, segregate people, or even put some people into institutions to prevent reproduction? Or even, as happened in Nazi Germany, attempt to annihilate a whole race of people because they were deemed inferior?"

"Well, it wasn't just Nazi Germany. In Canada there was a period of 40 years when a Eugenics Board approved almost 5,000 cases for sterilization; only about 3,000 were carried out."

"Are you kidding me? Why is this stuff not included in Canadian history courses?"

Martin shifted in his chair. "I've heard that Canadians were greatly influenced by American schools at the turn of the century. Did you know that in the 1920s there were hundreds of university courses on eugenics in some of the United States' leading schools? Imagine if thousands of students were taught that this was a progressive way of thinking. Imagine how many ways that could affect society: immigration policy, health care, individual rights, you name it. I remember reading that in the 1930s some of the big American foundations – Carnegie, Rockefeller, Kellogg – all funded activity in the eugenics movement."

"Today," Laura added morosely, "we associate it with racism and elitism at its worse. So Aleda…you thought your day was depressing. How would you have liked to discover that your own father was one of the last of a dying and recalcitrant breed of elitist bigots?"

"Oh, that's a little harsh," Aleda said, touching Laura on the arm. "Try to think of him as a man whose feet got cemented in a previous time."

Laura, Aleda, and Martin fell into a companionable silence for a moment and the music player in the living room made a clicking noise as it changed to a new CD. Suddenly, Martin jumped up. "The music! Do you two not hear this music? My wife made me go to ballroom dancing last winter! I'd ask you to dance Laura but you seem to have a broken ankle. That leaves you Aleda! Have you ever danced the tango?"

"Are you serious?" she laughed.

"My dear," he said, gesturing to the long polished hall. "It's perfect. Just follow me. I'll lead. You'll follow," and he held out his arms in a gallant gesture. "Slow, slow, quick, quick, slow…slow, slow, quick, quick, drag. Let yourself go, Aleda! Go crazy!"

And Aleda and Martin glided up and down the gleaming polished wooden floor of the hallway, dancing the tango, until all three friends collapsed in laughter.

22

Funeral

Y THE TIME ALEDA WALKED across to the church on the morning of the funeral, the church parking lot was already full. People had begun to park on the street and in the empty school yard. It would be a big funeral, she knew that. The women were busy in the kitchen, cutting sandwiches and setting out trays of squares, cookies, and Rose's cinnamon loaf. Roy had three large kettles boiling for tea, and the hundred-cup coffee maker burbled on the counter.

Aleda wandered through the basement greeting people, then put on her white cassock and purple funeral stole embroidered with a gold cross. She climbed the steps to the sanctuary and welcomed people as they entered. The church was filling up when several cars drew up together, letting out a group of teens, most of them boys. Savannah, who had come to stand beside her, said in explanation, "Dwayne's woodworking class."

"I didn't know that Dwayne did woodworking," Aleda said, surprised.

"Yes, he was quite good at it, or so Roy said. Sometimes he helped Roy in his shop. Roy once told me that Dwayne made some of the finest bevelled edges he'd ever seen."

"Really." Aleda had had no idea that Dwayne and Roy had worked together with wood.

A boy from the woodworking class approached, carrying something, and when he got to the top of the steps he stopped, unsure of where to go.

Aleda stepped forward. "Do you need some help with that?"

"It was Dwayne's," the boy said, holding out a birdhouse. "The last thing he made in class. I thought his family might want it."

Aleda reached out, thanked the boy, and turned to carry the birdhouse to the front of the church, intending to set it by the box of Dwayne's cremated remains. She stopped suddenly, realizing that these youth might not know what to do at a funeral, including where to sit.

"Savannah, there are two long rows empty on this side of the church. Will you please take Dwayne's friends to their seats?"

With her usual confidence, Savannah smiled at the self-conscious teenagers and said, "Sure. Follow me please."

Aleda set down the birdhouse next to the only picture of Dwayne that the youth could find; a photo that had been taken just a week before. It was plain to see that he was smiling as he held the hand of an equally unkempt Callum. Their heads were down, looking for treasures in the ditch, but they were holding hands and Dwayne was smiling. Yes, Dwayne was definitely smiling.

Aleda began to worry. Dwayne's grandmother and parents had not yet arrived. Aleda glanced at her watch again and rubbed her sweating palms on the side of her cassock. Then, just before the funeral was scheduled to begin, Aleda watched from the steps as an old car pulled away from Dwayne's grandmother's house and crawled toward the church. As Dwayne's family approached the bottom of the church steps, Aleda took the arm of Dwayne's grandmother and led the family slowly to the reserved front row of the pews. Aleda then nodded to Savannah, Victoria, Ashley, Jacob, and Michael. They picked up their instruments and began to play Pachabel's Canon.

As the music died away, Aleda walked up the stairs into the chancel, stepped behind the large pulpit, and took a deep breath. They were all there in front of her. Martin sat with Rose and his brother, James. Roy and the women from the Guild sat together under the clock; Laura was sitting with Grace. The woodworking class sat huddled together looking awkward and worried. Aleda recognized one of them as the boy who had lit her candle at the vigil. In the back row, looking out of place, was Officer Brennan. He will be pleased to hear the organist play both of the pieces he suggested, Aleda thought. Patrice and Robert sat next to the members of the church Board, while the parents of the teens in the youth group sat clustered together. Dwayne's parents, looking lost and confused, sat staring up at Aleda, but Dwayne's grandmother had her head bowed. The whole congregation sat quietly, waiting for Aleda.

Aleda took a deep breath. Through her mind flashed a story from one of her colleagues, who had told her about a time when he did the funeral for a member of his congregation who had committed suicide. "It was the strangest thing," he said. "I was halfway through the service and I thought in a moment of panic, 'No one is crying. This man has taken his own life and no one is crying.' Then I don't know what came over me. It was as if I had to do the crying for the people. I just broke down and sobbed. It was embarrassing, and I've never had it happen before or since."

Please God, Aleda prayed, help me to be strong. But even as this little prayer swept through her, Aleda recognized that she could and would be strong, for the church was full of people ready to grieve. She would not have to do it for them. Many were already crying softly, pulling tissues and handkerchiefs from their pockets, crying for the lost teenager, crying for lost things and lost people in their own lives, crying out of fear that this might happen to someone close to them. Dwayne's sudden and tragic death had touched everyone.

I can begin, Aleda thought, and in a firm, calm, and comforting voice she said, "Thank you all for coming today to honour Dwayne and to support one another in your grief and confusion. Thank you especially for supporting Dwayne's grandmother and parents today and in the days ahead. We have gathered to honour the life of a young man. At this sad time, we will not speculate on things that we do not understand. Instead, we come in faith to grasp the certainties of life, for these certainties come from God."

23

Lists

FTER SUNDAY WORSHIP WAS OVER, Aleda sank onto the sofa in her living room and fell into a deep sleep, untroubled by dreams or nightmares. She wakened some time later, stretching and yawning, then stumbled to her feet and made her way into her office where she grabbed a pad of paper and pencil from her desk. She wandered to the front porch, settled into the wicker chair, and began to make a to-do list. Whether she wanted to go or not, she had a plane ticket to Winnipeg sitting on the kitchen counter.

She would drive to Toronto tomorrow and board a plane from Terminal 1 at 2:30 p.m. By 4:40 p.m. she would be stepping off the plane in Winnipeg, a delegate to her national church's General Assembly.

"Should I bail out?" she had asked Robert. "It all seems a little overwhelming at the moment – first Eadie's death and then Dwayne's. The last thing I want to do right now is attend the General Assembly. My life has been in such turmoil lately, and I just can't imagine that I'll make any positive contribution at all." Even as she said this, though, her thoughts darted to the email from Ben. How could she miss the opportunity to see him again after all these years?

In the end, Robert had suggested that the time away might be beneficial and help her see things from a different perspective, and so Aleda sighed and reconciled herself to writing her list.

Find someone to look after Tracker. (Roy? Martin? Michael?)

Pack clothes. (What is the weather like in Manitoba in June?)

Pack the enormous red book of reports for the Assembly. (Why does it weigh so much?)

Check that all windows are closed and locked. (When had she last done that?)

Check refrigerator for perishable items. (When had she last cleaned out the fridge?)

Ask someone to pick up her mail. (Grace? Roy?)

Hey, wait a minute, she scolded herself. It's not as if you're going overseas for six months. You're travelling within your own country, and you'll be gone four days. Still, it was best to leave things in good order, was it not?

Aleda remembered a time – she was nine years old – when her father began to speak about going back to Hungary to visit. From the very beginning, it had seemed to her that her father was much more in favour of going than her mother. Aleda had never understood her mother's reluctance. Did she fear for their safety? Would a trip back to Hungary stir up memories too painful to face? In the end, her father had gone alone.

What she remembered most from the days before his departure were the lists. Her father had made lists including the name of his employer, the number of his life insurance policy, the street addresses of his sisters and mother in Budapest, the names and phone numbers of his best friends at work, the things to be done at the house before he left.

Her father had had a deep distrust of airplanes so he sailed to Europe from Montreal aboard a Greek ocean liner. On the day of his departure from Hamilton, a cold and rainy April morning, Aleda clutched her mother's hand at the train station, waving and calling, "I love you, Papa! Come back soon, Papa!" Her mother was quiet for weeks after that, going through the routines of her cleaning jobs – scrubbing, dusting, polishing. Aleda opened the mailbox every night hoping for a letter or postcard, but there had been only one that read, "Thinking of you both. I'm well. Reconnecting with old friends and family. Love, Papa/Ferenc."

Her father had been granted a three month leave of absence from the steel mill, and as the days slipped by and there were no more phone calls, letters, or postcards, Aleda could see that her mother was worried. The three months were almost gone, and there was no news of her father's return.

When school finished for the summer, Aleda spent her days at the home of her best friend, who lived next door. "Oh, I wouldn't even notice one more," her friend's mother had said, laughing, when Aleda's mother asked her to look after Aleda for the summer.

It was June 27 – Aleda remembered the date with clarity – when her mother announced that she had booked a flight to Budapest. She was to leave the next day, and she had made a lemon poppy seed cake for Aleda to share with her friends.

Now, 33 years later, as she sat making her own list for a brief trip to Winnipeg, Aleda thought back on that time. What had been going on with her parents? Had her mother feared that her father was not planning to return to Hamilton and had gone to fetch him home? Why had her father over-stayed his time? Had he attempted to set up a business in Hungary or find a new job there so his family could return to the land of his birth? Had her mother gone to persuade him that life was better and safer in Canada? It was impossible to ever find out, Aleda thought in resignation. It seemed to her that so many things from the past would remain unknown or unresolved.

When Aleda had finished her list, she rose and opened the front door for some fresh air. As she stood leaning on the doorjamb she spotted the police cruiser stopping behind her van. Constable Brennan swung his long legs out of the door. Aleda called out, laughing, "The neighbours will begin to think that I live a wicked life."

Constable Brennan smiled. "Just passing through. Wondered how you were doing after yesterday. That was a tough day, but you did a wonderful job at the funeral."

"Will you come in?" Aleda asked.

"Well…"

"Please."

The police officer pointed to the wicker chair lined with the pink afghan. "You take the chair and I'll take this," he said, settling himself onto a sturdy wooden stool. He sat quietly for a moment, looking at his clasped hands. "There's something on my mind," he then said, frowning slightly. "If you're open to it, I may need your help with a police matter."

Aleda turned her head sharply to stare at the face of the officer who continued to look down.

"I've had a request to investigate something, and it's making me a bit uncomfortable."

"You need *my* help?"

He began to explain that a man who had recently renamed himself Jacob, and his wife, Leah, had bought an abandoned old church south of Wiarton and were intending to renovate the building and live there with their eight children.

"But why are you investigating?"

The officer shrugged. "Not sure just yet. Just following up on a call from a real estate agent in Owen Sound, Doug somebody or other, who sold them the property. He had some reason to believe that the children or maybe the wife might be in need of protection."

Aleda shifted in her chair. "I have heard about them, and that the man had a sudden religious conversion and he and his wife try to model their lives after Jacob and Leah in the Bible. It does seem more than a bit peculiar – but there are lots of eccentric people in the world. Too bad they don't live in England. The British are so much more tolerant of eccentrics than Canadians. Despite all our boasting about multinationalism and multiculturalism, we do love all our folks to conform and live like everyone else."

Constable Brennan shrugged a little. "What I was wondering," he glanced at Aleda, "was whether you might come with me when I call on the family? You might have a better sense of whether they really do need some intervention, or whether we can just leave them alone to live in their own funny way. You might have a better sense of whether this religious belief has put the family in danger."

Aleda nodded slowly. "I'm heading to Winnipeg tomorrow for a few days, to our Church's General Assembly…perhaps when I get home. I'm not sure if I can be much help, but I'm willing to try."

Constable Brennan rose to his feet. "There's no rush. No rush at all. The family doesn't get possession until July 1, so I won't be checking in until later. I just thought I would mention it."

He turned toward the door and, standing with his hand on the doorknob as if deciding whether to leave or stay, he turned his head back toward Aleda, who had risen from her chair. "I was also wondering if you would be interested in coming with me to one of the Harbour Nights concerts in Owen Sound."

"Oh!"

Constable Brennan rushed on, "The concerts are very good. You just bring a lawn chair and there are great local and travelling musicians."

"Oh, yes, well…"

Constable Brennan turned to go, a look of confusion and embarrassment on his face. Aleda stepped forward and placed a hand on the sleeve of his uniform. "I'm sorry. It's just that so much has gone on lately, and your invitation caught me off guard. It sounds wonderful though, it really does. When I've returned from Winnipeg and things are back to normal, I'll let you know. Is that okay?"

As she stood watching the police car pull out onto Main Street, Aleda rubbed the bridge of her nose. What she hadn't mentioned – what she couldn't say – was that she would be connecting in Winnipeg with the one true love of her life, Ben Snell.

By nightfall her clothes were packed and her airplane ticket and the large red binder of General Assembly reports were tucked into her large tote bag. Tomorrow would bring its own challenges, but for now she would try to sleep.

24

Winnipeg

Y THE TIME SHE WAS ON THE AIRPLANE to Winnipeg, Aleda remembered again why she did not like to travel. It had taken her three hours to drive to Toronto and another hour to find the correct Park-and-Fly lot and catch the bus to the terminal. Yet another hour had passed by the time she had checked in for her flight and boarded the aircraft; then another delay as the plane sat on the runway awaiting its turn for departure. Aleda napped during the flight, but by the time the plane landed she wanted only to have a shower, change into fresh clothes, and find something to eat.

After locating her room in the university dormitory, she unpacked, showered, dressed, and slipped on her delegate's badge. She then went to the elevator and made her way to the university cafeteria.

She was late, and most of the delegates were already eating at long tables in a noisy, echo-filled room where the clatter of china and cutlery bounced off the walls. Aleda, feeling not hunger but tightness in her stomach, picked up an orange cafeteria tray and stood at the end of the food line. Two women in front of her were deciding between the shepherd's pie and the vegetarian primavera. As she stood waiting, she heard someone come up behind her.

"Aleda. Aleda Vastag," a man said softy. She turned around. "Ben."

"I was so excited to see your name on the list." Ben was smiling.

Aleda smiled back and nodded, clutching the tray in front of her. Please God, she prayed silently, don't let him hug me. Not after all these years. Ben, she noticed, was somewhat heavier, but had the same boyish good looks, the same outgoing personality, the same easy charm that she remembered.

"We'll have to spend some time together this week. It's such a great chance to get back in touch. I insist on taking you out to dinner. And not like the old student days, either," Ben laughed.

When they had been students at seminary, they ate once a week at The Noodle Factory, the cheapest sit-down café on campus. Neither of them had money for luxuries, but they did have to eat, they reminded each other. How they joked about their dining out, pretending that the almost non-existent beef in their beef lo mein was filet mignon, and that the free fortune cookies were sources of profound wisdom. They pretended that their glasses of water, with the cloudy ice cubes, were goblets of Bourgogne Chardonnay, or they reverted to the adolescent jokes they had shared with their friends in high school, adding a toothpick to the water and calling it a pine float. Aleda had once brought along a red-checked hand-kerchief to spread on the table, and an empty Chianti bottle holding a candle; they pretended that they were in the north of Italy having dinner. In a reckless moment Aleda even lit the candle, but a worried waiter came to the table to tell them that open flames were not permitted.

The cafeteria line began to move, and Aleda turned forward. She felt Ben's warm hand on her bare arm as she stood staring at the food in the stainless steel trays. "Aleda," he said softly from behind her, "I am really looking forward to getting back in touch with you. I've missed you so much."

Martin was working beside the barn as Callum came up the lane. The boy waved and then headed straight into the kitchen. He was always eager to see and feed Buddy. Callum scooped some kibble from the tin by the back door and dumped it into Buddy's bowl, but today Buddy could not be enticed to eat. The dog seemed rest-less and anxious, looking around as if trying to find a place to make a nest. Callum pushed the dog bowl in front of her, but the dog was not interested in her food.

Martin came up the steps into the house and stood in the open doorway watching the boy trying to coax the dog to eat.

"Is she sick?" Callum inquired.

Martin shook his head. "She ate this morning, remember?"

Buddy had gone to lie down on an old blanket in the corner and Callum moved forward again, setting the bowl in front of her. But the dog, who moved with difficulty because of the cast on her leg, rose almost immediately and began to pace around the blan-ket.

"I think we should just leave her alone for a while," Martin said, taking the boy by the hand. "I've got some work out by the barn. Maybe you could give me a hand."

Martin had never had the experience of seeing a dog have pup-pies. Should he call the vet? Should he take the dog to the clinic at Rockford? He handed the boy a hammer. "You any good at pound-ing nails?" he asked. "I'm trying to get these boards on the side of the barn."

After a couple of hours, Martin suggested that the boy go home for his supper. "Can't I just see Buddy for a few minutes?" he asked, anxious and eager.

"We'll just let her rest today," Martin said firmly. "Come by tomorrow morning on your way to school."

Callum turned toward home, scuffing the gravel with his shoes. Martin watched the boy amble down the laneway. Callum stopped now and then to look back over his shoulder and wave, or to pick up something from the long grass. When Martin could see that Callum had safely crossed the road and was walking up his own lane, he turned back to the house and walked up the steps into the back kitchen. Should he call the vet? When he entered the house, he saw that he no longer had to make a decision.

There, lying beside Buddy, was a small puppy, helpless and wet. Martin stood frozen, and within seconds the mother dog reached around to lick a sac from the puppy's face. Buddy was not gentle with the puppy, but soon the puppy was giving lusty cries and starting to move around. Martin watched, both horrified and fascinated, as the female dog briskly tore at the umbilical cord with her teeth. You seem to have things under control, old girl, he thought as he backed out the door and shut it gently.

It's a good night to visit Mother, he said to himself as he climbed into his truck and eased it out of the laneway and toward the village.

25

Puppies

ARTIN HAD SPENT THE PREVIOUS EVENING with his mother, asking questions as long as possible, encouraging Rose to tell him about the latest book she was reading: *The Arctic Grail* by Pierre Berton. What had she liked best about the book? Which explorer seemed the most credible to her? Did she understand the drive of Europeans to explore a dangerous frigid environment and search for the elusive Northwest Passage? Had the weather been similar to what she had experienced as a young nurse in Whitehorse?

Martin had lingered over the washing and drying of the dishes, then scrubbed off the stove and swept the kitchen floor. He suggested a cup of lavender tea on the back porch, and when it had begun to grow dark and the mosquitoes had come whining around their ankles and necks, they moved indoors. They watched an old movie on television, but by 11 p.m. his mother was yawning, so Martin rose to go home.

"To what do I owe this long and dedicated evening?" Rose asked, smiling.

Martin shrugged, grinned, and said, "You're such great company," but then, seeing the puzzled look on his mother's face, he relented and added, "There's a puppy birthing going on in my back kitchen and I thought it was better to get out of the way."

Because he could no longer delay, Martin headed home. As he put the truck into gear, he paused to look up toward Aleda's home that stood in darkness. Ah, yes, Aleda had gone to Winnipeg. The lights were out in the doctor's house also, and as Martin sat in his truck he remembered his mother telling him at dinner about her morning visits with Laura.

"You and Laura seem to have quite a bond," Martin had commented as he cut into his pork chop.

"She's a wonderful person, but why wouldn't she be? She had such a wonderful father."

"Laura is more like her dad than her mother?" Martin asked, surprised to hear his mother compare Laura to her father.

"Well, I'm not sure about that so much," Rose said, and Martin, noticing something different in his mother's voice, stared into her face for a moment until she said, "Now then. Tell me about your composting."

Martin twisted open the kitchen doorknob and tapped the light switch. He hung his keys on a hook, careful not to let them rattle, and then peeked around the corner at the blanket where Buddy made her bed. Martin slowly shook his head. There, lying contentedly it seemed, was Buddy with three puppies sleeping on her side.

Although he hated to disturb the little canine family, Martin began to clean up the birthing mess, not wanting Callum to see it in the morning. He knew the sight of it would trigger a hundred questions. How did the puppies get out? Did Martin see them come out? What did Buddy do when she first saw them? Did they come out all at once or one at a time? No, far better just to hide the evidence. Martin gathered up the soiled blanket and pushed it into a plastic garbage bag before setting down a clean one. Tomorrow I'll call the vet and ask if Buddy and the puppies need to be checked, he thought. Martin stood looking down at the puppies and the tired mother dog. Beautiful family, he mused, until a sharp anxious feeling, almost like panic, settled in his stomach. Who on earth is going to look after these puppies when I've returned to Guelph at the end of the summer? And who is going to see that this dog is spayed so this unnecessary scenario doesn't happen again?

Tuesday at General Assembly had been a busy and – Aleda admitted to a man who shared her table in the meeting room – often boring day for her. Some of the reports were long and tedious, while other innocuous reports seemed to elicit long and complicated debates. Some described topics that she neither comprehended nor much cared about.

Aleda sat at the table staring down at her binder, remembering how she and her first-year seminary classmates had been invited to that year's General Assembly. I suppose, she recollected, our professors thought that attending the conference would be a great educational opportunity. To her dismay, she had not enjoyed it at all. In her opinion, it seemed as if some clergy joined in a debate in order to hear their own voices, or show off their erudite debating skills. And it seemed that some topics unnecessarily became objects of great scrutiny.

A few days after their return, the students at her college were urged to attend a special seminar by Ninian Smart, professor in the Comparative Study of Religions at University of California, Santa Barbara. Aleda had not wanted to go – there were papers to write and she had fallen behind on practising her Greek cue cards – but in the end her sense of duty and obligation won out. She sat in one of the hard seats of the lecture hall and listened to Ninian Smart's gentle Scottish burr explain his seven-part definition of religion, and how all religions have certain recognisable elements that can be studied. Dr. Smart was making a point that although these seven dimensions varied in importance from religion to religion, it was possible to see the seven dimensions in all religions. Dr. Smart put up a list: doctrine, myth or story, ethics, ritual, experience, institutional care, and material.

Recalling the lecture with Robert once, Aleda explained that it was one of those moments when it seemed as if a light bulb had lit up in her head. "How could anyone possibly love all seven characteristics of religion? If a person did ... well ... that would be a very dull, boring, and over-focused person. I certainly wouldn't invite a person like that out for an evening of beer or bowling!" she declared.

"But," she continued in an animated way, pointing her finger in the air as the bemused Robert listened, "that lecture by Dr. Smart freed me in a most unusual way. There are parts of religion I love, like the stories and the rituals and experiences; and there are parts of religion that I am neutral about. For instance, I know that good doctrine is important, but I don't want to be the one to help form and shape it. I will leave that to others who care deeply about that task. And," she continued, "there are parts of religion that I just don't like – like the institutional care of the church. I'll go to church meetings and I'll take my turn going to General Assembly, but now I give myself permission to not like them!

"But it's okay for me not to like certain parts of religion because I know there are other people who love the parts that I don't, and they are willing to invest lots of time and energy in those parts. Why should I deprive them of something they love? It's such a freeing thought, don't you think, Robert?"

Robert, nodding and smiling, said, "I hadn't thought of it like that before, but that is what community is all about – using our different gifts for the good of all, supplementing and complementing."

During the afternoon break, when she had begun to feel groggy, she felt a gentle hand on her shoulder.

"How's the day going for you?"

Aleda lifted her shoulders to loosen tense muscles, then turned to face Ben, who had dropped into an empty chair beside her.

"Let me whisk you away from here," Ben said. "May I, Your Royal Highness," he said with a court-gesture flourish, "have the pleasure of taking you out to dinner tonight?"

"Tonight."

"Yes. Tonight. There's something on here – there was an announcement before lunch – but I don't think it's that important for all of us to be here. Besides, there's no voting tonight, just a presentation of some kind." Ben reached over to where Aleda's hand lay on her open binder and, with his thumb, caressed the flesh between her thumb and first finger, his warm hand pressed against hers.

Aleda hesitated, thinking of the presentation that she had looked forward to hearing. Ben, misinterpreting her hesitation, leaned forward and spoke in a low voice. "Look Aleda, it's not what you may think. I'm not a married man hitting on you. I've been divorced for ten years. My daughter – you remember my daughter, Sophie? – she's a university student at Mount Allison now. I had a brief second marriage that didn't work out, a few relationships here and there, but nothing serious. The truth is," Ben almost whispered, "I never really got over you. Whenever I was with another woman, it was you I thought about. I compared them all with you. You were – you are – so smart, so funny, so attractive, so adventurous. I made a mistake and I know it."

Ben stopped talking, and Aleda let out a long soft breath. She looked at him and said clearly, "I would love to go out to dinner tonight. Where shall we meet and when?"

As Aleda stood waiting on the dormitory steps, she spotted Ben coming toward her, smiling. He had changed into khaki slacks and a sky blue shirt that matched his eyes. He can still make my heart skip a beat, she thought.

"Where to, Madame? You have three choices. I've done my homework! We can go to the lovely grand old lady, the historic Fort Garry Hotel, built in 1913 and known for its sophisticated international cuisine using local products," Ben said, imitating a tour guide. "A bit of beautiful history and a good meal. Or we can go to The Forks, built upon another historic site where the Red and Assiniboine rivers meet. For at least 6,000 years this site has been the meeting place for First Nations peoples."

"Really! How do you know all this stuff?"

"Elementary, my dear Watson. I read the promotional literature that came with the red binder."

"Oh."

"And if we walk around The Forks Market, there are at least two good restaurants – Sydney's and The Beachcomber."

"Let's go to the Beachcomber. It sounds like fun! It's so warm out tonight and the idea of being a beachcomber has always appealed to me."

Ben reached over, gave her a hug, then slipped his hand around hers, joining their fingers. "Off we go then!"

I had forgotten how good this feels, Aleda thought as they walked along in search of a taxi. She felt happy and relaxed, happy to be back with a man who adored her, happy to be laughing and talking, happy to be experiencing companionship once again with someone who had been so important to her. She would not spoil the evening by talking with Ben about some of the angst in her life. No, not tonight, but perhaps she would have a chance to tell him everything soon.

At dinner, they lingered over mussels in ancho broth, then shared two dishes – wild Manitoba pickerel and bison short ribs. When the bottle of Merlot was empty, and they had both refused dessert and coffee, the waiter brought the bill, set it down near Ben, and said, "No rush. When you're ready."

Aleda detected some hesitation when Ben picked up the folder holding the bill. As he opened the folder, it occurred to Aleda that Ben might not have enough money to cover the bill.

"We've had a great time catching up," Aleda said. "So much talk about the old days at seminary. Do you remember when we were poor students and went out to dinner at The Noodle Factory?"

"Of course," Ben laughed.

"You remember how we agreed that, if we were to have a relationship of equality, we would each pay our own share of the bill?"

Ben nodded, grinning.

"Now," Aleda said, reaching for her shoulder bag, "we are going to keep up the tradition."

After dinner, Aleda and Ben climbed the six storey tower at The Forks Market and stood gazing out at the confluence of the rivers and at the expanse of green space where they imagined canoes laden with dried buffalo skins, pemmican, and beaver pelts.

Then they strolled through the marketplace, pausing to admire stalls of bread, meat, wine, fresh fruit, cigars, and displays of local art. "Look, Ben. This stall says that they specialize in fresh-from-the-oven organic sourdough bread." Aleda threw up her hands. "Ah, Ben. Me and sourdough…well, that's another story I have to tell you."

When the sun had dipped below the horizon, they stood looking out over the swirling eddies. Ben slipped his arm around Aleda and turned her to face him. Cradling her head between his hands, he kissed above her eyebrows; she felt his lips on her cheekbone before she lifted her face to his, their lips and tongues meeting, eager and soft, her hands pressing flat on Ben's back, holding him close to her.

Ben pushed Aleda back slightly, slid his hands up her bare arms and stood looking at her with his clear blue eyes. "Aleda," he said in a serious voice, "there's something I want to say. We had something very special 20 years ago. Can we pick up where we should never have left off?"

26

Secrets

ARTIN STOOD WAITING OUTSIDE, watching for Callum to meander up his lane on his way to feed Buddy. As he approached, Martin waved and called out, "Morning, Callum." When the boy was beside him, Martin reached out and grasped his shoulder. "I have some important news for you."

Callum looked up eagerly.

"It's Buddy. She had her puppies last night," Martin said, grinning.

"Puppies!" Callum shouted, turning toward the farmhouse. Martin tightened his grip on the boy's shoulder.

"Callum, listen to me," Martin said. "Buddy is tired out, and she is learning how to care for three little puppies. What she needs is quiet and calm." Martin saw the look of disappointment on Callum's face. "But we can go in to see the puppies. We just won't go close to Buddy while she's learning to be a mother." Martin smiled as he watched the intense little boy, wiry and eager, tiptoe up the steps to the back kitchen. Together, they crept to the doorway. When they peeked around the corner, Callum stood staring for a long time. Martin could see that the boy was working very hard to stay quiet, his small fists clenching and opening.

"In a little while," Martin whispered, "they'll be big enough to play with, but not now."

The boy nodded and watched as two of the puppies nosed their way toward Buddy's nipples and began to suck. The smallest one lay apart, snuggled into a fold of the warm blanket until Buddy nudged it forward with her nose so it could sense the warmth of her flank.

Martin and Callum stood together, watching, until Callum turned to Martin and whispered fiercely, "She's a good mother."

Martin dropped Callum off at school and drove to the store. He ran up the steps two at a time, calling out, "Morning, gentlemen, what's new?" to the two men sitting outside.

"Not much. Anything new with you? Still up to that crazy business at the back of your farm?"

"Yup," Martin answered in a cheerful voice. "You wait. It'll make me famous someday. But I do have a bit of news. We have a dog with three new puppies this morning. Know anyone who's looking for a puppy when they're weaned?"

"Not that I know of, but if I hear of anyone, I'll give your mother a call."

"That's the spirit." As Martin drove past Laura's driveway on his way home, he caught sight of Laura carrying some trash out to the dumpster. He pulled in and jumped out of the truck.

"Still cleaning out?"

"Oh hi, Martin. Glad you dropped in. Why don't you come in and have a look at the study?"

When they were inside, Laura waved toward the hall with its flung-open doors, and with a proud smile on her face, showed Martin the room that had been her father's office. "It cleaned up well, don't you think? The only thing left is Dad's old rolltop desk. David and I want to persuade Aleda to take it. She admired it and would make good use of it, don't you think?"

"She sure would. I can see some elegant sermons flowing from that desk."

"There's something else I've been wondering," Laura said to Martin. "Come across the hall with me." They stepped into the living room that was separated in the middle by French doors. Laura swept out her hand. "What do you see?" she demanded.

"Well…"

"Yes! Precisely. Heavy, dark, substantial old furniture. Maroon and green, velour and plush. Nice old pieces and no doubt worth something, but I'd like to get rid of them. Everything."

"Everything?" Martin asked, waiting.

"I'd like to fill this room with light. With white…and air…and freshness…and brightness! When you enter this room, I'd like it to feel as if you had just smelled lemons. I want it to say peace and comfort and wholeness and harmony. Most of all, I want it to be full of light, and white."

"You mean…in other words…men can be a bit obtuse about these things, you understand…you want to get rid of all these solid old pieces of furniture and refurnish in your own taste?"

Laura laughed. "I can certainly afford it, and why not make this into a pleasant space I would enjoy?"

Martin stood still, glancing around the room. "But surely," he said, "the carpet…"

The large area rug was thick and luxurious, a bright ocean blue patterned with shades of gold and white.

"Maybe I'll keep the rug. I see that it is beautiful, now that you point it out to me, but the rest of this stuff…" Laura hesitated. "Do you by chance know of anyone who would just take the furniture away? Is there anyone around who could use it?"

Martin, his arms crossed, shook his head slowly. "Can't think of anyone," but after gazing again around the room he said, "Well, if you're quite sure that this is what you want to do, I suppose I could ask Callum's father. They have an empty living room and an empty dining room too. Of course, having furniture might cramp that kid's style," Martin said, smiling. "Where on earth would he keep his beetle collection?"

"Thanks Martin. Have time for a coffee?"

"Sure thing, but when we're done I want you to hop into my truck and come up to the farm for a few minutes. I have a surprise." Laura set a carton of cream beside the two mugs of steaming coffee. "Martin," she said in a tentative voice, her eyebrows drawn together in a frown, "something very intriguing has come up while I was sorting out my father's office." She explained to Martin that she had come across birth certificates for both Martin and James in her father's locked box.

"I talked to David about it, but neither he nor I can make sense of it. Do you have any idea? Why did *my* father have *your* birth certificates locked in his file box? And why were you born in Guelph, not Owen Sound?"

Martin stirred his coffee and shook his head. "Mother never mentioned that. Maybe she had high risk pregnancies? I don't know. Perhaps Dr. Browning suggested that she go to a centre where there were specialized facilities for babies? Or perhaps Mother didn't want to have her babies so close to home?"

Martin and Laura sat in silence, each lost in thought. "You do know, don't you," Martin said at last, "that my mother worked with your father in the time before my brother and I were born? She worked as his nurse. I know that Mother and Dr. Browning were very fond of one another – my mother still speaks highly of your father…you know that…and they had what they called *adventures* going out into the country to deliver babies in the middle of snow-storms. Mother used to tell me how they heated bricks in the wood stove and set them under their feet in the cutter, then drove out to farm houses through drifts of snow. They kept warm under buffalo robes."

"But your mother was already married at this time?"

"My mother was engaged to my father before he went off to war, and when he came back badly injured I think she felt some obligation to marry him. But you know Laura, I know that my mother was devoted to my father, but I've always thought that she was in love with Dr. Browning. And that he was in love with her."

Laura stared at Martin, who sat clutching his mug.

"Martin, that's absolutely preposterous!" she said at last, her voice breathless. "My father was a married man, with children."

Martin shrugged. He glanced up at Laura. "Did you know that your father visited us every week? To check on my dad, or so we were told. The doctor always took a keen interest in James and me. I remember him spending a few minutes with Dad, but mainly he spent his time at our kitchen table talking to me and James and Mother. He would ask about school and how our sports were going. My mother always made sure that we were home when the doctor called.

"Did you know," Martin took off his baseball cap and mopped his forehead with his hand, "did you know that your father paid for our university educations? And, one time when I was doing those things that young kids do, I found a hatbox full of love letters tied up with ribbon in my mother's closet. I couldn't resist. I opened one. I'd seen your father's hand writing often enough on prescription pads. I recognized immediately who wrote those love letters to my mother."

The kitchen fell silent, apart from the ticking of the clock above the kitchen sink. Laura spoke at last. "Does this mean…are you suggesting…do you think it's possible that you and I are?…" Laura's voice trailed off into silence again.

Martin pressed his tightly folded hands onto his lips. "Look at us, Laura, just look at us. You, me, James. Tall. Thin. Blond. Built like your father. James and I don't resemble *our* father, not a bit." Martin set his hands flat on the kitchen table. Laura looked both pale and shaken.

"Laura, I'm sorry. I never meant to mention this. I know it's a shock to you, whereas I've had years to think about it. But do you really want to open up something that happened so long ago? Sometimes I think it's better to just let things be. Does it really change anything if we know for sure one way or the other?" Martin paused, gazing out the window. "Does it really matter in the long run?"

"Martin!" Laura exclaimed angrily, slamming her open hand on the kitchen table. "It matters! It matters a great deal. This is hugely important, and I just can't figure out how I feel about Rose now."

Martin gave Laura's hand a squeeze and in a quiet voice said, "Rose is a wonderful, wonderful woman; intelligent, caring, wise, and immensely loyal. I hope you will always see that. And, well, what the hell, I've always wanted a sister."

But Laura avoided his eyes. Oh, this is an unbearable secret, a burden too heavy to keep to ourselves, she thought. We have to find a time to talk this over with Aleda.

After what seemed a long time, yearning to restore some sort of equilibrium to their relationship after his shocking revelation, Martin suggested that Laura go with him to the farm to see his surprise. He led the silent Laura up the back steps and began to tiptoe into the kitchen. He waved Laura forward and she gave a small but audible gasp.

"Three!" she whispered.

"Can you believe this?" he said softly. "Not even 24 hours old and they're already named."

"Callum?"

"You bet. He told me on the way to school this morning that he would name two of the puppies after dogs that were in story books at school. That one is Clifford."

"Ah, yes. Clifford the big red dog."

"The little one, the runt, is Pokey."

"Uh-huh. Pokey the puppy. I know my kiddie literature. And the other one? The biggest one?"

"That one," Martin said, folding his arms and leaning against the wall, "that one is going to be called…" he hesitated, and Laura looked at him, her eyebrows raised. "That one is called Dwayne."

Martin telephoned Dr. Patel after driving Laura home and she had agreed to pop in that afternoon as she would be in the neighbourhood. Martin was using the front-end loader on his tractor to tidy up the stockpile of sawdust when she pulled into the yard. He shut off the motor and reached out to shake her hand. "Thanks so much for coming by," he said. "I think the dog did all the work herself. I just got out of the way."

"Good. Good. Puppies nursing okay?"

"They seem happy and content. One is a little smaller than the others, but even the runt is nursing with a little encouragement from the mother."

"That's often the case," Dr. Patel said in an absent-minded tone of voice. "I'll take a look. It could be that you should change the mother's food for a week or so in order to help her milk production. She was quite malnourished when you brought her in with the broken leg." Dr. Patel's voice drifted off and she stood looking past the tractor and beyond the grove of Scotch pine trees behind the barn. "I understand that you're experimenting with composting dead stock." She glanced at Martin, who nodded. "I would be very interested in seeing your operation," she said as she grabbed her bag from the back of the truck.

"Oh! I'm happy to show you," Martin said, his voice eager. "In fact, I'm more than happy to show you the system." They began walking toward the house. "Tell me, how did you hear about the composting? Are the local farmers talking about it?"

"Yes. Yes they are. I've heard about it quite often, in fact, and it made me very curious." Aha, Martin thought, at last I meet a woman who isn't totally grossed out by the whole enterprise.

"And what are they saying?" Martin replied as he held open the back door.

Dr. Patel set down her bag and removed her rubber boots. "Well, quite frankly," she smiled, "they think you're absolutely nuts. Crazy, in fact."

27

Home

BY THE TIME ALEDA HAD LANDED in Toronto and found her van in the Park-and-Fly lot, it was evening and she was tired and hungry. She had driven north on Highways 6 and 10 and turned west from Rockford. The sun had begun to set, and bands of gold and orange stretched across the horizon. It would be a beautiful night at the lake, Aleda sighed, wondering if Ben would enjoy Sauble Beach as much as she did. As she pulled into the driveway, she knew she needed to see Tracker, but first she wanted to check the mail and phone messages.

Home at last, Aleda bumped open the porch door, unlocked the inside door, and dumped her bag in the hallway. Have to open some windows, she thought. It's stuffy in here.

When she walked into the kitchen, she spotted a tidy stack of notes and letters on the table beside a neatly folded copy of the *Sun Times*. The message light on the telephone blinked red. Sinking onto a kitchen chair, she picked up the stack of paper and began to flip through it. Some bills, some flyers, and a card from a friend who had heard about Dwayne's suicide. There was a note in Roy's neat handwriting: *Tracker is just dandy. He's enjoying these warm days, but his ground meal is getting a little low.*

Aleda rose from the table and filled and plugged in the kettle before turning to the telephone with a small shudder brought on by fatigue and apprehension. Somehow paper messages seemed manageable and benign, but phone messages held the possibility of crisis and anxiety. But when Aleda listened to the messages – there were only two – she smiled at both.

The first was from Robert. In his calm deep voice he welcomed her home and said that he remembered how it had been for him when he returned from General Assembly and had to scramble to catch up on pastoral concerns. "I know you're a most capable woman," Robert continued, "but if it's helpful to you, I'd be happy to preach the sermon for you on Sunday. It would give Patrice and me a chance to take you out to lunch too. Give us a call when you're settled."

The second was the cheerful voice of Savannah. "Hi Aleda! We missed you, and hope you had a great time in the Peg. We have a band practice on Saturday – extra practice for the school trip – Mr. Hart is a slave driver – so we phoned around and cancelled the Saturday kid's camp. Hope you don't mind. And by the way, we thought that you might need a night off from dealing with us rowdies, so we also cancelled Youth Group on Friday night. Still on for the chocolate strawberries for the strawberry social though. Ciao! See you soon!"

As Aleda unplugged the kettle and reached for the teapot there was sharp rap on the front door. Oh please God, not tonight, she sighed as she padded to the front door in her bare feet, but to her delight it was Martin. She glanced over to the truck pulled in behind her van. Laura, sitting in the passenger seat, had rolled down the window and was leaning out.

"We won't stay. We know you're just home," Martin said. "Have a good trip?"

Aleda walked down the front steps and followed Martin over to the truck so Laura could be part of the conversation. "Yes. In fact, it was an extraordinary trip. What are you two up to?"

Laura grinned and looked at Martin. "While you were away, I decided to get rid of all the old furniture in the living and dining rooms and replace it with furniture that is more my style. We spent the day hauling sofas and chairs and tables up to Callum's house. They seemed happy to get it." Laura glanced at Martin. "Martin did most of the hard work."

"It wasn't so bad, really. Callum has already arranged all the furniture. He wants to have everything square so all the furniture is placed around the edges of the rooms. That boy…" Martin laughed, shaking his head. "He said it would leave room in the middle for his bowls of coloured stones."

"Honestly, Aleda," Laura said, "it's wonderful to have you home. I hope you and Martin are still on for dinner tomorrow night? Maybe I'll go furniture shopping tomorrow. With some luck, I might even have my new and improved living room set up to show you."

Martin jiggled his keys, thinking sheepishly that he and Laura sounded like two children eager for the attention of a parent who has been away on a business trip. "And while you were away we had some new arrivals. Buddy has three adorable puppies. You'll have to pop up to the farm house to see them. Are you in the market for another pet when the puppies are weaned?"

"Ha! That's all I need, another creature to look after. Besides, what would people say? The Reverend finally got a socially accept-able pet. I couldn't bear the shame."

Martin turned back toward the truck. "We'll let you get settled in then and see you tomorrow night."

But as he spun around to leave, Aleda called out, "Wait! There's something I need to ask, a favour, really. I have a guest arriving tomorrow. He's an old friend…well, more than an old friend. We reconnected in Winnipeg after many years, and he's coming here tomorrow for a day or two before he flies back to Fredericton." Martin and Laura stared at Aleda. "I'm a bit worried about the older people in the village. They talk, especially Ethel at the store…and Grace," she added, but the truth was that Aleda was most worried about what Roy might think. "I'm worried about whether I should have him stay here. You know what I mean. Will people think it *proper* for their minister to entertain a man overnight?" She threw her hands into the air, looking at Martin who had folded his arms and was leaning on the tail gate of the truck. Laura sat speechless, her mouth open.

"I was wondering," Aleda rushed on, "if one of you might be willing to host Ben overnight tomorrow, just to sleep I mean. I'll look after him the rest of the time."

There was a silence until Martin cleared his throat. "Would be glad to normally...but I really don't have an extra bedroom set up at the farmhouse, and with the new puppies..."

Laura said slowly, "Well, I suppose..."

"Thank you! Thank you!" Aleda said, beaming at Laura. "You two are wonderful, the best friends in the whole world. It means a great deal to me. You see," she hesitated, looking from one to the other, "it would seem that Ben wants to rekindle our relationship that ended 20 years ago."

When Martin pulled into Laura's driveway, she turned to him and said, "Would you like to come in for a drink? We could sit in my empty living room on some lawn chairs."

"I really should get home," Martin hesitated before continuing, "but I did give strict orders to Callum that he is not to come over tonight, so I suppose it would be fine."

"I've had more enthusiastic responses," Laura replied.

"I could use a drink. Where do I find the lawn chairs?"

When they had poured a drink and settled on the lawn chairs, Martin crossed one leg over the other and gently rocked the ice in his glass of Scotch. "What are your long-term plans for this house? It's a beautiful old home."

"I know. I know." Laura frowned. "I'll have to come to some decision soon. David keeps reminding me of that. After all, I have my condo in Toronto and when this comes off..." She pointed to her walking boot.

They lapsed into silence.

"Call me stupid," Martin said, turning to look directly at Laura. "But is it only me who thinks that this business of Aleda's boyfriend is a bit sudden?"

Laura took a sip of her wine. "We don't know Aleda that well, I guess. I mean, really…"

"None of us knows each other all that well, I guess. But we live in a bit of a bubble here and the news about Ben makes me feel a bit sad or uneasy, I can't tell which. I've spent my whole career in innovation. That's what the university pays me for, to invent changes and think outside the box. But it's funny Laura. This summer, connecting with you and Aleda and Callum, and spending time with my mother, and getting reacquainted with Roy, and Ethel at the corner store, well, for the first time in my life I find myself not wanting things to change."

"But Martin! You've just dropped a bombshell of a secret about your mother and my father. You of all people must realize that life is always changing!"

"Laura, I'm sorry. I really am. I know that it was a shock to you, but I have had years, decades, to get used to the idea." Martin and Laura sat immersed in their thoughts. "I've been wondering if it would help if you and I had a bit of a conversation with Mother?"

Laura said, slowly, "Let me think about it. It would be difficult. Let me think about that for a while." She sighed. "Shall I get us another drink?" she asked, looking down into her empty glass, having gulped down the wine far too fast. Martin's Scotch had also disappeared.

"I'd better be on my way," Martin said, slowly standing, but when he reached the kitchen door he turned back and said, "Laura, have you been wondering something, the same as me? Will we like this Ben guy?"

28

Ben

PAIR OF ROBINS HAD BUILT their nest over the light fixture by the front door of the parsonage early in the spring. The duo – and their large extended family, it seemed to Aleda – began their relentless singing in the maple tree as soon as there was a hint of light in the eastern sky. Aleda heard them warbling through her open window; a song that sounded like *cheerily, cheer up, cheer up, cheerily, cheer up*. The singing rose and fell in steady rhythm, paused, and began again.

Aleda's alarm clock read 4:43 a.m. Pounding her pillow over her ear, she drifted back to sleep, but before long she was awake again, making a mental list of the things she needed to do before she met Ben at the bus depot that afternoon: call Robert and gratefully accept his offer to preach on Sunday; prepare the rest of the worship service; print the worship bulletin (oh, how she envied her colleagues in big churches who had a secretary); buy another bag of food for Tracker; pick up some groceries; make something for the dinner at Laura's house. She wondered how Laura and Martin would respond to Ben.

What would she wear? She flipped through hangers in the closet, flicking from one garment to another until her hand rested on an orange sundress. When Aleda had worn this dress in the past she had always received compliments. She pulled it from the closet and held it against her, leaning forward to peer into the full-length mirror on her bedroom wall. The broad straps and diagonal slash gave it an impertinent flair, a certain *je ne sais quoi,* and the warm colour brought out the natural shine and warm glow of her skin. Perfect, she thought, as she headed for the shower.

Her work done by late morning, Aleda glanced at the clock. Panic and excitement rippled through her stomach. The awareness that Ben would actually be at her house, would be sitting in a lawn chair in her backyard, would be wandering around in her kitchen, filled her with both exhilaration and agitation. Yes, she was more than ready to have Ben back in her life, and she believed that, in time, their renewed relationship might even lead to the marriage they had planned together 20 years ago.

Aleda remembered she needed to prepare something for dinner. Should she run into the grocery store before picking up Ben? Should she make one of her many Hungarian specialities? She heard her mother's voice echoing in her head: *Aleda, my dear, stick to what you know best.* Okay, Mama, it will be *Bélszín Budapest-módra* with its stewed veal bones, tomatoes, peppers, mushrooms, and medallions of beef. But as Aleda thought through the steps of preparing this dish she realized that she did not have the time or the proper ingredients. She opened the refrigerator door and stood peering into the nearly empty space.

Recalling her mother's advice brought back a memory of another time – was she six or seven? – when her mother stood at the kitchen counter, rolling dough. Aleda, perched on a stool, watching, picked at bits of dough that clung to the edge of the bowl and popped them into her mouth. As her mother worked, she explained to Aleda that gingerbread cookies were a traditional gift in Hungary. "Many men will choose a gingerbread heart over flowers for their sweethearts," Mama had said as she sprinkled flour on the counter and turned the brown dough over to roll it again, making it thin and even.

"But Mama, why are *you* making the gingerbread? Shouldn't Papa be doing this? You said the men give gingerbread to their sweethearts."

"Oh, silly goose," her mother responded, smiling. "It doesn't matter who gives to whom, as long as you love each other."

Aleda flung open the door to the cupboard where she kept her baking supplies. Yes, she had everything she needed – molasses, ginger, flour, cinnamon, and, of course, the icing sugar and food colouring with which to make the fantastic designs on top. Where had she put the rolling pin and the cookie cutter that she had inherited from her mother? She pulled out her mother's brown earthenware mixing bowl.

She would make the tastiest, most splendid, most garish gingerbread for her true love Ben, and she would make cookies for two people who had become dear friends. As she mixed, stirred, and rolled, she remembered her mother telling a story about a Hungarian writer called Mikszáth who said that the art of gingerbread baking is watched over by Cupid. "Gingerbread is full of love, full of fun," her mother told the small child on the kitchen stool, a smudge of flour on her cheek. "Mikszáth said that the gingerbread-maker is not a tradesperson, but a veritable poet."

As the fragrant cookies cooled, Aleda prepared small bowls of icing – red, orange, pink, blue, and white. It was important to make the colour combination and pattern on each gingerbread gift unique, her mother had taught. Aleda began to create red hearts, white and pink sugar flowers, fanciful blue leaves. Around the edges she added delicate swirls of orange, curving around the hearts. She etched a deeper scallop of white icing on the borders. In the centre, Aleda made a square of fluted orange and pink icing, and inside the square, with a toothpick, she drew the initials for Ben, Laura and Martin. Standing back, satisfied, she laughed aloud, thinking that the gingerbread cookies were the kitschiest thing she had ever made. Yet she knew she would tell a flamboyant story that evening about the heritage of gingerbread as a token of affection for a loved one.

Dumping all the sugary bowls into the sink, Aleda glanced at the kitchen clock. She ran back upstairs, washed her hands, checked her face for flour, and changed into the orange dress. She had time to pick up some things at the grocery store – they would need coffee, fresh bread, salami, orange juice, butter – and then, with a shiver of excitement, she reminded herself that there would be just enough time to get to the bus terminal in Owen Sound to meet Ben.

She caught sight of him before he saw her. Beautiful Ben, she thought, gulping hard to swallow what seemed like a large lump in her throat. Holding a brown duffle bag in front of him, he swung out of the bus door, his hair rumpled as if he had been sleeping. When he spotted Aleda, his eyes crinkled at the edges as a smile lit his face. He put his free arm around her and pulled her toward him.

"Aleda, you're beautiful," he said. "I can't tell you how happy I am to have you all to myself for a couple of days."

Perhaps she would wait until later to tell Ben about dinner at Laura's house that evening. She turned her face up toward him and let herself be kissed.

When they got back to the parsonage Aleda asked Ben if he would like a cup of coffee on the back veranda. Would he like to meet her pet, Tracker? Was he hungry? Would he like a snack? Would he like to see inside her church? Would he like a stroll through the cemetery? Aleda knew that she was rambling, but she was nervous and couldn't seem to stop.

Ben stretched, took her chin in his hand, and turned her to face him. "Aleda, my darling, I've been cramped in a bus seat for four hours." Ben's hand caressed the back of her neck and slipped across her shoulder, moved slowly down her ribs, and lingered for a moment on the side of her breast. His hand slipped down until it cupped her buttock and he pulled her toward him. "What I want to do is take a shower and stretch out on a bed for a while. Will you join me?"

It was after six when Ben and Aleda walked back downstairs. "I'd really like to meet that horse of yours," Ben said. "Do you have anything to drink, by the way?"

"Chilled white wine. Is that okay?" and when Ben assured her that anything would do, they walked down the back steps toward the open door of the shed. "Poor Tracker," Aleda said, laughing. "He certainly got neglected today."

Ben stood back from the stall, watching as Aleda fed the horse his oats and his evening apple, filled his water bowl, and gave him a quick rub down with the brush. "You never were one to do things the ordinary way," he said as he kissed her. "How about a tour of the church?"

For an instant, Aleda hesitated. How would it look if someone noticed her entering the church with an attractive stranger, a glass of wine in her hand? As they walked through the grass alley, Ben halted in front of the steeple door. "Is this where…?"

Aleda nodded.

"May I?" he asked. Aleda shivered, but shrugged her shoulders. She stood back as Ben opened the door and squinted into the dark interior. He pulled on the dirty string that someone, years ago, had tied to the chain under the naked bulb, and stepped into the tower, looking up at the frayed rope. He walked around the small space for what seemed a very long time, occasionally pressing his hand against the stone walls before looking up again.

After he had tugged off the light and shut the door, he said, "Did you ever notice that there is a small trap door halfway up the back wall? If you had a step stool, it looks as if you could remove the door and crawl right into the church."

"Oh, that is creepy," Aleda said, shuddering and desperate to move away from the area that brought back painful memories. Then she blurted out, "Oh! That's how he got into the church that time he lived there for a few days."

"Who?" Ben demanded.

"Dwayne. Dwayne of course." Aleda turned toward the backyard where the two lawn chairs sat warmed by the late afternoon sunlight. "Come and sit for a while. We'll finish our wine and see the church tomorrow."

Martin and Laura were sitting in the back arbour when Aleda and Ben pulled up in her van. It was a beautiful evening – warm, moist, and golden. Aleda might have suggested to Ben that they walk to the doctor's house, but she was reluctant to be seen strolling along with Ben, for she knew that he would insist on holding hands, or walk with his arm around her waist, or perhaps even pause at the corner store to kiss her. No, it was better to drive.

As Aleda introduced Ben to Laura and Martin, they were polite and formal in their responses; but, in a half hour, when everyone had had a drink and some conversation, Aleda beamed as she watched Martin laugh at one of Ben's stories and Laura offer a third helping of the stuffed mushroom appetizer. It is usually me who is the lively one, the storyteller, the jokester when we get together, but tonight Ben has taken over, Aleda thought with a flush of pleasure.

Ben turned to Laura and Martin and asked, "If you were new to this area and had just one weekend, what would you want to see and do?"

Laura suggested a stroll through beautiful Harrison Park, a glass of wine in the new café overlooking the river in Tara, and a trip to Sauble Beach to see the splendid crashing waves of Lake Huron. Martin suggested a trip up the Bruce Peninsula and a picnic overlooking the harbour at Tobermory, perhaps a tour to see the ship wrecks preserved in the deep icy waters of Georgian Bay, maybe even a boat ride to Flower Pot Island.

"But what did you do already today?" Martin asked, and watched as a flush crept from Aleda's neck up into her cheeks. At once regretting his question, Martin jumped up and said, "Time to go in. The mosquitoes have arrived."

Laura announced cheerfully, "Yes, time to move indoors. And, ta-dah!" she said with a flourish. "I'm proud to announce a new arrival – my white living room, just born and delivered this afternoon."

It was late by the time dinner was over. Ben and Martin had taken coffee into the living room, joking about how they felt inclined to trip and fall into the new white sofas. Laura and Aleda lingered in the kitchen, scraping and stacking the dishes. "Well, what do you think?" Aleda whispered to Laura.

Laura smiled and shrugged. "He's charming. I can see why you have fallen head over heels in love."

"Again." Aleda replied. Laura looked over at the shining face of her friend and nodded. She had never seen Aleda so radiant, so glowing, and for a moment she was stabbed with jealousy, longing for such a moment for herself.

Close to midnight, Martin glanced at his watch. "Aleda, you must bring Ben up to the farm tomorrow to see the puppies. Laura, I should be getting home, but I'll give you a hand with the dishes before I go."

"No, no," Laura insisted, leaning on the arm of the chair to lever herself to her feet.

Ben hopped up. "You stay and chat with Aleda," he said to Martin. "I'll give Laura a hand. I'm the best dish dryer ever invented."

Aleda longed to ask Martin his opinion about Ben. Somehow, what Martin and Laura thought of Ben seemed very important to her. She wanted their approval, wanted to hear that they thought he was as wonderful as she believed him to be. Speaking with Martin was not so easily done though, not like whispering with Laura in the kitchen. Aleda slipped off her sandals, tucked her feet under her legs, and curled into the softness of the sofa.

"Well, since I've been talked into staying on a bit," Martin said, stretching out his long legs, "maybe I'll have that nightcap."

"Let me," Aleda said, jumping up, eager to be in the kitchen close to Ben. "What will it be, Scotch on the rocks as usual?"

She bounced out of her seat, stepped into the dark hallway, and froze.

Aleda had a clear view of Laura and Ben doing dishes together at the kitchen sink. Laura was washing the plates and passing them to Ben, who stood, with patience, holding a dishtowel. But as he waited for Laura to finish rinsing a plate, Ben reached over and caressed the back of Laura's neck. Aleda watched in horror as Ben then slipped his hand across Laura's right shoulder, slid his hand down Laura's ribs, let his fingers linger for a moment on the side of Laura's breast. She watched as he lowered his hand until it rested lightly on Laura's waist. Then his hand slipped down until it gently cupped her buttock and he pulled her toward him. Startled, Laura looked at Ben, her mouth open, and he bent forward with his lips parted as though to kiss her.

Aleda took a step back into the hallway. She stood in the dark listening to the sound of her breath, Martin's empty mug pressed between her breasts. She spun around and stepped into the washroom beside the office, turned on the water, and leaned on the sink, staring at her face in the mirror. She took one deep breath, then another, and when she had composed herself, she flushed the toilet and went back into the hall, calling out, "Another drink for Martin, please!"

Laura swung around toward Aleda, reaching for the empty coffee mug, then abruptly turned back to the sink, removing the plug although only half of the dishes had been washed. "That's it," she said to no one in particular. "We'll finish these in the morning."

When Laura – who had suddenly become very quiet – and Ben returned to the living room, Martin noticed that Aleda looked ashen and pale. "You okay Aleda?" he asked, frowning.

She nodded, but then said suddenly, "Oh, I'm afraid I'm not feeling well at all. Martin, would you mind driving me home? A bad headache. Ben, I'll see you in the morning. Laura, thanks again for hosting us and for giving Ben a bed tonight. I'll pick up my van in the morning."

When they were pulling into her driveway, Martin glanced across at Aleda and frowned. "You sure you're okay, Aleda? I'll see you to the front door."

"No, no. I'm fine. Just need to take some painkillers and sleep this off," she said as she shut the door of Martin's truck. She turned and ran across the front lawn and up the stairs into the porch.

She slammed the front door behind her, snapped shut the lock, and ran up the stairs to her bedroom. She yanked off her dress, ripped off her underwear, tugged her oversized T-shirt over her head, and dropped into the bed, kicking at the crumpled bed covers. It was when she pulled the sheet up around her face and smelled Ben on the bedding that she began to sob. She sobbed until there were no more tears left, and when she caught a glimpse of her red and swollen eyes reflected in the alarm clock, the tears flowed again.

Eventually, exhausted, Aleda went into the bathroom and poured cold water over a towel. She twisted it fiercely, then returned to bed, lay down on her back, folded the towel into three, and laid it over her swollen eyes.

In the early-hours air of June, she raised her arms in the air and wailed into the darkness, "Are you there, Mama? Can you hear me, Mama? He has broken my heart. Again! He has broken my heart again."

29

Spilled Tea

LEDA WOKE SLUGGISH AND SOLEMN on Saturday morning. Her need to cry had been replaced by a steely determination, a solid, flinty anger. She went through the routine of opening the shed door and feeding Tracker. "No outside today, old chap," she said, slapping his rump gently.

Aleda grabbed her purse and headed out the front door. She did not care that Grace, who was hanging laundry on her clothesline, glanced up as she saw Aleda stride down Main Street to the doctor's house. Aleda unlocked her van, still in the driveway from the previous evening, backed out of the driveway, and headed to Owen Sound.

When she returned home from her errand, she marched into the kitchen and dialed Laura's number.

"Oh, Aleda. I'm so relieved to hear from you! You looked so pale and sick when you left last night. Are you okay?"

"Yes, thanks. Much much better. Thanks for asking." Aleda could hear a quality of polite formality in her own voice. "I was wondering if Ben is up yet."

"No. Not yet. Not sure what time he went to bed." There was silence for a few seconds until Laura continued, "Aleda. It's about Ben. I think you and I need to talk about Ben."

"Oh, Laura! I can be so impulsive at times. I realize now that I put you in a terribly difficult position. I'm just so sorry. I should never have asked you to host Ben overnight. I put you in a very difficult position."

Laura broke in. "Aleda, Aleda, it's okay. It turned out fine in the end. Martin came back here after he dropped you off. I met him in the driveway because I was upset about something that had happened in the kitchen. I explained that I didn't feel comfortable having Ben alone in the house with me, so Martin offered to stay over too. Thank goodness I have lots of spare bedrooms!"

"Laura, you need to know that I saw how Ben touched you in the kitchen. I was in the hall, coming out to get another drink for Martin."

"Oh, Aleda!" Laura gasped. "I hardly know what to say." Aleda could hear the anguish in her friend's voice. "I felt so...well, is violated too strong a word? But mainly I felt angry that he was your boyfriend and yet felt free to try to seduce me when you were out of sight."

Aleda could feel sadness rising up, threatening to overwhelm her. Then she reminded herself that she was determined to be strong about Ben.

"When do you think Ben will be up?"

"I have no idea. Shall I call you when he's up?"

Aleda could hear something different in Laura's voice; a gravity, a hesitancy, a sadness that was not usually there.

As soon as Aleda had finished her call with Laura, she picked up the phone again. When Patrice answered, Aleda blurted out, "Patrice, will you and Robert be home this afternoon?"

"Yes, I expect we will be here, won't we Robert? Is there something wrong, Aleda?"

"No...well, yes. Yes, there is something wrong." Then she added in a gloomy voice, "Oh my, Patrice, do I only call when there is something wrong?"

"Of course not. Come along. We are always glad to see you."

A few minutes later, the phone rang and it was Ben, cheerful and upbeat. "Laura said I was to call and let you know when I had surfaced."

"Yes, I'll be right up."

When she arrived she could see that Laura had made Ben scrambled eggs and toast. They sat at opposite ends of the kitchen table drinking coffee. Aleda noticed her own tote bag resting on the floor beside the kitchen counter. A plate on the buffet held the remnants of the gingerbread cookies. Ben's cookie laid there, one bite out of the corner, the rest of the cookie shiny and resplendent in pink, yellow, blue, red, and white.

"Coffee, Aleda?"

"No. No thank you." Aleda glanced at her watch and said in a calm clear voice, "Laura, thank you so much for having Ben overnight. Ben, do you have your bag together? You'll be staying somewhere else tonight."

"Really?" Ben said. His chair scraped back and he jumped to his feet, grinning. He began to move toward Aleda, but she had stooped to collect her tote bag and said, "If you're ready, Ben, get your bag and we'll be off."

When they reached the driveway Aleda turned to Ben and said firmly, "Ben, I saw what happened last night in the kitchen, how you touched Laura."

Ben raised his eyebrows in surprise, then grinned and waved his hand, "Oh, Aleda, it was nothing. The wine, a good time…"

Aleda continued in a slow calm voice, "Listen to me carefully, Ben. There will be no relationship between you and me in the future. Relationships are built on trust and mutual understanding. I would always be plagued with worry that this would happen again. And now," she continued, waving a bus ticket in front of him, "I am going to drive you to the bus terminal in Owen Sound. Here is a one-way ticket to Toronto. There are lots of places to stay in Toronto." And as she moved toward the driver's seat she said, "Get in."

Once or twice on the way to Owen Sound Ben tried to talk to her, but Aleda stopped him each time. "Enough talking," she said, and snapped on the radio, turning the volume so loud that it reverberated around the van.

When they reached the bus terminal, Aleda hopped out of the vehicle, unlocked the tailgate, set Ben's duffle bag on the sidewalk, then reached out to hand him the bus ticket.

"Aleda, Aleda" he said, looking mournful and remorseful, holding out his arms. Aleda took a step backward. At arm's length, Ben put one hand on her shoulder and placed the other on her cheek until Aleda turned sharply, hurried back to the van, and drove away.

Patrice answered the door. She was dressed in a lilac silk pantsuit and high-heeled sandals trimmed with glittering rhinestones, and her thick white hair was swept back in a French roll.

"Oh my gosh, Patrice. However do you do it?" Patrice smiled and pulled Aleda into the dining room where she had already laid out a tray with paper-thin bone china cups, a teapot painted with gardenias, and some chocolate wafers set on a crystal plate. Robert wandered into the dining room from the back of the house.

When they had settled and Patrice had poured out the steaming amber tea, Robert said, "Okay my dear. What's up? You know that we're to spend some time together tomorrow so I'm surmising that you have something on your mind."

"Oh, you are such good friends to me," Aleda gushed, repeating, as she had done so many times before, "I honestly don't know what I would do without you." They nodded, smiled, and waited.

"Well," Aleda continued slowly, "it's Ben, you see," and she told them the whole story of how she and Ben had reconnected with a passion in Winnipeg; how he had suggested that they resume the romantic relationship they had enjoyed 20 years ago, claiming that he had always been in love with her; how he had come from Toronto just yesterday to spend time with her. Then Aleda told them about the incident in the kitchen.

"It wasn't just a touch, you have to understand that. It was a sexual caress, and the worst of it was that he had done the same thing with me just hours before." Aleda could feel her calm reserve evaporating.

"Damn it all!" she almost shouted, slapping her hand hard on the table. "How can you trust a bastard like that?"

Startled, Patrice looked down as the tea from their china cups splashed into their saucers and across the white linen table cloth.

"Oh, Patrice, I'm so sorry, so sorry," Aleda said, jumping up.

"Don't worry. I'll get it," Patrice said, jumping up too and turning to the kitchen.

"I'm just so angry," Aleda said to Robert. "I'm angry at Ben for being such a jerk. I'm angry because now I have this great personal disappointment and grief while I'm still trying to make sense of Dwayne's death. I'm angry at myself for being so stupid. I'm not a teenager! How could I have fallen for this?"

Patrice's high-heeled sandals click-clacked as she returned to the dining room, set the tea tray back on the buffet, whisked the linen cloth off the table, and said, "Nothing that a little laundry detergent won't fix." From under her arm, Patrice unfolded a vinyl picnic cloth, laid it on the table, smoothed out the fold lines, then turned back to the buffet and lifted the tray onto the dining room table.

"Now then," she said. "Shall we try this again?"

On the way home, Aleda reminisced about the conversation of the afternoon. At one point Robert had said, "Aleda, it's okay to be angry. You have every reason to be angry. You have been betrayed by someone who you thought loved you. And when you think about it, many wonderful things happen when people get angry. But don't hold on to anger until it turns bitter, my dear. It will turn to a stone in your belly. Turn it into something positive. Think of how you might use this strong energy you have."

"But what form would that take?"

"I can't tell you that. You have to work that out for yourself. I know that unless you do something with anger it becomes like a cancer in your life, or it flips you into a slough of despond, as John Bunyan said so well. Neither is good."

"I feel like such a fool over this."

Patrice had been listening quietly. "Oh, but you mustn't feel that it was your fault Aleda. It was simply a matter of a relationship gone topsy-turvy. As they say," she said, glancing sideways at Robert, "it takes two to tango. Even Robert and I have our tiffs at times, and I admire how you deal with things. When he makes me angry, I wish I could slap my hand down hard enough to spill the tea."

"Really?" Robert tilted his head toward Patrice, frowning. "When do I make you angry?"

"Oh really, Robert, it's not important now."

"No, really, Patrice. It *is* important. You must tell me these things. When do I make you angry?"

Aleda's head swung from left to right. "Hey, hold on a minute!" she said, throwing up her hands. "Do I need to recommend a marriage counsellor for you two?" For a moment, there was silence, until all three began to laugh together.

Back at home, Aleda threw open the shed door and called out, "Come on old soul. You have been neglected too long. You need some fresh air and what's left of the sunshine. Out you come."

30

Picnic

FTER WORSHIP WAS OVER on Sunday morning, Robert, Patrice, and Aleda stood for a moment on the front lawn of the parsonage watching as the farmers pulled away in their vehicles and the villagers walked home.

"If I didn't know better," Robert said, "I would say that this is an idyllic situation. Good people staying to chat on the church lawn, good people looking out for each other, good people going home to eat a roast dinner at noon. A little church that is still the centre of village life."

"Sometimes I wonder," Aleda said, dryly. "There is an underbelly to this village and community, it seems to me. But still, it's a good life. And now then," she said, turning with a smile toward Robert and Patrice, "I think I'd like to change out of these clerical duds before we go out for lunch."

"Oh yes, please do," Patrice urged. "And if you don't mind, may we use your guest room? Robert and I brought along a change of clothes too."

"Of course," Aleda said, looking up in surprise.

"Dress casually," Patrice called out. "We're going on a picnic. A beautiful picnic will take your mind off things for a while."

While Patrice set up the meal in the picnic area, Robert and Aleda went to watch the Sydenham River pouring over Inglis Falls. Clear water splashed over graduated steps of escarpment rock, darkening the exposed and gnarled roots of century-old trees, while other verdant trees and shrubs clung with tenacity to clefts in the rock. Ferns on the banks rustled and swayed in the cool humidity, a study in green.

"Over there," Robert was saying, "is the Bruce trail. And up there," he gestured, "you'll find glacial potholes and the remains of an old grist mill. Doesn't this place invite you to slip back in time and imagine that you've come to this spot to buy some ground meal for Tracker? Or maybe you have chickens that need crushed corn."

"Or," Aleda said, finding the spirit of Robert's imagination quite contagious, "maybe I've come here because it is a sawmill and I need lumber for my new henhouse."

"Or could it be that this is the location of the flour mill? Do you need some flour for your bread making, Madame? Do you want the bran, too?"

Aleda laughed. "Or perhaps you've come to find some spun clothing that is more becoming to an early Canadian countryman. Would you like to purchase a tweed coat, sir, or perhaps some new flannel long johns?"

They laughed quietly and stood in silence for a time, leaning on the wooden rail, and when Aleda spoke again her voice was full of awe. "How can it be that I have lived in Milburn Corners for a year and never visited here before? It's amazing. Cool. Beautiful."

Judging by the number of baskets and coolers they had carried from the car, Aleda had deduced that it would be a grand picnic, but when they turned around, Aleda gasped. "Oh, my gosh!"

Robert laughed as he watched his elegant wife. "Patrice loves picnics. She really gets into them. Sometimes I think she fancies herself as part of that famous painting by Édouard Manet, the one where the remains of a lavish picnic are spread out on a blue blanket, and two men in dark suits are in serious debate. Do you remember? In the background, a young woman looks as if she is harvesting nuts or mushrooms, but in the foreground beside the men is a woman looking pensive, holding her chin in her right hand, and totally nude!"

"Yes! I remember! Totally nude. Which woman do you think Patrice would be?"

"Not sure," Robert said, laughing heartily. "What do *you* think, my dear?"

Patrice was setting out the last items for the picnic. "You two are being silly," she scolded, feeling self-conscious with their attention focused on her. "Come. Our feast is ready."

"Wait!" Aleda cried out. "I must have a photo."

How little did Aleda realize at the time that she would look at that photo for so many years to come, and that it would be so saturated with memories. Patrice stood smiling under the trees in the dappled sunlight, the light shimmering off the soft drapes of her long white dress, the scarlet scarf falling over her left shoulder and on to her bare arm. The picnic was spread in front of her, the crystal dishes and bowls glittering in the filtered light. A scarlet lace tablecloth dropped into pleats at the corners of the picnic table and the edges puddled gracefully onto the ground. Patrice had placed a candelabra in the centre of the table. A decanter of orange juice, a bottle of champagne, smoked salmon with angel sauce, Italian croissant bites, white bean tapenade, orange and sesame salad, and rich chocolate truffles on a silver pedestal plate filled the rest of the space.

Robert and Aleda approached the table shaking their heads in amazement, but as they were about to sit down, Patrice put up her hands and said, "Stop! I forgot something." Reaching into a picnic basket she pulled out three black silk bow ties, each with an elastic neck band. "We shall picnic in style," she said, passing them around.

Minutes later a small group of tourists came around the corner to peer over the rail at Inglis Falls. One of the tourists took a photo of the three friends dining, and Aleda knows that somewhere in Japan there is a photograph that shows a handsome older man in a white polo shirt; a short, curly-haired younger woman with high cheek bones and a radiant smile, wearing Bermuda shorts and a blue T-shirt; and an elegant older woman, her luxuriant white hair tossed back and tied with a scarlet scarf, offering a crystal bowl full of olives. All are smiling at the camera in the dappled light of Inglis Falls, and all are wearing black silk bow ties.

Aleda had driven her own van to the picnic because Inglis Falls was halfway between Milburn Corners and Owen Sound and it didn't make sense to Aleda for Robert and Patrice to backtrack to Milburn Corners when the picnic was over. After they had packed up the hampers and coolers and stowed them into Robert's car, Aleda hugged them both, repeating her thanks and appreciation. It had been, she raved, the most splendid, amazing, spectacular, delicious, interesting picnic she had ever experienced. She waved a final goodbye and drove away.

How will I spend the rest of my day? she wondered. Lately, life had been a rollercoaster of good and bad. As she sped along she remembered that she had always considered that life was just that – a rollercoaster – but of late she had come to think of life as having two parallel tracks where good and bad things happened simultaneously and it didn't seem to matter if you, yourself, were good or bad. This is just the way life works out. Her mind flicked to that mysterious verse in Matthew's gospel: *God makes the sun rise on the evil and on the good, and sends rain on the righteous and on the unrighteous.*

Ah, Aleda sighed as she hurried home, I know how I will spend the rest of my day. I will let Tracker out to hang his great shaggy head over the back fence, and I will pour myself a tall glass of lemonade and add lots of ice cubes. I will grab my novel and bask in the sunny spot in the backyard.

Aleda's thoughts were disturbed by something flashing in her rear-view mirror. "Oh shit!" she said aloud when she spotted the blinking red light of a police car behind her. She pulled over onto the gravel, rolled down her window, and was reaching for her wallet to find her driver's license when she heard a male voice at her window.

"May I see your driver's license, please?"

She spun around. There, peering through the window only inches from her face, was Constable Brennan, a slight smile playing around his mouth. "You were speeding, ma'am," he said, suddenly serious.

"I was? Surely not," Aleda murmured. "Well, you see, Officer Brennan," she stammered. "Well, you see, Officer Brennan," she repeated. "Oh, what the heck," she said, throwing her hands up in the air. "There's no excuse for speeding."

"I'll just give you a warning this time," he said in a stern tone; but was that a twinkle in his eye?

"Thank you. Thank you so much." Aleda wondered if the officer would ask her again about going with him to a concert, but he seemed to have forgotten about that invitation. Instead, he slid his hand along the shiny surface of the passenger door and said, "I recognize this van, and sometimes see it around Owen Sound."

Aleda nodded. "I do go to Owen Sound often. I'm always running out of things and need to go to the mall or the grocery store, and that's where I get my ground meal for Tracker, and of course I have friends there." I'm babbling, Aleda thought as her words spilled out. She inhaled deeply. "What's so unusual about this van?" she asked.

"Oh, not the van. It's the license plate I noticed. It's an occupational hazard of being a police officer. I notice license plates."

"The license plate," Aleda said flatly. "It's the plate that Service Ontario assigned me. D zero one, Z one N."

"Exactly. Step out and have a look with me."

Aleda hopped out of the van and walked to the back of her vehicle. "Like I said," she repeated, "D zero one, Z one N."

"Don't you see it?" Constable Brennan asked as Aleda took two steps backward, squinting at the license plate. "Plain as day," he said laughing and reading it out so that it clearly sounded like, "Do I sin?"

"When I noticed that vehicle around town, I used to think that maybe it was the joke of the priest at St. Mary's church – he has a great sense of humour – but now I think the joke is on the minister of Milburn Corners Community Church who didn't even notice that she had it."

Aleda folded her arms and pursed her lips. She couldn't decide if he was scolding her, teasing her, reprimanding her, or making fun of her.

"Off you go, then," he said with a wave of his hand. "And slow down this time. You don't want to hit a stray dog or get stopped by a less sympathetic cop."

He turned back to his cruiser, climbed in, turned off the red flashing light and swung out past Aleda. For the next eight kilometers to Milburn Corners she followed the cruiser, the speedometers in both vehicles resting exactly on the speed limit. But when she slowed to pull into the driveway of the parsonage, she detected a wave from the window of the police vehicle as it suddenly picked up speed, flew up over the knoll, and tore out into the open countryside.

31

Rain

I<small>T WASN'T THE ROBINS</small> that wakened Aleda on Monday morning: it was the steady splash of rain on the front porch roof and the relentless dripping from the window sill. Aleda opened her eyes wide enough to squint at the sky, but all she could see was grey. Good day to roll over and go back to sleep, she thought, relieved that she didn't have to weed her perennial beds. Maybe I'll make Hungarian stew when I get up.

Many people disliked rainy days, but Aleda recalled wonderful rainy weekends when her father would stay indoors, unable to clean the eaves troughs, mow the lawn, or re-tar the driveway. At the kitchen counter her mother would chop onions, dice beef, and grate carrots while Aleda, a curious and contented child, sat on her father's knee at the kitchen table, a map and a picture book of Hungary spread out before them. Papa pointed to the picture of herdsmen with their gray long-horned cattle grazing on wide marshy steppes.

"That's what the word *gulyás* – goulash – originally meant, Aleda – *herdsman*. This dish your mother is making refers to both the herdsmen and the meal they used to make. Not much wonder that the Hungarian word for *cattle* is the same as the word that means *wealth*. The more cattle a Hungarian had, the more good goulash he had, and he became stronger and wealthier as his herd grew." They would sit together poring over the pictures while Mama would fill the kitchen with the aromas of paprika and frying onion.

By noon, Aleda's own kitchen was filled with the aromas of

frying onion, paprika, braising meat, and tomato. As the goulash simmered, Aleda removed a loaf of French bread from the freezer, wrapped it in foil, and set it in the oven to warm. She had managed to have a good night's sleep two nights in a row, and she felt rested and content.

As she was about to take the bread from the oven, she heard a knock on the front door. Aleda glanced at the kitchen window. The rain still beat against the pane in a steady sheet. She hurried to the front door, knowing that whoever was there would be standing under a steady shower from the porch eaves.

"Roy! Come in. Come in," she said, stepping back, waving her hands, and motioning him into the porch.

"Land's sake, that's a downpour."

"Dump your rain gear here, Roy, and come on into the kitchen."

"Don't mind if I do," Roy said, removing his rubber boots and shedding a large yellow rain poncho. "It smells good in here."

"And you shall join me for lunch," Aleda declared. "Hungarian goulash. My mother taught me how to make it the old country way."

Roy shuffled into the kitchen behind Aleda. She motioned him to a chair at the end of the table and set a spoon and knife on a placemat in front of him. She unwrapped the warm loaf and set it beside a serrated knife on the board in the centre of the table. Using a large silver ladle, she scooped spoonfuls of tender beef, tomato, onion, carrot, and green pepper in rich tomato-paprika-butter sauce into bowls.

When she had set down the soup bowls filled with steaming goulash and settled herself at the table, Aleda smiled at Roy, who sat waiting, his hands folded at the edge of the table. "Roy, would you give thanks for this food?"

"It would be an honour." There was a pause as they bowed their heads, then Roy's calm and even voice said, "God, we give you thanks for this day, and for every blessed day that you send to us. When things are right and good, we thank you for this blessing.

And when things go wrong, we thank you that you give us strength to meet the challenge. We give you thanks for this meal that Aleda has prepared. May this food be used to strengthen our bodies and renew our souls." There was a pause, then Roy concluded, "And, Lord, may you always have mercy on us. Amen."

"That was a beautiful blessing," Aleda said quietly, picking up her spoon.

"Well," Roy responded thoughtfully, "if a man is an elder in a church and can't even say a blessing, of what use is he to anyone?"

Aleda smiled and set her spoon down. "Since we're eating Hungarian-style today," she said, "we might as well follow Hungarian tradition about the bread. In our family – and in most Hungarian families – the man has the honourable task of cutting the bread. Will you saw us off a great hunk, Roy? It is simply impossible to eat Hungarian goulash without a big slice of bread with which to mop up all these fantastic juices."

As they ate, Aleda told Roy about the novel she was reading. She told him about the amazing picnic that Patrice had prepared. She even told him about her night terrors, re-living the scene of Dwayne's shoes hanging in front of her. But she avoided mentioning her troubles with Ben. The betrayal was still too fresh and raw, too personal.

When the bowls were empty and the loaf half gone, Roy sighed and said, "That was the best meal I've had all year, Aleda. A mighty fine meal."

Aleda jumped up and began to fill the kettle with water. "I'll make us some tea."

"Oh, don't bother, Aleda. I've taken up enough of your time," he said, but he didn't stir from his end of the table. After Aleda had set some mugs, milk, and sugar on the table, she sat down to wait until the kettle boiled.

"Actually," Roy said slowly, "there's something on my mind." Aleda raised her eyebrows and waited. "It's the rain."

Aleda nodded. "Yes?"

"I was up to Spence's Berry Farm yesterday and there's a problem. They're having a bad year with strawberry mildew."

"Strawberry mildew."

Roy nodded. "It happens from time to time. Mildew sometimes occurs when it rains at night and stays cool into the morning so that there's no warmth to dry the plants, like we've had this June. First, a fine white film forms on the leaves, then the leaves just roll up. When the strawberry fruit appears, it's small and hard. Inedible, really."

"But Roy! For weeks, people have been saying that it will be a great season for strawberries. I've heard all the farmers saying that."

"Yes, well – the vagaries of weather, you know."

"So," Aleda said, pouring out the tea, "there is a problem with…"

"Yup. Getting enough strawberries for Saturday night."

"Oh." Aleda set down her spoon. "Should we tell the women?"

"Why don't we wait a day or two until…" He gestured to the window and the two of them sat sipping sweet tea and watching the rain beat against the pane.

After lunch, Roy zipped up his windbreaker and slipped into his rubber boots, then picked up his yellow hooded poncho that he had spread out on the floor of the porch.

"That's a splendid poncho," Aleda said.

Roy nodded. "When the missus took sick with cancer, but before she got real poorly, I took her on a little holiday to Niagara Falls. She had always wanted to go on that boat, the *Maid of the Mist*, and sail right up to the falls. They gave us these big ponchos to wear and there we were, tucked up in our rain gear, so close to the thunder of the falls, the mist all around us. Pretty amazing. You could buy the ponchos at the end of the trip and so we did. I've kept them all these years. It's right handy for gardening in the rain."

"You garden in the rain?" Aleda laughed.

"Oh, there are lots of garden things you can do in the rain," Roy said. "Prune the roses or tie clematis to the trellis. Yep. Mighty fine poncho."

When Aleda had rinsed the soup bowls and wiped the table, she lay down on the couch in the living room to read, but her mind was restless and her body was full of energy. With a sigh, she swung herself onto her feet and stood looking out the window. The rain had lessened but still fell heavily. Maybe I'll take a drive into Owen Sound and have a wander in the mall, she thought. Maybe I can find a poncho like Roy's. It would be handy to pull on over my clothes when I'm heading out to feed Tracker.

The mall was quiet, almost deserted. Two young mothers, one with a rose-shaped tattoo on the side of her neck, the other with an eyebrow piercing, pushed two sleeping babies in strollers. For a moment Aleda wondered what that would be like to have the care of an infant 24 hours a day.

She wandered from store to store. In one she found some rain ponchos for children, and in several there were windbreakers that were rain resistant, but she didn't come across any splendid yellow ponchos like Roy's. Aleda was thirsty and longed for a cold drink but didn't want to sit alone in the food court, so she hurried through the rain back to her van. As she was driving up Second Avenue on her way home, she glanced at the movie theatre marquee. A matinee was scheduled for that afternoon. In ten minutes she was sitting in an almost empty movie theatre, a bucket of buttery popcorn in her lap, a soft drink in the holder beside her. And for the next two hours, Aleda munched her way to the bottom of the popcorn barrel, licking her fingers and watching *Star Wars: Attack of the Clones.*

32

Café

THE NEXT MORNING, Aleda opened the back door and stared up through the rain. When would this let up?

She was so intent on looking at the sky that she failed at first to notice a brown paper package on the back veranda. The package was protected from the rain by clear plastic, and when Aleda squinted at the note on top she recognized Roy's handwriting. She picked up the package and stepped back into the kitchen.

Dear Aleda, the note read. *When I got home I got to thinking that the wife's yellow poncho from our trip to Niagara Falls is still on the shelf in our bedroom. You might find use for it. Roy.*

Well, bless his heart, Aleda thought, shaking out the folded poncho to release the creases. She slipped it over her jacket and stood admiring her wavy reflection in the shiny face of the tea kettle. She smiled, then turned toward Roy's house and said aloud, "Why, thank you, Roy. Just what I needed."

After Aleda had settled at the computer in her office and opened her Bible to Philippians in order to ponder the scripture passage that she would use for her Sunday sermon, her attention was caught by two seemingly insignificant sentences: "I urge Euodia and I urge Syntyche to be of the same mind in the Lord. Yes, and I ask you also…to help these women, for they have struggled beside me in the work of the gospel…"

Of all the letters in the Bible, Aleda considered the book of Philippians her favourite. Sometimes she would think glibly, it's just so full of flippin' joy. How could Paul be in jail facing certain death and still talk so readily and easily about joy? Paul was prone to scolding other struggling new Christians for divisions and in-fighting in their communities, but here he is urging two women to get along with each other. Even though they are squabbling, he praises them for being part of the struggle of the early church. Very odd.

Aleda pondered the reality that conflict in the church was as old as 2,000 years. And it was still a difficult issue. She thought about the time when the church Board had brought up the issue of the contemporary music favoured by the youth. "We just don't care for it," one elder said. "It's not what we're used to. We don't like it at all." It was a simple as that.

"Oh, my," Aleda had replied mildly. "I wonder if adults used to say that back in the '30s. All that big band racket the young people are dancing to. We just don't care for it. It's not what we're used to. We don't like it at all." Sometimes, Aleda reflected, she was able to diffuse conflict by being calm and saying something she hoped was a bit wise.

When she had been a minister for a few years, she had visited Pastor Fazekos, her minister at the Hungarian church in Hamil-ton when she was a teenager. They had begun to discuss conflict in the church and she remembered his advice: "Be a bit playful, if you can. That way you don't get sucked in to taking sides or taking the conflict too seriously – if in fact it's something that shouldn't be taken too seriously.

"Let me tell you a little story," Pastor Fazekas had said as he crossed his arms and sat back in his desk chair. "Shortly after I came here – how old would you have been?"

"Seventeen. I remember it well. I was so angry that our wor-ship services reverted to Hungarian from English."

"Yes. Yes. Well – you weren't the only one who was upset," he said with a wave of his hand. "The children didn't want to come to church anymore. The parents wanted their children here, but it was hard to force them to sit for an hour through something that they didn't understand. So the parents petitioned the older people for an English Sunday school. The older leaders refused and said that the children needed more discipline. The only thing they would agree to was to set up a time for lessons on Saturday so the children could learn Hungarian." Pastor Fazekas shook his head, "It was a mess. I was about ready to sail back to Hungary."

"How did it get resolved?"

"Well, it was curious really. One of the younger elders had a friend who was a therapist. The elder got the idea that this friend would come to the church on a Friday night and have some kind of a program to build some bridges. Were you there?"

Aleda shook her head. "I don't remember this at all."

"I met the therapist for half an hour before the program and explained things to her. She had an idea that she would do four activities, each building a bit in intensity; by the end of a couple of hours she hoped there could be some meeting of minds among the three generations."

"It must have worked," Aleda said with enthusiasm. "The church is still here."

"It sort of worked, and it sort of didn't work. The therapist never got past the first activity."

"No! You mean people just walked out?"

"Oh, no. Nothing like that. I was there so I saw what happened. The therapist had a ball of yarn. She explained that she was going to hold the end of the yarn and toss the ball to someone in the circle. She would ask that person a question; they would answer, then toss the ball to someone else in the circle and ask them a question. Then that person would hold on to the string and toss the ball of yarn across to someone else, until the whole thing looked like a big spider web."

"That seems a bit complicated for Hungarians," Aleda laughed.

Pastor Fazekas smiled. "Oh, everyone got the hang of it, and that was the problem. The therapist tossed it to young Aron – you remember that active kid who used to annoy everyone by kicking around a ball during refreshment time after worship?"

"Of course. Everyone remembers Aron."

"The therapist asked his name, and then she said, 'Aron, what did you do at recess at school today?' And when he had answered, she invited him to toss the ball of yarn across the circle to someone else and ask a question. You remember how all the children called the older men *nagypapa* and the older women *nagymama*?"

Aleda nodded.

"I think he was just trying to be smart, but Aron whipped the ball of yarn across the circle to an older man and said, '*Nagypapa*, I want to ask you how you met *Nagymama*.'"

"Oh, no! Was *Nagypapa* angry?"

"Well, that's the curious thing. He wasn't, really. He very seriously told Aron about how he and his sweetheart planned to get married before the war, but they became separated and it was in 1945 as the war ended that, by chance, they ended up in the same village, both trying to buy some very wrinkled turnips at a market. They couldn't believe it when they found each other. It was like a miracle to them, and they fell in love all over again." Pastor Fazekas shook his head at the memory. "You could tell that young Aron wanted to hear more, but the therapist asked him to let everyone have a turn. So the old man threw the yarn to your father, Aleda, and asked him what he had found hardest about coming to Canada as a young man."

Aleda sat forward on her chair. "How did he answer?"

"Don't remember that. I only remember the question. But as I said, the therapist didn't get past the first exercise. Back and forth that ball of yarn flew, and every time the therapist tried to quit the children would cry out, 'No, no, we haven't heard from...'" Pastor Fazekas shook his head again.

"Did it help? Did it solve the tensions in the church?"

"I think so. Improved communication is never wasted. But you know, Aleda, there is always the potential for conflict in every church, every family, every marriage. It's just part of life, so we have to deal with it wisely when it occurs. I often find it helpful to be a bit playful. When the elders complain about how noisy the children are in the church hall, I sometimes say, 'Oh, you should be at fellowship time over at St. Raphael church. They don't have any kids in their church. Not a child in sight. Nothing to listen to except the church mice.'" Pastor Fazekos locked his hands together behind his head and smiled.

Sitting in her office, staring at the unrelenting rain, Aleda recalled this conversation and thought, thank you Pastor Fazekas, for your sage advice about playfulness and for so many other things.

Aleda was heating some soup for lunch when the telephone rang. She frowned when she saw Grace Stone's name on the display panel.

"Aleda, we have a problem."

"Oh, good morning Grace, and hello. How very nice of you to call, and how are you today?"

"We have to have an emergency meeting of the Ladies Guild. Tonight," Grace replied sternly.

"I'm fine, thank you, Grace. It's quite a stretch of rainy weather we're having, isn't it?"

"Did you not hear me? I said that we need to have an *emergency* meeting of the Ladies Guild and we need to do it tonight. There's a big problem with the strawberries. Roy tells me that Spence's farm will have to plow under their entire five acres of berries. They have strawberry blight or mildew or something and the berries are just wizened up, green and hard. Now where on earth will we find strawberries to feed 100 people on Saturday night? We can hardly have a *strawberry social* without strawberries."

"But surely these are not the only strawberries in the world." Careful Aleda, she told herself. Take a deep breath. Be playful.

"We are *not*, and I repeat *not*, going to buy those watery, expensive strawberries imported from California. That would be a public disgrace. We would never get over the shame of it. No,"

Grace said firmly, "people expect our sweet local berries. It surely is an emergency. Maybe we'll have to cancel the social this year, but what would we do with all the other food? We've already got the meat and dinner rolls on order, and I know for sure that Margaret has already grated 12 heads of cabbage. What on earth would we do with that much coleslaw? Oh, it's a real emergency."

"I think," Aleda said slowly, "that it would be good for all of us to have a night out at the church tonight. We all have cabin fever with this rain keeping us indoors. Why don't you call the Ladies Guild members and invite them to the church to discuss the strawberries. Is 7 p.m. okay?"

At 6:45 p.m. Grace paused in the doorway of the church hall, staring in amazement. In the centre of the room, small tables had been draped with the white linen cloths that were only brought out for special occasions. In the centre of each table was a flickering candle in a glass bowl. Each table had been set with small plates and dessert forks. A red napkin sat on each plate, topped with a bearded iris bloom.

Roy, wearing his white apron, a white towel draped over his arm, stepped forward, smiling. "Welcome to Esterházy Café," he greeted Grace. "Won't you please follow me to a seat, ma'am?"

Grace meekly followed Roy to a small table where two other Guild members sat. Aleda appeared from the kitchen carrying a silver pot. "May I offer you some freshly brewed dark roast coffee? We have both regular and decaffeinated. Which would you prefer?"

When the evening was over and all the women had gone home, Roy and Aleda sat down at a table and grinned at each other.

"It was the best meeting ever!" Aleda declared, and then she began to hoot with laughter. "Oh, Roy, you were too hilarious for words. 'Madame, may I offer you our house specialty? It's a fine Esterházy gateau with yellow buttercream between layers of our finest almond sponge, filled with orange custard and iced with fine sugar and topped with candied fruit and flaked almonds.' What a great description for a humble cake mix! That was totally brilliant. I couldn't have done that in a million years."

"Been reading too many of the wife's old *Chatelaine* magazines I suppose," Roy chortled. "But the meeting; that was the best part, don't you think?"

"Absolutely. Utterly amazing how that went. Grace didn't put up one word of protest. She just went along with the whole scheme."

"Well, it helped that I planted the idea in Rose's head earlier. Rose carries a lot of clout in this village. She doesn't speak up and assert herself much, but when she does, everyone listens. They know that she's a wise woman, and they're all fond of her."

"Well done, Roy. It was a great coup. World War III is averted, and we have a new dessert compromise – fresh rhubarb cobbler with local farm cream, topped with one beautifully decorated choco-late-dipped strawberry, imported from who knows where and pre-pared by the youth. It was a brilliant solution, Roy. Hats off to you!"

Roy grinned, pleased but also bashful about receiving Aleda's exuberant praise. "And I have to say hats off to you, Aleda. It was your idea to do the café, and it was so…"

"Playful? But it didn't hurt either that you pointed out that there is lots of rhubarb in gardens around this community, that rhubarb is a community favourite, and that it would save the women $150 on strawberries!"

"I say we done a fine job, Aleda. If only we had a little apricot schnapps for a toast, it would finish off a perfect evening."

"Roy, Roy, Roy," Aleda groaned with mock sadness. "How you underestimate me!" and she reached into her tote and plunked a round bottle in front of the surprised man. "It's better than apricot schnapps! Hungarian *pálinka*! It's the national drink of Hungary. We Hungarians use not only apricots but also plums and apples for our wonderful *pálinka*. It's usually served in special tulip-shaped glasses, but tonight coffee mugs will have to do!" And, with a flourish, Aleda poured the smooth, sweet liqueur.

Later, talking the evening over with Robert, she said, "Perhaps it was the *pálinka*, maybe it was because we were in such high spirits. But really, it was Roy. It was Roy who helped me out of this depressing funk I've been in about my work not being meaningful. It was such an important moment, really; one of those moments in life that seem like a breakthrough, that seem like you've just turned an important corner. Do you know what I mean?"

"I do. I do. I've had a few of those moments myself. I knew that you'd been worried about a number of things and I knew that you had been going through a period of doubt about your ministry, and that can be very upsetting. What was it that Roy said that helped you so much?"

"We were just sitting there, quietly sipping our *pálinka*, and I don't know what got into me. I just blurted out all my worries about whether or not what I was doing with my life was of any value. I told him that I was seriously wondering if I should change careers, if I should find work that would really make a difference to people's lives. I said to Roy, 'Honestly, I can't even be a strong spiritual leader in this community. You remember that fiasco on the day of Dwayne's death? First I fainted, and then, when I saw all those people on the church lawn, I turned into a blubbering idiot for the whole world to see.'"

"And what did Roy say?"

"You know Roy. He just sat there quietly, listening, and then he finally said, 'Well.'"

How clearly Aleda remembered that evening. "Well you know, Aleda," Roy had said when she had finished speaking, "there's the matter of your sermons."

"My sermons! What on earth are you talking about?" Aleda's head jerked up. She had just confessed the dark angst of her soul and he wanted to talk about her sermons?

Roy didn't seem to notice. He just chuckled. "Oh, there's no forgetting your sermons. That one about potatoes. Never heard a preacher deliver a sermon about potatoes before." (Aleda noticed with relief that Roy had not pronounced the word as *badaydas.*) "Yup, that sermon on potatoes was something else. If I remember correctly, you went on to talk about world hunger, and you told stories that made us want to cry. The next day it was raining so the farmers weren't that busy. A few of them got together and phoned the guy from the Canadian Foodgrains Bank to see if they could help. That's when they started working that shared field up by the town line, so's they could send the profits to feed the world's hungry."

"Oh. I didn't know."

"Then there was that sermon about considering the lilies. I liked that one a lot. It was the first time that I had ever thought of my gardening and woodworking as anything other than hobbies. But there you were telling us that the things we do – growing day lilies, making pies, raising sheep and calves – are noble callings. You said that God calls us to add beauty to the world and do good work. It's not just ministers whom God calls. We all have important work to do for God." Roy shook his head. "Life doesn't happen from Monday to Saturday, then church on Sunday. We each get a chance every day to make a difference. That sermon even had some of us scrambling to dust off our Bibles."

"Oh. Really."

"But the sermon that was the real stinker, pardon the expression, was the one about the importance of spreading manure." Roy leaned forward on his chair, laughing and coughing. "We wondered where that one would go for sure. But then, before you know it, you had us all thinking about how life is a cycle, a circle; how the waste from the land renews the land. And you had us realizing that, pardon the expression, sometimes there's shitty stuff in life, but when we work through those times we end up stronger. I do believe that sermon helped all of us who've ever had to change a baby's dirty diaper, or clean up after an incontinent person, or clean up the calf pen after the calves get the scours."

"Really Roy. Surely that was not my finest moment."

Roy seemed to pay no attention to her comment. "And your sermons are one thing, but your example is another."

"Really?" Aleda's mind flashed to the many times she had committed a *faux pas* in Milburn Corners: walking around the village at night with a glass of wine in her hand, repeatedly feeling annoyance with Grace, remaining stubbornly belligerent about turning the shed into a stable for Tracker.

"Yes, your example. You're such a welcoming person. We all noticed when you befriended Laura and Martin, and how you welcomed all those wonderful young people."

"Oh, but surely that's not noble of me. They give me far, far more than I give them."

"Well that may be, but the truth is you have a warm spirit, and that has wakened a warmer, kinder heart in some of us. Why else would Grace start baking cookies for Callum? And why else did Eadie put her trust in you? And why else did I, for that matter, take Dwayne under my wing, doing woodworking and the like?"

"Oh. Oh. I didn't know."

"Then there's that thing that Rose said to me." Aleda looked up in surprise, her eyebrows raised. "She told me," Roy said, speaking more quietly, "that she had a heavy burden on her soul – she didn't say what it was – but she told me that she had one good heart-to-heart with you and she felt as if a great trouble had been lifted from her life."

"Oh. I see. I didn't realize."

"No. I guess that's the thing of being a minister, Aleda. I can replant my dahlias, and the Robertsons can plant a corn field, and Grace can make a cherry pie, and we all see what we have done. But it can be hard to see the results of your work."

Aleda sat staring at Roy, her left hand absent-mindedly brushing cake crumbs from the tablecloth.

"What you give us," Roy said, leaning forward, "is exactly what we need. We need you to remind us that hope is a firm and steady anchor for our souls. And that's in the Bible. I didn't make it up. You can look it up if you like." Roy smiled.

Aleda's eyes were shining with tears, but the tears rose from feeling a gratitude and peace of mind that she had not experienced for a long while. "Roy," she almost whispered, "I can't tell you how much this conversation has meant to me."

"Aleda, if a man is an elder in the church and can't even talk about these things with his own minister, well, of what use is he anyway?"

Roy rose slowly to his feet. "Now git some good hot soapy water in that sink. We got some dishes to wash, and I'm gonna need all the help I can git, cause I'm feeling a little tipsy."

33

Flood

THE RAIN HAD CONTINUED into the morning. Even the robins nesting over her porch light were quiet.

"It's unnatural," Aleda said to Laura when they chatted on the phone later in the morning. "Maybe this has happened before, but honestly, I don't remember a time when it has rained continuously for three days and nights."

"Why don't you come up for a coffee this morning?" Laura inquired.

"Love to. I really would. I'll get at my sermon right away. Does eleven work?"

"That would be great. See you then. And – oh, Aleda – there's something I'd like to discuss with you. You don't mind, do you?"

Laura hobbled to the kitchen door when she heard the van arrive. Aleda jumped out of the vehicle and ran to the house through the unrelenting rain. When they had settled at the kitchen table, Laura drummed her fingers on the tabletop until Aleda said, "Laura! For heaven's sake! What's on your mind?"

Laura had not had the opportunity before now to talk with Aleda about Martin's conviction that Laura's father and Rose had had a love affair, and how she, Laura, seemed unable to accept the fact – if Martin was correct – that her father, a strong, important, and stern presence in her life, had secretly helped to raise two families.

"It's just too much to take in," Laura cried, wiping her eyes. "And worst of all, what do I do about Rose? I've grown so fond of her, and she's so good to me. She felt like a second mother to me until this happened." She stopped, took a deep breath, grabbed a tissue, and stared at Aleda, who sat nodding and saying nothing. "How can you be so calm about this, Aleda? Wouldn't you be upset if this happened to you?"

Aleda raised her shoulders slightly in a shrug. "Well, Laura, I already knew all this."

"You knew!"

Aleda nodded. "One day Rose and I went to visit Eadie in the hospital. Rose needed to talk about all this."

"You knew, but you didn't tell me?"

"I know how shocking this must be for you. It certainly surprised *me* when Rose told me. If I had learned something like this about one of my parents I would have been more than a little astonished."

"I can't believe that you didn't say something to me about it. Isn't that how friends help each other?"

"Laura, Laura." Aleda covered her friend's hand with her own and squeezed lightly. "It's just that in ministry, people tell me things in confidence, and it would be wrong to go around blabbing about it."

The two friends sat at the kitchen table in silence, still holding hands, until Aleda said, "I think that this was on Rose's mind a lot. She truly loved your father with a passion, but she also didn't want a scandal in the village. And," Aleda said emphatically, "she was adamant about not wanting to disrupt the lives of your mother, you, and David. She acknowledged to me that the doctor was the father of her beautiful sons, but she had been able to push the complications of this situation out of her mind until you came along this summer. She could see that you and Martin were becoming close friends. Perhaps she worried that you and Martin would become involved with each other, not suspecting that you were related."

Both women sat trying to make sense of the new reality that seemed to have dropped upon them without warning. A minute later, the telephone rang. "It was Martin," Laura said after she hung up. "He wonders if we would like to slip up to his farm to see the puppies."

Aleda sat waiting, and in a few moments Laura rolled her head from side to side and sighed. "Well, let's go see those puppies. I could use a distraction just now."

Martin greeted them at the back door, helping Laura up the steps. "Welcome. All is quiet here at the moment," and when the women peeked around the corner they caught sight of the three puppies snuggled close to Buddy. "She's doing a good job," Martin said. "Seems to have all the instincts of a good mother. Too bad it will be her first and last litter."

"Callum's father has agreed to have her spayed?"

"Not sure yet. It will happen somehow though, because she can't continue to have litter after litter. I can't imagine Callum's dad looking after a bunch of puppies every year. Nor Callum for that matter. I hate to sound like I'm indispensable, but I don't think these puppies would have survived at Callum's farm."

"You've been wonderful," Laura and Aleda both exclaimed, but Martin waved off their praise. Aleda wondered what had motivated Martin to help in this way.

As if he read her mind, Martin said, "Callum and his dad just seem like lost souls, really. There's not a lot over there to soften life for them, and helping with Buddy has been my small contribution."

As they stood watching the puppies, one wakened and crawled closer to his mother's belly. "That's Clifford," Martin said, crouching down. "That one," he said, pointing to the smallest puppy, "is Pokey. He's smaller than the others but seems to be doing well." As if they knew that they were the focus of attention, the puppies roused themselves from the pockets of the blanket and began to nurse. Buddy lay grooming the puppies as they fed. "And you remember that Callum called this other one Dwayne?" Aleda nodded and Laura laughed softly. "There is a bit of a problem with that," Martin said as he stroked its ruffled fur. "He's a girl."

"Well, then," Aleda said slowly. "Perhaps that pup will have a special bond with Buddy. A female dog called Buddy and a female puppy called Dwayne."

Neither Laura nor Aleda had been into Martin's kitchen before. It was a big square room with a pine table set in the centre. Against the south wall there were old cupboards, a sink, a fridge, and a gas range. A pot-bellied wood stove stood on a brick platform in the northwest corner and along the north wall under the window was an old buffet that was the repository for Martin's files on old buildings. The only other piece of furniture was a large rocking chair set between the wood stove and the window. Aleda noticed a large stack of books sitting on the floor beside the chair.

Martin set down cream and sugar. "What do you think? Does this place need softening up? That's what my mother says. I like it as it is. I call the design style *postmodern-rural-man-doesn't-really-give-a-shit.*"

The women laughed.

"Your wife and daughter never come here?"

"They did in the beginning, but neither of them much likes farm life. Too quiet for them."

"You never get lonely or bored?"

Martin laughed. "Lonely? Bored? Are you kidding? I never have enough hours in my day for all the things I want to do."

While they sipped coffee and chatted, the puppies finished nursing and Pokey and Clifford nestled in close to their mother on the blanket. The puppy called Dwayne ventured away from the blanket, her short legs skidding out from under her on the hardwood floor. Closer and closer she crept, curious and timid, until she was at Aleda's shoe. She reached out a paw and touched her shoelace.

"Seems like you have a friend," Martin said softly.

"I told you before…" Aleda protested. "But look, can you believe this?" Puppy Dwayne had put her head down on the top of

Aleda's shoe and was closing her eyes. It lasted only a moment. The puppy soon realized that Aleda's shoe was not as warm and comfortable as her mother and the blanket, so back she skidded to safety, warmth, and security.

Oh dear. Aleda looked tenderly at the creature, her heart stirred by the puppy's overture. After a moment or two, she turned to Martin and said, "The least I can do is inquire around to see if there is anyone in the area looking for a dog – when the puppies are weaned, of course. It's been a while since I've had those rubber boots on. It's a great excuse to get out visiting on some farms…to see if they want a puppy, I mean."

Aleda glanced at her watch, saw that it was noon and said, "I must be going. I have a worship service at the nursing home in Owen Sound in an hour. I'll drop you off if you like, Laura."

It was late afternoon when Aleda returned to Milburn Corners. As she parked, something at the west side of the church caught her attention. Jumping out of the van, wearing her new yellow poncho as protection from the rain, she hurried around to the parking lot and stopped, astonished and confused. The side door to the church basement was propped open with a chair, and near the door stood a tall white pail full of gloves and goggles. Aleda could hear the steady chug of a motor and noticed a black plastic hose lying on the basement steps. The hose ran across the church parking lot and out to a drain in the street. Aleda took in these unusual sights, then turned and ran toward the parsonage. She unlocked the front door and hurried to the telephone.

"Roy! What on earth is going on at the church?"

"Oh you're home Aleda. I've been trying to get hold of you all afternoon. It seems that we have a flood in the church basement."

"A flood!"

"I went up to the church this afternoon to check on the tea supplies for the strawberry social, but as I was going down the stairs to the church hall, I noticed the bottom two steps were under water."

"Oh my gosh!"

"I called the chairman of the Board, and he called a plumber who came and installed a sump pump. Either the drains in the basement are clogged or the ground is just so saturated from the rain that the water couldn't drain away and started flowing into the basement."

"Has this ever happened before?"

"Not to my knowledge. The first thing we had to do was turn off the power in the church. Then, from what the plumber tells me, we have to go slow in pumping out the water. There's a lot of water pressure in the soil outside the basement walls and the water inside kinda acts as a balance. If you pump the water out too fast the walls can crack or break down." For the first time since she had known him, Aleda heard Roy sigh.

"This is going to take a couple of days to dry up. Then we have a big clean up job. We'll have to scrub and disinfect the floors, walls, and furniture. Then we'll have to keep the fans blowing until it is really dry down there.

"You do understand, don't you, that there is no possible way that the church basement will be in any shape for the strawberry social on Saturday night? We may not even have the power back on by then. This time, Aleda, we have a *real* emergency, and we won't be able to solve it with a Hungarian café."

34

Shed

LEDA AWOKE TO SEE that the rain had stopped at last and the sun was emerging over the horizon. Thank God for small mercies, she thought, before drifting into a light sleep.

As she finished dressing for the day, the doorbell rang. Aleda glanced at her watch: 8:14 a.m. Who on earth was dropping in at this time of the morning? She padded down the stairs in bare feet and headed to the front door, where Roy and Grace stood waiting.

"The rain has stopped at last!" Aleda greeted them in a cheerful voice.

Grace uttered a word that sounded like *humph*, but Roy said in a level and calm voice, "Grace here wants to talk over our options for Saturday."

"And I say we have no options," Grace declared sharply. "We have to cancel. We'll just have to figure out what to do about the ticket sales, and the potato salad, and the coleslaw, and the cold cuts. There's no way we can get the basement in shape for Saturday."

Aleda swallowed and took a deep breath. "Why don't you come in?" she said. "I'll put on some coffee and we'll talk about it."

When Aleda had brewed a pot of coffee, she turned to Roy and Grace. "May I serve you a slice of Hungarian walnut cake?"

"No, no, really, it's far too early in the morning," Grace said with a shooing motion of her hand; but when Roy didn't answer Aleda cut a thick slice for him and one for herself. She added a little whipped cream on the side and sprinkled blueberries on top.

As Aleda placed the plate in front of Roy, she saw Grace glance at the cake, look quickly away, then glance back again. Aleda set her own piece in front of Grace and turned back to the counter to cut a third slice for herself.

"Now then," she said after setting down three mugs of steaming coffee. "What is to be done?"

Grace set down her fork with a clatter. "We have no choice. We have to cancel – and the sooner the better."

"Is there no other option?" Aleda inquired. "The school gym? The arena? It does seem a terrible shame to cancel when everything has been ordered."

"No," Grace declared emphatically. "There's no other option. The school gym smells like sweaty socks and the arena has no atmosphere. No one wants to enjoy a strawberry social in either of those places. We have to cancel."

Aleda nodded and stirred her coffee. Roy took the last bite of his walnut cake and slowly set down his fork.

"Well," he said.

Grace and Aleda looked over to him, waiting.

"Well what, Roy?" Grace said brusquely.

"Well...I've had a bit of a thought."

Grace leaned toward Roy, an impatient frown on her face. "Well?" she demanded loudly.

"When we're done, I'll show you."

It had been a God-sent golden day, Aleda reflected as she crawled into bed that night. An absolutely fantastic, God-sent golden day. It was the only way to describe it. She smiled as she remembered how Roy had led them around to show them the state of the church basement and methodically explained what would be needed to restore the basement to its safe and normal state, as if to reinforce that the situation was impossible.

Then he led them around the north end of the church. He stood for a moment and looked at the cemetery behind the shed.

"A beautiful cemetery," he declared. "One of the most beautiful cemeteries in the province of Ontario."

Grace, whose late husband rested in the cemetery, nodded. Aleda searched out the places where Eadie and Dwayne now lay, the earth still mounded and raw. No one spoke.

Roy turned from the cemetery toward the shed. "Now, this shed," he said, "is as old as our cemetery. Such beautiful carved wooden doors. Not to boast, but my grandfather handcrafted them doors. He wanted doors on both ends of the shed so the horses could come and go more easily and not have to back up and turn around in cramped quarters. At least that's what he told us, but between you and me I think he just wanted a good excuse to spend a winter doing what he loved most – carving wood."

"These doors are exquisite," Aleda agreed, running her hand over the surfaces, "and so well preserved."

"I refinish them every year," Roy said as he stroked the wood. "For the old, this shed has memories; for the young, it has intrigue. I'll bet that some of our young 'uns have never even been inside this shed."

"You're probably right, Roy."

Roy turned to Grace. "For Aleda, this shed is a home for Tracker. And this shed is where the strawberry socials *used* to be held in the olden days. Those were the days before the church basement was made into a hall. People would just walk right up to the cemetery gate and turn right, right into the shed."

"No kidding!" Aleda exclaimed. "You held the strawberry social in the shed?"

Aleda could see that Grace was nodding her head but also wondering, no doubt, what Roy was getting at.

"What are you meaning Roy?" Grace demanded.

"In those old days, even if the church basement had been properly finished there simply wouldn't have been enough room for everyone, so we set up trestle tables in this shed. We men got together and cleaned it up once a year. We swept it out, whitewashed the walls, cleaned the windows, and opened all the doors so it got properly aired out. It was a grand time. Then we lined the walls with paper streamers and hurricane lanterns." He pointed to Tracker's stall. "That's where the women laid out the dessert. The old-timers told us that it felt like a proper old-time threshing bee."

"So, Roy you are suggesting…?"

"I'm suggesting," Roy answered in a loud clear voice, "that we go back in time and have an old-fashioned strawberry social. I'm suggesting that today and tomorrow we gather people to clean up the shed, and then have the strawberry social right here." Roy hesitated, then added, "The farmers will help. It's much too wet to work on the land just now."

"It sounds like a workable idea, Roy. Maybe even a great idea." Aleda glanced at Grace, who was shrugging as if to say, "Well, what choice do we have?"

"I have one concern, though," Aleda said. "What will I do with Tracker?"

35

Work Bee

S SOON AS ROY HAD REVEALED his plan, Aleda, Grace, and Roy drew up lists of people who might be willing to help with cleaning.

"Hasn't had a proper clean-out in years," Roy declared as they looked over their lists. "It'll be good to do it."

They divided up the phone lists, and by the time Grace and Roy were back home Aleda had already called Laura and Martin. She asked Laura if she could help prepare drinks and sandwiches for the work party. "I'll ask Rose to help you, and I'll give you sit-down jobs so you won't have to stand on your ankle." As she spoke, Aleda realized that perhaps Laura might not yet be ready to work alongside Rose, and that perhaps there would be tension and strain.

But Laura answered, "That would be fine, Aleda. It might give us a time to chat."

"Martin," Aleda said when he answered the phone, "I have a most unusual favour to ask." Aleda explained Roy's scheme. "Would you consider keeping Tracker in your barn for a few days until the strawberry social is over?"

"Not a problem. I'll come down and get him this morning. Just round up his food."

"But how will you transport him? I'm quite sure that it won't work to put him in the back of your pickup."

"No, that wouldn't work at all." Aleda thought that she could hear a smile in Martin's voice. "I'll just put on his halter and lead him up the road to my farm. I hear that sort of thing has been done before in the streets of Milburn Corners." A blush crept into Aleda's cheeks.

The church parking lot had filled with pickups and cars. Roy had been right. The farmers in the area were eager to help. The trucks were loaded with shovels, push brooms, large garden buckets, and stout sticks that looked like they had once been broom handles. Aleda could see a couple of wheelbarrows, two large boxes stamped *Mason Lime*, and a box of paint rollers.

Grabbing her keys, she jumped into the van and drove the short distance to the store. To the surprised and always curious Ethel she said, "I'll take your whole shelf of bread, three pounds of butter, eight tins of salmon, three dozen eggs, two jars of mayonnaise, and two pounds of ham. I will also need two large tins of coffee and two litres of cream. That's it!"

"Goodness gracious!" Ethel exclaimed. "What on earth is going on?"

"You got your ticket to the strawberry social yet?"

Ethel nodded. "Never miss it. It's the only day of the year I close up early."

"Well, you're in for a surprise and a treat this year. We're changing the venue. We're clearing out the church shed and making the social like it was in the old days."

"Oh my! Should I…" Ethel gestured in a wide circle.

"By all means. Tell the whole world!" Aleda exclaimed. Oh dear. Perhaps that was too blunt, she thought, but Ethel didn't seem to take offence.

"This food would be for the work party then," Ethel said. "The folks who've come to clean up the shed."

"You got it," Aleda smiled.

"Then I'll give you a hand getting it down the steps and into your van."

By 2 p.m. Aleda's kitchen was full of women peeling hard-boiled eggs, slicing ham, draining tins of salmon, spreading butter on bread. She hadn't needed to worry about finding extra help.

While the men were busy cleaning up the church shed, women drifted over to the parsonage and offered to help with the refreshments that they would all enjoy mid-afternoon. Aleda was kept busy scurrying around providing bowls and utensils. "It's a pity that I didn't think of paper cups for the drinks," Aleda said.

"No problem," said Margaret, looking up from the table where she and Laura were buttering bread. "I have plenty in my pantry. Here Rose, you take over this job and I'll slip home and get them."

Rose slid into a chair beside Laura. From across the kitchen, Aleda heard Rose say to Laura, "Now, my dear, it's wonderful to have some time with you. I haven't seen much of you in the past few days. Is everything okay with you?"

Laura sat poised, a slice of bread in her hand. "I think so," she said slowly, nodding to Rose. "Yes, I think that in the long run everything will be fine."

Later, Aleda told Laura and Martin that she had never seen the women of the church so animated, so full of energy and suggestions, so willing to help. And, if the truth were told, eager to be inside the parsonage kitchen where their minister cooked and ate. For the first time they had a legitimate reason to pull open the drawers and cupboards to have a good look inside.

At the end of the day on Thursday Aleda and Roy stood together in the centre of the shed, Aleda with her arms crossed, Roy leaning on a broom.

"It looks wonderful. So clean and inviting," Aleda said.

"You ain't seen nothin yet. Wait 'til we git that whitewash on in the morning. It makes a world of difference. You won't know the place."

"Roy, I hate to plead ignorance, but I have no idea what whitewash is. Is it a kind of paint?"

"Oh, no, not at all. It's lime."

"Lime? As in gin and tonic?"

Roy laughed. "Mason lime. We mix the lime with water and salt until it looks about like pancake batter. That's why we need the women to help us. They let us know when we've got the mixture just right. We just roll it on with those paint rollers over there."

"Is it just a cheap form of paint?"

"Oh, it's much more than that. It sure does brighten up the place, and there's no strong paint smell either, but whitewash has antibacterial properties too, so it keeps animals healthier. It'll be good for Tracker. But the main reason we whitewash is to kill insects. You don't want a spider dropping into your potato salad tomorrow night, do you?"

"Roy, you're pulling my leg. Who do you think I am, a dumb city girl?"

But Roy only laughed.

As they were turning to go, Aleda wheeled around and said, "Roy, there's something else I've been wondering. There's no electricity in the shed, and the power is still turned off in the church. I didn't think about this until now. How did the women brew the coffee this afternoon, and how will they cook the peas and carrots on Saturday?"

Roy looked at Aleda and his shoulders swayed slightly. "Generators my dear. This is a farming community, remember? Generators."

When Aleda returned to the house she had a message from Savannah to let her know that there would be no youth meeting Friday evening. The youth were meeting at Jacob's house. Jacob's mother had purchased luscious – it was Savannah's word, luscious – strawberries from California. They were going to spend a fun night together creating 100 chocolate-coated strawberries to be used to garnish the plates of rhubarb cobbler.

Friday evening, before she set off for her weekly dinner with Martin and Laura, Aleda walked over to the shed. During the day she had noticed Roy and a couple of the men, all wearing tall rubber boots, carrying chairs and tables from the church basement out into the parking lot, where they were wiped down with disinfectant. She had been busy preparing for Sunday worship service though, and had not visited the shed.

Aleda flung open the door and gasped. The inside glistened; the walls and Tracker's stall were transformed by dazzling brightness. A table set with red cloths and gleaming cutlery stretched the entire length of the building. Wide vases filled with plumes of red astilbe and the lime-green froth of lady's mantle had been placed down the centre of it. Along the west wall of the shed were serving tables waiting for their platters of ham, pans of potato salad and coleslaw, and the inevitable hot peas and carrots. On the north wall a table held large silver urns for coffee and tea. The door of Tracker's stall had been thrown open and tied back with wide bright-red ribbon. Someone had created a sign that said *Desserts* and hung it on the side of the stall. Looped along the side walls of the shed were garlands of greenery hung with red Chinese lanterns.

"Amazing," Aleda said aloud. "Simply amazing."

Aleda could see Laura and Martin sitting in lawn chairs in the arbour when she arrived at the house. "Go in and help yourself to a drink," Laura called as Aleda swung her tote bag out of the passenger side of the van. Aleda waved, entered the kitchen and slid a foil pan of frozen lasagna – there had been no time to cook – into Laura's oven. When Aleda returned to the arbour, red wine in hand, Laura rose from the lawn chair, held out her arms, and said, "Do you notice anything different about me?"

Aleda gazed at her slim attractive friend. Her silver-blond hair was pulled to the side and held in place with a black clip. She wore large gold hoop earrings and a long black-and-gold-striped summer dress. "Tonight you look absolutely beautiful, as ever," she said, but as she looked down, she caught on. "Your feet! You're wearing sandals. You're no longer wearing your walking boot!" Laura laughed as Aleda gave her an exuberant hug.

"I start physiotherapy on Monday. Oddly, I still walk with a limp. Habit, I suppose, but the doctor said that will improve with time. Now, bring us up to date since yesterday."

Martin, swirling the ice in his drink, gazed at the two women who had become such an important part of his life and felt an enormous sense of well-being. He glanced over to where they sat. "Did you know," he said, "that this is the first day of summer?"

For a moment there was silence. Then Aleda said with enthusiasm, "Well, isn't that wonderful! We have the whole summer to look forward to."

"Exactly." Martin said. "Precisely."

After dinner they moved into the living room. They settled into the sofas, choosing places where they could set their mugs on side tables.

"I've something on my mind," Laura said, crossing her long legs, "and I'd love to hear your opinions on this. I know you will be honest with me." Aleda and Martin looked at her, waiting. "You see…I've been considering taking early retirement and staying on in Milburn Corners."

"Really," Aleda said in a neutral tone. Martin nodded slightly.

"I won't make a secret about my age," she continued. "I'm 52, two years older than you Martin, as you remember from our school days." She hesitated. "I came here reluctantly. I was used to my lifestyle in Toronto and my teaching career, but now that I've been here a few weeks I find that I don't miss either Toronto or teaching at all." Laura paused while Aleda and Martin waited in silence. "I can afford to retire. Money is not an issue. I never thought that I would enjoy village life so much – getting up when I feel like it, reading novels that I've always meant to get from the library. And now that I have made this room my own I feel very much at home here. I've even been thinking of getting a grand piano for the other half of the room." Aleda and Martin turned their heads as if to imagine a piano in the large open space beyond the French doors. "I used to play as a child, and I would like to take it up again. A little Chopin, some Mozart, some ragtime."

Laura paused and looked at her friends. "To be honest, I realize that part of my decision comes from being able to set aside my angst about my father, but the biggest factor really…" Laura suddenly looked shy. "I've had a wonderful time developing friendships with the two of you. Somehow I can't imagine myself back on St. Clair Avenue. I'd be wondering all the time what the two of you are up to. Aleda, your life always seems full of interesting things, and Martin, I never tire of hearing about those old buildings you're researching, and the puppies, and your adventures with Callum. The composting business is a different matter," she teased.

"The truth is, I would miss going down to the corner store to catch the latest newsreel from Ethel Aylmer, and I would miss chatting with Roy when I go to pick up the mail, and I would even miss Grace shouting *ya-hoo* to her little dog. Who else in the world summons their dog with *ya-hoo*? I would miss your mother's visits, Martin. Who else but Rose would bring me a pan of fresh cinnamon buns every week?"

Laura sank back into the sofa cushions. "What do you think?" she asked, looking from Martin to Aleda. "Do you think it's a good decision to take early retirement and just stay on here and enjoy life?"

Martin glanced at Aleda, and Aleda sat for a moment gazing off into a corner. "What do you think, Martin?" Aleda asked.

Martin shrugged and turned toward Laura. "I think it's your decision. You have to do what seems right to you."

Laura nodded, then turned to face Aleda directly, an expectant look on her face. "What do you think, Aleda?"

Aleda pressed her index finger against her lips before speaking. "I agree with Martin," she said. "It *is* your decision, but it has always been my experience that it's often hard to come to a decision without talking things over with trusted friends and colleagues. So I will be honest with you, Laura. I'm not sure that it's such a great idea."

"What! Why do you say that?"

"Things won't stay the same as they are this summer. Whether we like it or not, things will change. Roy and Grace will grow older and die. Ethel is getting older too, and in time will probably sell the corner store, and it may sit boarded up for years. Maybe they will even rip it down if it becomes a fire hazard. Tracker – God rest his soul – will die and have to be composted in Martin's God-forsaken bin. Then I'll be free to move on to another parish. I can't stay here forever."

Aleda might have added that Savannah and the other kids would leave the village and go off to university, and who knew where Martin would be in ten years, but she could see that Laura's face had become drawn and sorrowful. Perhaps I was too honest, too direct, Aleda thought, so she said gently, "Laura, things will change, and here you will be when the winter snowstorms move in from Lake Huron and Georgian Bay and keep you housebound for two or three months. Are you up for that?"

Laura pursed her lips, staring straight ahead at her outstretched legs. Aleda took a deep breath. "Having said that," Aleda continued, "I agree with you totally that this village – maybe any village – teems with life. Sometimes there are annoying things, but mainly life in Milburn Corners is healthy and good. It may not be perfect, but it is real. Changing and challenging, but always real. You know what I think, Laura?"

"I did ask your opinion. I want to hear what you think."

"I think it might be wise to request a year's leave of absence from your teaching position. It would give you a wonderful break and, at the same time, give you a chance to discover if this might be a good long-term solution for you. That's it. That's my opinion. For better or for worse, I've given it."

Aleda sank back into her corner of the sofa while Martin lifted his mug in salute and said, "Well spoken, Aleda."

Laura smiled and took a sip of her cold coffee.

36

Strawberry Social

N SATURDAY, AS ALEDA HURRIED around to the north parking lot at the church, she noted that someone had again changed the signboard at the front of the church. It now read *Strawberry Social Saturday in Church Shed 5:00 p.m.*

"God has blessed us with a beautiful day," Aleda called out to the men and women unloading bags of dinner rolls, coolers of ham, and buckets of potato and cabbage salads. They paused in their work, waved a greeting, and looked up into the sky, smiling.

In another hour this place will be buzzing with activity, Aleda thought. Children will be playing with the hula hoops and skipping ropes that had been set out. The women would be stirring the simmering peas and carrots, setting out the serving forks, cutting plates of butter, taking the dinner rolls out of their plastic bags, and setting out dishes of Anna's bread-and-butter pickles. Roy would have the coffee percolating; the teenagers would be delivering their chocolate-covered strawberries and setting up their instruments for the after-dinner music. Bessie and Anna, wearing their best Sunday dresses, would be at the door of the shed, standing at a little table collecting tickets, saying over and over as they smiled, "We hope you enjoy your meal. There's lots of good food."

It had become Aleda's habit to act like a butterfly at church dinners. She had discovered that if she got her plate and sat down with someone she would be there chatting and eating for a half hour. There was nothing wrong with that, but it meant that she

missed opportunities to chat with others. She could count on being asked to say a blessing, and when that was over she simply
circulated, adopting the role of friendly hostess moving from group
to group, spending a few minutes here, a few minutes there.

The sun was dipping behind the tops of the spruce trees by the
parking lot when people began to stream into the shed. As they
passed through the doors there was a chorus of *oohs* and *aahs*. Aleda
heard someone exclaim, "I remember this from when I was a child!"
Even the young people were delighted with the space. "Awesome,
cool," Jacob called out when he entered with his mother.

The tables were filling up. Aleda moved to where Martin stood
in line with his empty plate. "Hi Aleda!" he said. "Have you met
Paul, Callum's father?"

"Pleased to meet you Paul. We have so much enjoyed getting
to know your son," Aleda said warmly. "Such an interesting…" Her
sentence was interrupted when they noticed Callum move toward
Grace and tug on her apron. "Oh my," Aleda said. "I don't even
want to think about what he's going to ask her."

Aleda moved on to the middle of the table where Laura sat
with Rose. It was hard for Aleda to believe that just a few days
eirlier Laura had worried about her feelings for Rose. Today, it
seemed, over ham, potato salad, and strawberries, they were friends.
Rose was telling Laura about a novel that had just been released –
Atonement by Ian McEwan.

"What do you think, Aleda?" Rose asked as Aleda came up to
them. "Laura and I have just been discussing the possibility of starting a book club. There are so many wonderful new novels out this
year." Aleda smiled and held out her hand as if to say, "Why not?"

Aleda spotted Eadie's daughter and granddaughter and moved
toward them. Nestled in the curve of her mother's arm was the
plump baby, dressed in pink. "My goodness," Aleda enthused, "I
can't believe how she has grown." She laid a finger on the side of
the moist pink cheek.

Eadie's granddaughter smiled up at Aleda. "It's funny," she said, "I know that you baptized her Eden, but all of us are in the habit of calling her by her nickname – little Eadie."

Aleda laughed and clapped her hands together. "Wonderful. Your grandmother would have been so pleased. Enjoy your dinner, and it's great to see you again."

Aleda saw that Martin and Michael had settled down at the table together and were talking in an animated way, using hand gestures that suggested they might be describing some piece of electronic equipment.

On the other side of table, Jacob's mother had turned to Callum's father and was telling him something while pointing to her plate. Callum had settled beside Grace. As Aleda passed them, Grace looked a little embarrassed and said, "I wouldn't normally have sat down, you see. But they have lots of servers and Callum here asked if he could sit with me."

"Oh."

Callum turned to Grace, his mouth full of potato salad, and said, "Mrs. Grace, did you know that you have hairs up your nose?"

Aleda froze, wondering what would happen next, but Grace only smiled and looked down at the rumpled boy. "Goodness gracious child. The things you say."

Aleda paused to say hello to Ethel Aylmer, who was engaged in an animated conversation with a farmer from the town line about the price of soy beans and why she could not get fresh local lamb for her store.

Aleda turned to greet Patrice and Robert, who had filled their plates and were seated opposite Murta. Although it was a warm evening and Patrice wore a gossamer summer dress, Murta wore a knit shawl around her thin shoulders. But before Aleda could speak, Murta had engaged Patrice in a vigorous discussion about the pattern of her shawl. "Knit one, purl two," she was saying as Aleda moved away.

Aleda walked toward the west end of the shed where people were still streaming in. She stopped in surprise. A large man, wearing a brown sports shirt and tan pants and looking self-conscious and slightly ill at ease, waited in line with his empty plate. "Constable Brennan!" she exclaimed. "How wonderful to see you. What a surprise!"

He grinned and said, "I caught sight of the sign on the church lawn when I was passing through earlier, and I'm off duty today. Please call me Neil."

"Neil. Yes. Neil. May I introduce you to Savannah?" Aleda turned to the girl who stood waiting in line behind him.

Savannah reached out her hand and said, "Hi! I'm Savannah. If you're new here, you can sit with me."

Aleda turned to leave, hesitated, then turned back. She stood on tiptoe and leaned close to Neil's ear, placing her warm hand on his bare forearm. "About that concert," she said quietly, her head turned away from Savannah. "I'd love to."

Aleda edged over to where Roy stood close to the urns of coffee and tea and waited beside him for a moment or two, neither of them speaking. Then she said, over the hum of happy diners, "It's the community of saints, Roy." A sweep of her hand took in the cemetery gates and church shed. "It's the community of saints."

When the last mugs had been washed, the cutlery stacked into boxes, and the tables folded and set against the walls, people drifted home. Grace and Ethel lingered near the door, talking intensely. "You're such a wonderful pie maker, Grace. Oh, my word, I would say that you are more than a pie maker. You are a pastry artist!"

"Oh, really, no, no, no," Grace said. "And, honestly, Ethel, I don't think I could make six pies a day."

"Well, how about six pies on Friday and Saturday? I'll put out a special sign on the sidewalk to advertise. Maybe you could even make some of those wonderful butter tarts of yours, those lovely runny ones with walnuts and raisins. What do you think?"

Aleda helped Savannah, Michael, and Jacob pack up the music stands and instruments. The youth were flushed and excited by the praise they had received for their music. They were also proud that they had mastered renditions of the latest hits.

As the teens had belted out "A Thousand Miles," Aleda listened to them singing about longing to see someone and being willing to walk a thousand miles to do so. Would she walk a thousand miles to see someone she missed? She glanced at Laura and Martin. How she would miss Laura if she decided to return to Toronto, and how she would miss Martin when he returned to Guelph at the end of the summer. She glanced at Dwayne's grandmother and wondered if this song of longing pained her. Aleda looked across at Eadie's daughter and granddaughter and the baby asleep on her mother's breast and wondered if they longed to have Eadie back with them, just to see her one more time.

And when the youth had swung into "Ain't It Funny" Aleda reflected, with a twinge of bitterness, on how in just one moment things can change. She thought about that moment in the dark hallway and how her dreams of sharing a life with Ben had been dashed. And when Savannah and her friends sang out *I locked away my heart and you just set it free*, Aleda glanced over to Callum and Grace. Callum, sated and content, was leaning against Grace's shoulder fast asleep. Grace had her arm protectively around him, and her head was turned so that her lips almost touched the top of his tangled hair.

For their final song – a tribute to summer – the youth had chosen "Soak Up the Sun" to give everyone hope for good things ahead.

The sun had gone down when Roy swung shut the shed door. "I'll get the other door," Aleda called out to him. She watched Roy wander down the street for a moment. Then she turned back toward the house and entered the kitchen.

Restless and still full of energy, she reached into the cupboard and took out a flashlight. She stepped off the back porch and made her way to the cemetery gate and under the archway that read *Community of Saints.*

Night had fallen and she turned on her flashlight, strolling from grave to grave and reading as she went. She paused beside Eadie's grave. Then she then turned toward the place where Dwayne's ashes were buried. She stood remembering for a moment, and then turned back and walked through the cemetery until she passed through the archway.

Watching from his back porch, Roy could see a dark figure wandering among the gravestones with a flashlight. He turned and strolled down the narrow pathway between his bungalow and garage. He paused in front of his climbing roses and stood gazing at the lush blooms. The deep pink and red blooms were almost invisible in the faded light, but the white blooms seemed to shine. Roy touched them with tenderness, thinking *sleep well, my beauties.*

From her living room, Grace stood behind the sheer curtains covering her windows and gazed at Roy. She folded her arms around herself in a hug and watched Roy gently touch his roses.

It was close to ten o'clock. The village was quiet, and there had been no cars through for a while. The only sound was the incessant *riddip-riddip* of the frogs in the swamp.

Then came the unmistakeable clip-clop of horse hoofs. Someone was leading an old horse down the hill past the doctor's house, past the darkened village store, past the green mail boxes and the Victorian street lamp in front of Roy's house, and up the knoll toward the parsonage and the church. Then the man and horse disappeared into a grass alley.

ALEDA'S RECIPE FOR HUNGARIAN GOULASH

There are many versions of goulash, but Hungarians agree on one thing: Be generous with the meat, potatoes, and paprika.

Preparation time: 20 minutes

Needed: Large cooking pot with lid

Cooking time: 1 hour 15 minutes on low heat on stovetop or in 300°F oven

Serves: 6

3 tbsp	oil
1 lb	beef, cubed
1	cooking onion, chopped
1 tsp	caraway seeds
2 tsp	ground sweet paprika
2	cloves garlic, crushed
1 cup	water or beef broth
1 cup	red wine or tomato juice
1 each of:	carrot, parsnip, tomato
2 each of:	green peppers, stalks of celery, potatoes
2 tbsp	cornstarch dissolved in 2 tbsp water (optional)
2 tbsp	butter
	Salt and pepper to taste

1. Heat oil in large pot over medium heat on stove top.
2. Add cubed beef and chopped onions, stirring until brown (about 5 minutes).

3. Stir in caraway seeds, paprika, and garlic. Cook for 1 minute.
4. Add water/broth and wine. Stir well.
5. Raise heat and bring to a boil, then immediately lower the heat so the goulash is gently bubbling. Cook for 1 hour on stovetop or in the oven (see above).
6. While the meat is cooking, chop all the vegetables into bite-sized pieces.
7. After an hour, add vegetables to the meat in the pot. If boiling has stopped from opening the lid, raise heat until the goulash boils again. Then lower the heat, cover the pot, and let the goulash gently bubble for 15 minutes.
8. If you like a thick broth, dissolve the cornstarch in water and stir into the bubbling goulash.
9. Before serving, add butter, salt, and pepper.

ALEDA'S HINT

This is a bowl of Hungarian history! Serve the goulash in a small kettle as a reminder that this dish is the traditional outdoor meal of the proud Magyar herdsmen in the Carpathian Basin.

ROSE HART'S INSTRUCTIONS FOR SOURDOUGH STARTER

Preparation time: 10 minutes

Needed: Large glass or ceramic bowl, cheesecloth or clean tea towel

Resting time: 1 or 2 days

3 cups	warm distilled water
	(do not use water that contains chlorine or fluoride)
2 tbsp	sugar
1 tbsp	dry yeast (granular)
1 cup	white flour
1 cup	whole wheat flour

1. Pour the warm water into a large bowl. Stir in sugar until dissolved.
2. Sprinkle dry yeast over the sugar water and let sit while you measure the flour.
3. Stir the sugar-yeast-water mixture to dissolve the yeast. Mix in white and whole wheat flours. The starter should be the consistency of pancake batter.
4. Cover bowl with cheesecloth or a clean tea towel. Let rest in a warm place for at least 1 day. See Rose's hints below for how to tell if your sourdough starter is ready to bake with.

ROSE'S HINTS

In a day or so, test your starter to see if it has enough carbon dioxide. Do this by scooping out a spoonful and dropping it in a glass of warm water. If it floats, you're ready to bake. If it sinks, put it back into its warm place until the starter floats when tested again.

When it is ready to use, your sourdough starter should smell slightly sweet. Remove half the batter and use it as the basis for your cinnamon rolls. To refresh your starter (so you can continue using it) stir in 1 cup flour and 1 cup water until it looks like pancake batter again. This feeds and strengthens your sourdough. Stir well.

ROSE HART'S INSTRUCTIONS FOR CINNAMON ROLLS

Preparation time: 20-25 minutes

Needed: Mixer with dough hook and large bowl (Don't have one? Use a large bowl, then mix and knead by hand.); buttered 9 x 13 inch baking pan

Rising time: 2 hours or so

Oven temperature: 350°F

Baking time: about 20 minutes

Serves: 8

DOUGH

1 cup	sourdough starter
1 cup	water
2 tsp	salt
1 cup	flour + up to 3 cups more

FILLING

	margarine or soft butter
1 cup	brown sugar
2 tbsp	cinnamon
	Raisins or chopped nuts (optional)

1. Combine the sourdough starter, water, salt, and 1 cup flour in a large bowl and mix until smooth.
2. Add remaining 3 cups of flour 1 cup at a time, adding the last cup only as needed. The dough should be thick, sticky, and elastic.

3. Knead the dough for 5 minutes with your mixer and hook. If kneading by hand, sprinkle flour on the board to keep dough from sticking.

4. Let your dough rest for a minute while you wash and dry your mixing bowl. Coat inside of bowl lightly with oil. Add dough and turn to coat with oil. Cover with a clean tea towel.

5. Let rest in a warm place until doubled in size (about 2 hours).

SHAPING THE CINNAMON ROLLS

1. Return the dough to the countertop and use a rolling pin to create a rectangle measuring about 9 by 13 inches.

2. Use a kitchen knife to spread lots of soft butter or margarine over the rolled dough.

3. Sprinkle with brown sugar and cinnamon. Add raisins or nuts if using.

4. With the long side in front of you, roll the dough away from you until it looks like a jelly roll.

5. Pinch the seam together and rock gently to seal the edges. Pinch shut the ends of the roll.

6. Use a serrated knife to gently saw into 1 inch slices and set (with the brown sugar cinnamon showing) into a buttered 9 x 13 inch baking pan. Set the rolls slightly apart (not touching), as the dough will rise and fill in the spaces.

7. Let dough rise again in a warm place until doubled. Bake in 350°F oven for 20 minutes or until golden brown.

ROSE'S HINT

Drizzle a white glaze (made with icing sugar and water) over cooled buns.

THE AUTHOR

DOROTHY BROWN HENDERSON

Dorothy Brown Henderson lives in Exeter, Ontario, with her husband, John. Henderson has enjoyed a variety of careers: music teacher, mental health worker, writer, Christian educator, leadership developer, and, most recently, minister of Caven Presbyterian Church in Exeter, Ontario.

Henderson holds an ARCT in piano (University of Toronto), a BA in Religious Studies, a MA in Religion and Culture (Wildred Laurier University), and a MA in Religious Education (University of Toronto). In 2006, Henderson received the *Educator of the Year* award from the Association of Presbyterian Church Educators.

Now retired, Henderson enjoys spending time with her three grown children and their spouses, and her two grandchildren, especially at the family cottage on Lake Huron. She also enjoys writing, reading, cooking, running community culinary camps for children, growing an ever increasing garden, saving seeds, and community activities. She is member of the board of South Huron Communities in Bloom, and of the Kirkton Horticultural Society.

Besides *The Season for Strawberries*, Henderson is also the author of the cookbook *Loving It Local: Preparing Delicious Fresh Local Food* (2014).

PHOTOGRAPH BY BONNIE SITTER

THE ARTISTS

SARA F. GALLAGHER – COVER ART

The small town of Milford, Delaware has an annual Strawberry Festival, which inspired the painting on the cover of this book.

Sara F. Gallagher is an award - winning artist whose beautiful paintings come from her imagination and from direct observations of rural scenery and local events, as well as gardens. She works primarily in Watercolors, but as well as acrylics and oils. She moves freely between traditional and nontraditional techniques.

Gallagher continues to put her Masters in Art Education to work as she devotes time to teaching privately as well as for art groups. She sells and paints in galleries, as well as from her home studio. She also accepts comissions. She can be contacted at sarrahart362@yahoo.com

RANDY JONES - MAP

Randy Jone's art has appeared in *The New York Times*; *The Wall Street Journal*; and *National Lampoon*; as well as in books published by Houghton Mifflin; Random House; St. Martin's Press; Little, Brown and Company; and most recently, Post Hill Press/Simon & Schuster. His most recent books are *Monsters of the Ivy League*, by Steve Radiauer and Ellis Wiener, and *Trumpitude*, an illustrated look inside President Trump, by Ellis Henican.

A NOTE CONCERNING THE TYPEFACES USED IN THIS BOOK

The text face is Caslon, a serif font first designed by William Caslon in 1722 and used extensively throughout the British Empire in the early eighteen century. It was also widely used in the early days of the American colonies and was the font used for the U.S. Declaration of Independence, but fell out of favour soon after. It has been revived at various times since then, in particular during the Arts and Crafts movement. It continues to be a standard in typography to this day, and many typographers follow the rule of thumb, "when in doubt, use Caslon". This particular version, which includes a wide variety of swash characters, was designed by Carol Twombly for Adobe in 1990. The display fonts are a combination of Caslon and Old Style Bold Outline, which was introduced by Monotype in 1901. The ornamental initial letters were revived, from an unknown late nineteenth century source, by Lanston Type in 1977.

WOOD LAKE

IMAGINING, LIVING, AND TELLING
THE FAITH STORY.

WOOD LAKE IS THE FAITH STORY COMPANY.

It has told
■ the story of the seasons of the earth, the people of God, and the place and purpose of faith in the world;
■ the story of the faith journey, from birth to death;
■ the story of Jesus and the churches that carry his message.

Wood Lake has been telling stories for more than 35 years. During that time, it has given form and substance to the words, songs, pictures, and ideas of hundreds of storytellers.

Those stories have taken a multitude of forms – parables, poems, drawings, prayers, epiphanies, songs, books, paintings, hymns, curricula – all driven by a common mission of serving those on the faith journey.

WOOD LAKE PUBLISHING INC.
485 Beaver Lake Road
Kelowna, BC, Canada v4v 1s5
250.766.2778

www.woodlake.com